ROGUE

A SCI-FI SUPERHERO ORIGIN STORY

A JACK HAMMER ADVENTURE
BOOK ONE

TOBY NEIGHBORS

Rogue: A Sci-Fi Superhero Origin Story

Copyright © 2026 by Toby Neighbors

ISBN: 978-1-968189-24-2 ebook

978-1-968189-25-9 print

Mythic Adventure Publishing, LLC

Idaho USA

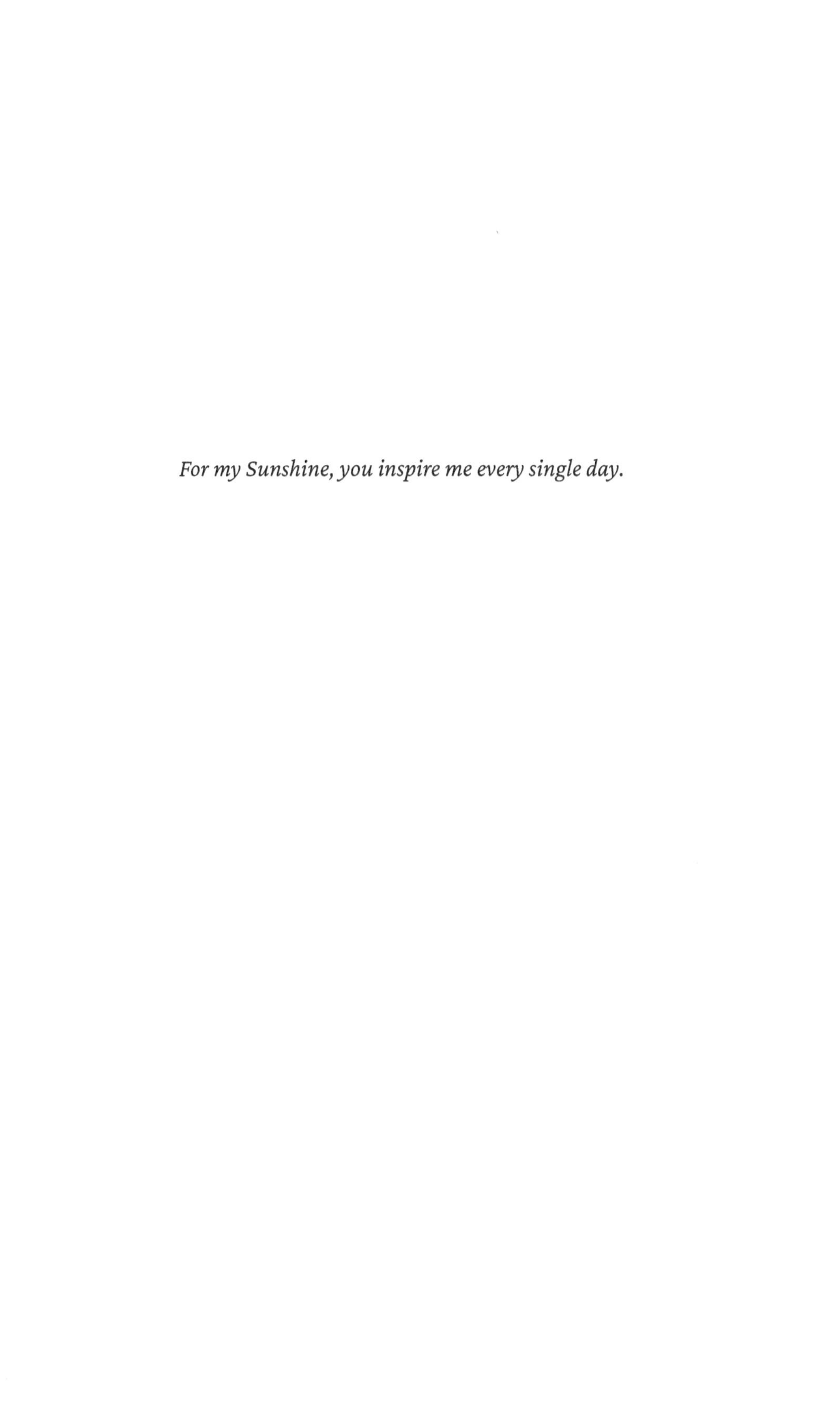

For my Sunshine, you inspire me every single day.

Appear weak whne you are strong,
And strong when you are weak.

— SUN TZU, THE ART OF WAR

PROLOGUE

"Captain, we have a problem," the science officer said.

His voice was calm, but the words were not what Captain Kittle wanted to hear.

"What is it?"

"I'm picking up a gamma flux surge. It's some kind of strange coronal mass ejection from the system star."

"And we're in its path?"

"Negative, Captain. By my calculation, when the gamma surge reaches us in eight minutes, we'll be far enough around the planet to be shielded from the radiation, but the last shuttle from the planet just launched."

"Who's on board that vessel?" Kittle asked.

"Sir, that's Marine platoon Delta, with one casualty. Looks like a Marine was trampled by some type of indigenous creature. They recovered the Marine alive and have him on the shuttle."

Captain Kittle did a quick calculation. He had two officers on board the drop ship and a platoon of Marines. In his mental equation, he didn't care about the Marines. That was the hard truth. People who didn't command starships might not understand, but

Marines were expendable. They weren't highly trained aviators or aerospace engineers; they were trigger pullers. And he still had five more platoons on board the *Intrepid*.

What he didn't like was losing a drop ship and two good pilots. They were much harder to replace than Marines.

"Is there any way to save them?"

"Negative, sir," the science officer said. "They're in a pre-calculated ascent, and there's no time for the shuttle to reach safety before the gamma surge reaches the planet."

"Very well," Kittle said with a frown.

"Should we alert the crew, Captain?" First officer Bingham asked.

"To what end?" Kittle demanded. "There is nothing they can do except despair. And who knows, we might be able to salvage that drop ship if they can get it back to the ship in one piece."

Bingham looked ill, and the rest of the officers on the Bridge exchanged glances, but none were foolish enough to argue. Kittle was a tough captain, the type who considered any alternative point of view a challenge to his authority. He often belittled and humiliated anyone who questioned his orders.

The first officer, Terrance Joshua Bingham, was, in Kittle's view, a sorry excuse for a starship commander. He was younger than his superior by almost twenty years and, like many of his generation, he thought his job was to protect the people under his command. Bingham would abandon the mission if he thought that it might get people killed. To Kittle's mind, the worst thing about Bingham was that he actually believed that the lives of Marines and crew were more important than achieving mission goals. Captain Kittle did not have any such compunctions. He believed that nothing, not life or property, was as important as the mission objectives which were handed down from Space Command. Likewise, if the choice was between saving lives or saving equipment, he would always choose military assets over his crew. They were all replaceable. Space Command recruited thousands of new crewmen and Marines every single year. Many would serve less than a decade before rotating back out to live their lives under the umbrella of safety that Space Command afforded. So, no, Kittle didn't value the lives of the drop ship's crew and passengers more than the aircraft itself.

They waited. There was no physical sign that the drop ship was affected by the gamma surge. It washed over them, and more accurately, through them. Half an hour later, the transport vessel landed safely in the *Intrepid's* hangar bay. Two flight officers, one Marine officer, and thirty-two enlisted Marines were all taken immediately to quarantine. The drop ship was checked and had to be discarded from the *Intrepid* due to high levels of radiation. It was just one of the many ways that things could go wrong in outer space.

Captain Kittle entered the loss of the ship into his log and continued on with the mission he had been assigned. It didn't matter that of the thirty-five people exposed to the gamma radiation on the return from their assignment on the planet's surface, only one would survive. What would come to his attention later, and what he would leverage as an unexpected, but highly valuable outcome of the mission, was the strange properties exhibited by that lone survivor.

This is his story...

1

Pain... that is what he remembered. For a time, he thought that he was dead. There was no more pain, no light, no sounds. But after a few moments, he began to hear a slight hum. He didn't believe that there would be a mechanical hum in the afterlife.

He didn't worry about it too much. He had been hurting, but wasn't any longer, and for a while that was good enough.

Then the beeping started, followed by a gentle red light. Hell, maybe, he thought. Maybe he really was dead and just in a sort of cruel soft beginning before being dumped into eternal torment.

But that didn't explain the beeping. Suddenly, between the row of soft, red lights, a shadow appeared through what looked like a window. The shadow was conical, which made no sense. It hovered, barely in view for a few seconds, then a sound assaulted his ears.

"Sergeant Hammer? Can you hear me?"

That was his name, Hammer, Jack, Sergeant First Class with the Space Command Marine Corps, Rock Jockeys as they were some-times called. He hadn't realized that he had forgotten his own name, but it came back to him in a rush.

"Yes," he responded. His voice sounded thin, weak and raspy. He realized his mouth was very dry. His tongue felt thick and sticky.

"How are you feeling, Sergeant?"

He thought about the question, but there wasn't much to say. "Don't feel much," he responded. "Thirsty."

"Yes, I suspected as much. I'll lower the hydration tube. It's right above your head. Can you reach up for it?"

Jack didn't know. He tried to move his arm and saw it move up past his face, but didn't feel it moving.

"Why can't I feel anything?"

"You were injured, Sergeant. I don't know the details, but your back is broken. We have you in a hyperbaric chamber now."

The lack of light and sound suddenly made sense. He wasn't thrilled to hear his back was broken, but he was still too groggy to make much of that terrible fact.

He pulled the hydration tube toward his face. It went into his mouth, soft plastic and sweet water. It was cool and flowed over his tongue like a river. He wanted to suck hard, but stopped himself. Instead, he filled his mouth about halfway, then let the cool water reach into the spaces between his cheeks and gums, let it wash over the roof of his mouth, and soak into his tongue. Only then did he swallow and allow himself another mouthful.

He could feel the water washing down his parched throat.

"How long was I out?" he asked.

"Five days," the voice said.

He could see something through the little window at the top of the hyperbaric chamber. It wasn't a face, though. It didn't even look like a person.

"Who are you?"

"I'm Doctor Zeldin, the ship's surgeon."

There were too many questions and not enough answers. Jack released the tube and closed his eyes. It felt good to let go, and before he knew it, the chamber was dark again. Time had passed. If the strange thing looking down at him was still there, he couldn't see it.

But his foot itched and he needed to deal with that. He rotated his feet together and rubbed them for a few seconds, then drifted back to sleep.

In Doctor Cal Zeldin's little office on board the *Intrepid,* a chime sounded. He looked up at his display wall. The little video feed from inside Sergeant Hammer's hyperbaric chamber expanded over the other open data windows. The doctor nearly jumped out of his chair as Sergeant Hammer rubbed his feet together.

"He shouldn't be able to do that!" Zeldin said

He was forty-eight years old and near the end of his twenty-year stint with Space Command. They had put him through medical school and, in exchange, he had worked on interstellar vessels for a decade. The work was more administrative than medical. Healthcare had become automated. Scans could detect a defect, injury or disease within minutes, while generative AI could diagnose and dispense treatments faster than any human being. Robots could perform surgery without getting tired or losing focus. Humans were no longer needed in the medical field, but they were still involved in the research and development industry. AI could concoct new drugs, yet humans were still involved in discovering how the human body functioned and imagining new ways to improve life.

His plan had been to retire from Space Fleet and join a medical laboratory on Europa or Titan. His experience overseeing military medical facilities would be in demand. While his work involved filling out reports and keeping tabs on the automated medical systems, he had worked hard to keep current on the latest updates in the medical field. Which was how he knew that despite trillions of pecuniary credits that had been spent on regenerative medicine, none had ever shown favorable results.

He slid his finger across the touch-sensitive control display on his desktop. It brought up the contact for Captain Kittle. He held it down until the name turned red, indicating that he was urgently requesting communication with the ship's primary officer.

"Go for Kittle," the captain said, his voice carried through the small speaker on Doctor Zeldin's desk.

"Sir, we have a situation here."

"Who died now, Cal?"

He said it in a jocular way, as if he was making a joke. Zeldin didn't think it was funny and never did. It was his duty to report the death of a crew member, but he knew his Captain well enough to know that it would not rise to the importance of an urgent communication request, not to Captain Kittle.

"Sir, as you know, Sergeant Hammer is the last remaining member of his platoon."

"And he's gone?"

"No, sir, he's very much alive. Surprisingly so. I'm looking at his vitals now and they are strong across the board."

"Get to the point, Cal. I don't have all day."

"Sir, you are aware that he had a complete fracture of his spinal column at the C-7 location. It undoubtedly occurred when his platoon mates moved him. He was paralyzed from the neck down and not given a favorable prognosis."

"That tracks," Kittle said. "But he's hanging in there?"

"Sir, I just saw him move his feet."

There was a full ten-second pause before the Captain responded.

"What are you saying, Doctor?"

"Captain, I am reporting that Sergeant Kittle is experiencing an unprecedented recovery, sir. Not just healing, but regeneration of the nerves in the spinal column. I'm running full scans now, with an emphasis on his nervous system."

"Unprecedented, as in never done before?"

"That's right, Captain. There is no natural explanation for his recovery. Except..."

"The Gamma surge? That's what you're saying? The same radiation that killed everyone else in his platoon is somehow affecting him differently?"

"It's the only thing I can think of. Sergeant Hammer suffered a cut on his back during a training exercise. It required thirty-one stitches, administered by an automated field unit. He had standard follow-up care. I checked it to see if he showed any signs of heightened healing ability in his prior medical history, because his vitals were growing stronger while everyone else exposed to the gamma radiation succumbed to the usual effects of exposure."

"What is your assessment of the situation?" Kittle asked. "Are you suggesting we do something different?"

"No, sir, but what we have on our hands is incredibly rare. My advice is that we keep him quarantined and continue tests … you'll want to add this to your report. I can guarantee you that if he continues to recover, Sergeant Hammer will be the most valuable person in the entire fleet."

"Noted," Kittle said. "Be sure and keep me updated on a regular basis, Doctor. If anything changes, I want to know about it immediately."

"Aye, Captain," Doctor Zeldin said.

He lifted his finger off the transmit button and leaned back in his chair. The medical scan had just finished and the results popped up on his display wall. There were still fractures in the C-6 and C-7 vertebrae, but no fracture in the nerve cluster. Somehow, despite the injury, his nerves had reconnected.

A few taps on his command panel brought up the scans from when he was first brought on board. It showed a complete break. There was a gap all the way across the spine between the broken vertebrae. It was a life-altering kind of injury that left people in medical facilities for what remained of their abbreviated life span.

What's more, the spinal fluid had risen back to the normal level after a good bit had leaked out of the break site and been absorbed by the rest of the body. It wasn't just the nerves and spinal fluids that were healing. The disks above, below and between the broken vertebrae looked healthy. They were made of soft tissue and allowed the spine to move. Normally, in even the slightest overextension, the disks were prone to bulging and swelling, which caused severe pain.

But, Sergeant Hammer's disks showed no signs of injury whatsoever. The spinal ligaments were intact as well. How they had reconnected without surgical intervention was a mystery.

Doctor Zeldin had an incredibly rare opportunity on his hands. As the doctor of record, with at least two more weeks of medical oversight to conduct while the ship completed its primary mission and returned to the Sol System, he was in a prime position to record and analyze what was without question the most valuable medical case in the history of Space Command. It might even be possible to discover the secrets to healing, physical enhancement and extension of the human lifespan just by studying this one case. It was like Doctor Zeldin had won the occupational lottery. He would be included in the records and history books that would undoubtedly be written about Sergeant Hammer. He would be able to leverage that into the most lucrative post-military careers one could dream of.

Sergeant Hammer was a rising wave of opportunity and Doctor Zeldin intended to ride it as high and as far as he could.

2

A few days later, Jack awoke with much more mental clarity than before. He was still in the hyperbaric chamber, but he could feel the padded bench he lay on and the neck stabilizer around his throat. There were also sticky patches on his chest and back with wires that he guessed connected to a computer that was keeping tabs on his vital signs.

Jack was less interested in where he was than in how he got there. His memory was a bit foggy. Everything was probably from pain meds. He didn't hurt, but the memory of his pain was vivid in his mind. He had never been hurt like he had on the planet. He racked his brain but couldn't remember the name of it. Most unexplored planets didn't have a real name, just a code designation. He was a member of Delta Platoon. They had been sent planet-side to explore and release drones that would collect scientific data about the planet.

Exploring sounds good, but in reality, it usually involves getting dirt, air and flora samples, if there are any to collect. All of which is really redundant work since the drones and satellites get the same information, only faster and, in some cases, more reliably. He was just one man, after all. Just one of the many who volunteered for the Space Marines because there wasn't anything else to do. There were no jobs available for people without specialized skills. He had two choices in life: live off the government in a single room apartment among thousands of other people with no real future, or join the Marines, where he would at least get to see planets outside the Sol system.

He had been taking a soil sample with his rifle slung across his back when the ground opened up beneath him. He fell and slid down a tunnel. He remembered that even though it happened so fast, he really just remembered the feeling of falling for a split second, followed by the pain of landing hard on his back. His armor probably had saved him from a serious injury in the fall, but then some kind animal had come charging past him. He remembered it, vaguely. He felt the rumble of the big creature, but never really saw it in the darkness. Heard the grunting as it charged at him. Then the impact as it stepped on him was sudden and terrible. That was all he could remember before waking up in the hyperbaric chamber, days ago. Since then, he had been in a dream state, sometimes waking up, but never for long. The memories of those days were even more shadowy than it had been in the tunnel he had fallen into.

He was awake and ready to make some changes. Getting out of the chamber would be a good start. He knew he needed a shower and something to eat. The red lights came on again and, after a few seconds, the strange conical thing appeared above the chamber. Jack turned his head and discovered a side window. Through it, he saw that the thing above him had legs.

"What is going on?" Jack asked.

"You're in recovery, Sergeant," the doctor said. "How do you feel?"

"Confused," he said. "How's a grunt like me getting seen by a real MD and not a scan bot or med droid?"

"That's a good question. You were hurt pretty bad. How do you feel now?"

"Tired of being in this tin can," Jack said, his temper flaring. It was a persistent problem he had never been able to conquer. "When are you going to let me out?"

"That's a good question. You're in quarantine for now," the doctor said. "Your scans look very promising, though. Are you in pain?"

"No," Jack said. "Am I on narcs or pain meds of some kind?"

"Negative, Sergeant. You haven't been on anything for days, but you suffered a traumatic injury. Are you sure nothing hurts? What about ringing in your ears or halos around the lights?"

"No, sir," Jack said. "But I'm feeling restless. I want out."

"Can't do that, not for a few more days, I'm afraid."

"What about food?"

"Can't do that either. Are you hungry?"

"Starving," Jack said. "Never been so hungry in all my life. Look, doc, I appreciate all you've done, but I'm fine. Can you just let me out? I want to rejoin my platoon."

"All in good time, Sergeant. Delta Platoon is in quarantine. You encountered an alien life form during your time on the planet. Do you remember that?"

"Pretty hard to forget getting stepped on," Jack said. "I don't remember much else about it."

"That level of contact requires two full weeks in quarantine, followed by another ten days in isolation. It's for the good of everyone on board. I'm sure you can understand that."

"Two weeks in here?" Jack asked, his irritation showing.

"Fraid so, Sergeant. The good news is you've been in there for ten days already. Just four more to go, and then you'll have a room all to yourself. Nothing wrong with that, I imagine."

It was rare to get any time alone in a space vessel. Marines typically lived, trained, ate and even showered together. Platoons were tight that way. Jack's closest friends were all in Delta. They had been on the Intrepid for nearly six months. They would rotate off the next time they were in the Sol system, where they could enjoy a couple of weeks leave before shipping out on another Fleet vessel.

"And I can't eat?"

"There's no way to get food into your pod and no place for your body to dispose of waste either. So, you'll get all the nutrients you need via the hydration tube. I'll load up a protein mix now. That should take the edge off your hunger."

It was far from what he wanted, but it was better than nothing. The doctor activated the hyperbaric chamber's entertainment screen that was built into the lid of the pod. Jack could watch movies or read. There were audiobooks, too, and videos of exotic places. He could load a beach scene and watch the waves rolling over the white sand for hours at a time if he wanted.

What he didn't have was the usual access to the ship's network. He couldn't message friends or read his email. Searching the ship's computer archives and information net was also off limits. The pod wasn't big enough to do much in. And the only respite was sleep. But he had slept enough in the last ten days to last him a long while.

Frustration set in hard. More than once, he screamed until his throat ached. Not that anyone could hear him, or cared. He sometimes pushed against the walls of the chamber. It was just barely big enough for him to roll over and lie on his side if he turned, shifted, slid back a little, then turned some more. But on his side or stomach, he couldn't see the entertainment screen. Nor could he see if the doctor came back in.

The doctor was his only chance to interact with another person. Jack had always thought of himself as a loner, but years of living in close contact with his platoon mates had changed him. He found himself yearning for conversation. His hunger was another issue. It hounded him day and night. He could drink down the protein mix the doctor loaded into the hyperbaric chamber's hydration system, but it did little to satisfy his appetite. It did fill his stomach and, while he was certain the taste of it was bad, he was so hungry it didn't matter. He sucked it down with gusto whenever it was available. Strangely enough, he didn't feel himself getting thinner. In fact, it was the opposite. He wasn't getting fat, but he could feel his muscles growing. It was strange. He could actually feel the tissue pulling apart and then regrowing.

Maybe it was all in his head. He chalked it up to a lack of intellectual stimulation. Plus, the hyperbaric chamber was meant to force more oxygen into his cells. It created a high-pressure, oxygen-rich atmosphere that promoted healing. Jack was certain that it worked because he felt better than he ever had in his whole life. Perhaps that came from the chamber, but he felt it was more likely an emotional response. He had come close to death, yet somehow he had survived. He would have to thank his platoon mates, who had pulled him out of the hole he had fallen into just as soon as they let him see and speak to people again.

Eventually, his liberation day arrived.

"Sergeant, we're going to let you out of the hyperbaric chamber," the doctor said.

"Where are you?" Jack asked, unable to see the physician through the chamber's windows like he normally could.

"I'm speaking to you from an observation room. You're still under quarantine."

He hadn't realized until that moment how much he longed to see another person. It just didn't feel right being so isolated. He had heard of people in solitary confinement going insane, but he never thought he would mind being all alone. He was wrong. The isolation was bothering him much more than he ever expected, but it was partly because he felt so good. He wanted to get up and move, to talk, to run and jump, but he felt completely stifled in the hyperbaric pod.

"The room has been arranged for you. We'll introduce solid foods if you feel up to it."

"I could eat a horse, doc," Jack said. "Bring it on."

"Alright, we'll start with the room lighting. I'll keep it on dim, but it might be a bit of a shock at first."

Light flooded through the windows of his hyperbaric chamber. Jack closed his eyes, expecting the light to hurt, but it didn't.

"I'm fine, doc. Open this thing up," he said.

There was a sudden, sharp, burning sensation in his groin. He instinctively reached down and felt the catheter slide out of him.

"Ouch, hey, you could have warned me," he growled.

"Sorry, Sergeant. We find it's best to just do it as quickly as we can," the doctor said. "You can remove the leads on your chest and back, too."

The pod opened with a hiss as Jack began to pull the sticky pads from his body.

"You'll feel your ears pop as your body adjusts to the air pressure in your room," the doctor explained. "I advise you to take things slow. You suffered a tremendous injury on PB 4827. There's no need to rush things."

"You can put a rush on that food," Jack said.

He sat up easily and waited for dizziness or a sense of unsteadiness, but there was none. In fact, he felt good. With a twist, he swung his bare feet out over the side of the chamber. Standing up felt surprisingly good. He looked around, unimpressed by the size of the room. But then everything on a starship was usually designed to be compact. The hyperbaric chamber was against one wall. Opposite that was a small bunk. There was a single padded chair next to a small desk. And at the other end of the tiny room was a shower stall and toilet. Jack thought it seemed more like a prison cell than a hospital room. He was starting to question if he was in quarantine or the brig.

The door to the room was oval with a thick locking bar that was visible on his side. There was no handle or controls for the door and Jack guessed they would be on the opposite side. Next to the door was a transfer drawer. It was opened from the outside, then sealed shut before he was allowed to access it. The drawer was designed to be germ-free, with harsh UV lights, and one-way air flow that passed through a series of medical-grade filters.

On the bunk, there was a set of neatly folded, almost paper-thin scrubs. He pulled them on and then paced in his room for a few minutes until the food arrived. It was standard shipboard fare, but there was plenty of it. A bowl of oatmeal, protein wafers that looked like sausage and tasted a little like meat. There were reconstituted eggs, toast with butter, and a fruit cup. There was also a sealed bottle of orange juice, a package of instant coffee, another of powdered creamer, and several packages of sugar.

"Is there hot water for the coffee?" Jack asked as he dug into the food.

"The water from the wash basin gets very hot," the doctor said. "You'll find a mug in your locker, but you'll want to wash the utensils that came on your tray. We don't want to clutter your space up too much with items that can be reused."

Jack ate everything on the tray, even the syrup his fruit had been packaged in. Then he made himself a cup of coffee. The doctor was right about the hot water. It was steaming and satisfyingly warm as he drank it down. His appetite was ravenous, but his stomach had shrunk in the ten days he had gone without solid foods. It took a while for his digestive system to work through what he put into it, but he felt satisfied after his meal.

"How do you feel, Sergeant? Any cramping or nausea?"

"No, sir," Jack said. "I'm right as rain, doc, and ready to get back to my platoon. I want to get back to training."

Looking down at his body, he could see that things were different. He had always been lean, but the muscles in his chest, abdomen, thighs, and arms were somehow larger and more pronounced. He was ripped and that surprised him. Even during boot camp, he had never had so little body fat. Jack could see not just muscles, but veins and even striations on the larger muscles such as his pectorals. He wasn't big like a bodybuilder, although he had somehow gotten buff in quarantine.

"There will be time for that," the doctor said, "but you've got four more days of quarantine yet. And when that's over, we'll be back at Titan."

That was a bit of a surprise. Jack hadn't realized he was so close to the end of his current deployment, but he didn't mind either. He was anxious to get out in the open and put himself through his paces.

"And Sergeant, we need to have a discussion about your platoon."

"Sure," Jack said. "Are they all in quarantine too?"

"They were," the doctor said. "But your drop ship was exposed to a burst of heavy gamma radiation on the flight back to the *Intrepid*. Are you familiar with radiation exposure?"

Jack was. Part of his basic training had been learning to recognize symptoms of exposure to certain elements. At the time, he found it boring. But the information suddenly came rushing back and he considered how he felt. Maybe the euphoric mental state was a side effect of the radiation that was masking a breakdown of his body's vital organs. But that didn't make any sense. They wouldn't have let him out of the hyperbaric pod if he was dying.

"Yes, sir," he replied.

"Are you experiencing any of them?"

"No, sir," Jack said. "I feel good. My mind is clear. No vision impairment. My skin is free of blisters or boils. I'm not nauseous, or cramping, or bleeding from my nose or gums. Sir, I feel exceptional."

"That's good news, Sergeant. Unfortunately, that was not the case with your platoon mates. Gamma rays are photons with the shortest wavelengths and highest frequencies in the EM spectrum. Because they don't have mass, the photons penetrate and pass through most materials, including the hull of the drop ship. We've studied the effects of these rays for decades, Sergeant. In almost every circumstance, they are harmful to humans. They can damage DNA inside your cells, sort of scramble the code, if you will. Most people either exhibit radiation sickness or develop cancer within days of exposure. For some reason I can not yet explain, you seem to have avoided both of those outcomes."

Jack felt like the deck was falling out from under him, just like the ground had done when he was caught in the sinkhole from the collapse of the underground tunnel. His heart was thundering in his chest, not from fear for his safety, but for that of his friends.

"Delta Platoon?" he asked, his voice thick with emotion.

"They're gone, Sergeant. As are the pilots who flew the drop ship. You are the only survivor."

The words were like physical blows: *only survivor*. It didn't seem real. How could it be? Tony, Picard, Franzitti, and Mason were dead? Lieutenant Spade and Staff Sergeant O'Neil hadn't survived? He sat down on his bunk for the first time since getting out of the hyperbaric chamber.

"Are you okay, Sergeant?" the doctor asked.

The answer was no. He was shocked, angry, frightened, and frustrated. He wanted to tear the door off his isolation room and go find his friends. They couldn't be dead, it didn't make any sense. And if they were, how had he survived?

Jack nodded. In the Marines, if you weren't dead, you were okay. Pain could be ignored. Injuries could be overcome. Grief could be felt later. A Marine didn't quit.

"Yeah, I'm okay," he lied.

"That's good, Sergeant. I know the news is a lot to take in, but you've got time to work through it. When we reach Titan, you'll be moved to a medical transport and taken down to the Space Command's research facilities."

"Am I showing signs of radiation sickness on the scans?" Jack asked as fear's icy breath blew cold against the back of his neck.

"Negative, Sergeant. There are no signs of radiation contamination or cellular disruption in your medical scans. In fact, your body has healed much more quickly than expected."

"Then why am I being sent to a med lab?"

"Please, try to understand, Sergeant. You and your body's reaction to the gamma radiation exposure is highly unique. Your service to Space Command and, ultimately to the entire human race, is to allow us to learn what makes you special."

"I don't feel special," Jack said.

"That's to be expected. Don't let your grief overshadow the incredible opportunity you've got here, Sergeant. The change in your cells could lead to breakthroughs that change the course of humanity's future. I, for one, am thrilled to have the opportunity to learn from you."

Jack slid back on the bunk and pulled his feet up onto the edge. It felt good to bend his knees and hips as he wrapped his arms around his knees, but he felt guilty for that. How could he feel so good when all his friends were dead? If they hadn't been forced to rescue him, would they still be alive? Despite the way his body felt, his emotions wracked him. And for the first time since waking up, he was glad he was alone.

3

The next four days passed slowly. Jack spent time between breakfast and lunch exercising. Sit-ups, push-ups, squats, stretches, anything he could think to do in his little room. There wasn't much space, but with nothing better to do and a high amount of energy to burn, he stayed in motion.

Afternoons, he napped, even though he didn't feel the need to. After dinner, he ran in place. The second day of his wait, Doctor Zeldin supplied Jack with a resistance band. Like most Marines, he had made fun of people using them, but he put his to work with as many different exercises as he could dream up. Any sort of resistance helped, and the band was long enough to use in a variety of ways.

When they reached orbit around Titan, his wait to get out of the tiny room ended. Doctor Zeldin and a technician arrived with what looked like an Egyptian sarcophagus.

"What's this?" Jack asked.

"It's for your protection," Zeldin said.

"That's hard to believe," Jack replied.

"I told you that you are the most valuable asset to Space

Command, maybe ever," Cal Zeldin said. "This is just a safety crash case."

"For what purpose?"

"In case the transport crashes."

"Do they do that often?" Jack said. "I've never heard of it."

"Well, it isn't impossible," the doctor continued. "And, it will keep you from catching any sort of bug or germ on the way through the *Intrepid*."

"I get the feeling that it's to keep me from spreading anything to the crew of the ship."

"Believe me, if they knew what you've got, Sergeant, they would all give their right arm to get it," Zeldin said. "Now, get inside. That's an order."

Orders... Jack had always obeyed them. It was the Marine Corps way; you did what you were told, when you were told and how you were told. It didn't matter what it was; Marines always got the job done. Even so, Jack was starting to get a bad feeling. He was no one special, despite what the doctor thought. His survival was a fluke; they just hadn't figured that out yet. Soon enough, he would be sent back to the front lines to do what he was best at.

Fighting had always come naturally to Jack. As a child, his mother insisted on calling him by his middle name, Dominic, or Dom for short. She wasn't keen on the allusion of his name to the old power tool used to break rocks and concrete. His father, on the other hand, wanted his son to be strong. The population controls on Earth only allowed for one child per couple. His parents would get no second chances, so they named their son to be strong under any conditions.

The Marine Corps hadn't tried to stifle Jack's naturally violent tendencies. In fact, they valued them. Instead of changing Jack's sometimes contrarian instincts, they simply steered him in the direction he wanted to go. And Jack had never complained or even so much as questioned that direction... until he was told to get into the strange-looking pod.

Outside his medical room was a rather dull-looking hallway with doors on either side that looked the same as his own. It was the med bay quarantine section, sterile and boring. Jack had the instinct to run. He could have easily pushed past the med tech and Dr. Zeldin. Neither were armed. But where would he go? Even if they had lied to him about everything, he couldn't just return to his platoon. He was on a military ship and there was no safety for someone who disobeyed orders on board the *Intrepid.*

He stepped into the pod and turned around. It had a thickly padded seat. The med tech closed the doors, which sealed. There were controls on the outside. Dr. Zeldin made the portion directly in front of Jack's face transparent so he could see what was happening. Then they wheeled him through the ship. It was an odd sensation. They passed other members of the ship's crew, even a group of Marines. They paid him no attention. It was as if the med tech was moving a piece of equipment and didn't garner any curiosity from the people they passed by.

They wound through the ship's many corridors and took a lift down to the hangar bay. There, Jack was loaded into a medical ship, which launched almost as soon as his pod was secured. As the flight crew worked to put him in the proper position, Jack saw Dr. Zeldin with Captain Kittle. They spoke to one another, both men laughed, then, to Jack's surprise, they got on board the medical transport. He couldn't see where they sat. He was in the rear section and there must have been either a passenger section or room in the cockpit.

The ship took off and made the insertion into Titan's highly altered atmosphere. What had once been mostly nitrogen, with methane and ethane gas, had been filtered to extract the unbreathable gases. The methane was used in a process called "Cracking", as fuel for the furnaces, which heated the ethane to convert it to ethylene and propylene where fashioned into plastics for all sorts of applications, both on Titan and in space. Saturn's moon also had massive stores of underground water and ammonia. There were still big refineries working to convert the moon's massive deposits of liquid methane into propulsion fuel for munitions and ammonia into a wide variety of chemical applications, including fertilizer. Titan, cold and distant, was covered with greenhouses that produced most of the food, which was used in space travel both in and outside the Sol system.

There was little chance of the transport crashing. It was commanded by two veteran pilots, who had little to do as the ship's autopilot did most of the flying. The computer system was in perfect sync and had much faster reaction times to the myriad amount of data that was collected by the ship's external systems, as well as the constant data stream from ground control stations, satellites and orbital stations. The transport descended swiftly and landed smoothly. Jack was soon wheeled out and through a different set of winding corridors in Space Command's sprawling network of buildings. They bypassed the medical facility and went instead to the research and development laboratories.

Jack was put into another sterile room, this one a bit larger and without a hyperbaric chamber taking up a large portion of the available space. It had a proper bathroom and shower. He was given sweat pants and sweat shirts, along with athletic socks and Marine-issue running shoes. The food was slightly better, with Titan having large meat-growing machines that produced a variety of artificial animal products. There were also fresh-grown vegetables instead of freeze-dried and rehydrated vegetables that required chemicals to maintain their taste.

His room had the standard desk and rolling chair, but it also had a recliner and an entertainment console. Still, the trappings of a better prison didn't put the idea of being confined to a space not of his choosing out of his mind. Nor was he happy when the officers, all non-combat personnel, but still outranking him, began their battery of tests.

The first day was filled with simple scans and blood draws. He was required to collect his urine and provide stool samples. There was no doubt that he was being watched around the clock and, when he exercised, it was only in a space with medical sensors, and while he was attached to various probes, from one that fit over his mouth and nose to measure his oxygen intake, to little devices that measured the salt content of his sweat.

The second day was worse. DNA swabs weren't enough; the researchers began taking biopsies from his major organs and samples from his bone marrow. To ensure purity in the tests, no analgesic or pain medication was administered either before or after the samples and biopsies were taken. His body was shaved from head to toe against his consent, and despite the painful tests, he was forced to run ten miles on a treadmill, and then forced to sleep naked and without sheets or blankets so the wounds could be observed as they healed.

It was the one saving grace in the situation. His body was changing. He knew it had healed rapidly after the incident on PB 4827, but he hadn't known the extent of his injuries or how much the hyperbaric chamber had aided that recovery. But after the painful samples were taken, he was still able to complete the ten-mile run in record time and could see the incisions the researchers had made in their collections from his body healing up. By morning, there was hardly even a visible mark where the cuts had been.

So began a more invasive, undeniably sadistic series of tests. Jack was cut open in various places on his body, in varying lengths and depths. The researchers collected his blood and shaved off portions of skin and muscle tissue. It was all for research, all for the good of mankind, Jack was told, but it was hellacious torture to him.

On the fourth day, he fought back. The researchers were expecting his outburst; in fact, they were measuring how much he could take before he turned violent. By that point, Dr. Cal Zeldin was sick over the treatment of Sergeant Jack Hammer. The man had done nothing to deserve such harsh treatment, yet the researchers were treating him no better than a science fair project. Their scientific measure of his tolerance to pain seemed more like frat boys taking bets on who would beat their football team first.

And to his horror, Captain Kittle joined right in. In fact, at one point, he asked if he could perform the test. Only it wasn't a test, it was torture. The power that Sergeant Hammer had lay in his altered DNA, and they had plenty of that from the non-invasive tests taken the very first day he arrived. As for the deep issue samples, they were a crude way of confirming what the body scans had already shown. His muscles had greater density, more like an ape's than a human. His bones were more dense too, so hard that only diamond-tipped drills could penetrate them. His heart was stronger, his vessels and arteries larger, and perhaps more importantly, his red blood cells were more capable of transmitting oxygen throughout his body. The results were greater strength, speed, and stamina. But what the researchers really wanted to know was how his healing had become faster and more complete.

The human body was an amazing collection of interactive systems in various states of synchronization. Almost every part could heal, including the brain, which was one of the most flexible organs humans possessed. In that way, even though a machine analogy was helpful in understanding the basic processes of the human body, it failed to account for the way that humans could adapt to all sorts of environments and physical maladies.

What the body couldn't do was regrow parts they lost or that got damaged. A break would heal, a cut would seal back up, creating new tissue in the process. But if a person lost a finger or a limb, it wouldn't grow back. If a person broke their spinal column, causing damage to the nerve cluster, it couldn't self-repair. Nor could man, in his best efforts, create a workable substitution. Sergeant Hammer should have been bedridden for the rest of his life. In fact, Dr. Zeldin believed he should have died before he even reached the *Intrepid*, and before he was ever exposed to the gamma radiation. The break in his spine had been complete, like a tree limb that is snapped in half. No nerves from the base of his neck down were getting input from the brain, which should have kept him from breathing on his own, and more importantly, kept his heart from beating. Of course, there were documented cases of brain-dead patients taken off life support who lived for hours, sometimes days, without input from the brain. So, it wasn't miraculous that he had lived, but it was still surprising.

And the regrowth of those nerves was truly unbelievable. How each nerve found its mate and reconnected, he didn't know. It was a mystery. Even if they could find the exact changes to the Sergeant's DNA that put his body in regrowth mode, it didn't explain how it managed to reconnect the right way. There were millions of nerves in the spinal column, each one like a wire in a computer. You couldn't just randomly connect them. If even just one percent were mismatched, it would have been game over for Sergeant Hammer, yet his body had fully recovered.

And it continued to recover, first from the deep tissue samples taken without any sort of pain management. Then the even more sadistic tests. A deep, eight-inch gash took two days to heal. The shallow ones were even faster. Even more interesting, they left no scars and seemed to regain his blood volume overnight.

The only thing the researchers did in favor of their test subject was feed him. Hammer was eating a dozen eggs for breakfast and a quart of oatmeal. At every meal, he was eating three times the normal amount. And yet, despite the dramatic increase in calories, he gained no body fat. His muscles grew and his body healed. It was one of the most interesting parts of his transformation. If the researchers did nothing else but crack the code of his new metabolism, it would be worth trillions. Humans had always obsessed about their weight and looks. Likewise, the increase in strength, speed and stamina was enough to radically change the military. Enhanced soldiers that could fight longer and harder would be in great demand. Since humanity's venture into space, they had discovered a thriving galaxy full of intelligent, space-faring species. And, like one might expect, many of those species were in open conflict with one another. Space Command was supposed to be a defensive force, but for decades, humanity's leaders had traded military help for technological secrets. If the researchers could gain enough understanding of what had changed Sergeant Hammer into a super soldier, they could replicate that result in thousands of active duty Marines, creating an even greater demand for humanity's services in the galactic wars that raged across the stars.

But, despite all that, they seemed more focused on what he could endure. And when Jack Hammer finally fought back, Dr. Zeldin was silently cheering the Marine on.

Nor was he the only one.

4

Astra was not happy. As a native Titan, she had jumped at the chance to work at the Space Command headquarters. She had begun her career in janitorial, but had worked her way up to supply supervisor in the Research and Development department. Officially, she was an independent contractor, but her work with Space Command came with all the benefits that Marines and flight crews were eligible for. And for a long time, she enjoyed helping the various research teams conduct their work.

All that had changed with the arrival of Sergeant Hammer. There were still dozens of teams doing work on all sorts of development projects that she had no objections to, even though some were weapons creation that had the potential to kill thousands. They were a military R&D division, so it only made sense that they would develop the tools necessary to wage war. But what they were doing to Sergeant Hammer was not that.

She just happened to be in the medical lab restocking their supplies when Jack was brought in. They had him in a wheelchair, but it was obvious that he was in bad shape. Astra had heard the rumors. The subject was supposedly some type of super soldier with amazing regenerative abilities. She had seen the focus of the entire R&D division shift to this peculiar Marine. If the rumors were true, money had started pouring in and the medical researchers involved had become the superstars of Space Command. Nothing had been denied them, she knew that much, as new equipment worth billions of credits had been ordered and approved.

But the Marine in the wheelchair didn't seem like a super soldier to her. He seemed like a very sick man on the verge of death. He was naked for one thing, which she felt was uncalled for. She wasn't modest, but she felt that being stripped of one's clothing was humiliating. There were three researchers in the exam room where she was putting away the medical paraphernalia that was used every day to treat patients, carry out exams and do a wide array of medical research. Everything from IV tubing to microscope slides needed to be replaced. She had her back to the researchers and their victim in the wheelchair, but she was watching them in the reflection of a polished paper towel dispenser that she was slowly refilling.

The researchers pulled Hammer to his feet, which is when she saw the angry red lines across his chest, abdomen and each thigh. At first, she thought they were lines drawn with markers, but then she realized they were cuts as blood oozed from one of the lacerations. The patient's skin was very white. His body had no hair except for stubble on his head and across his square chin. They stood him up against an exam table with hydraulic controls that could raise into an upright position. She saw thick straps used for holding the patient down, and then she noticed Hammer's eyes. His body seemed weak, although his eyes were like those of a caged tiger.

With a sudden lunge, he pushed the two physicians holding his arms back. The third was bent low, reaching for a strap that was meant to be placed across the patient's ankles and hold his legs down to the table. Hammer drove his right knee hard into the researcher's face. Blood exploded from the physician's nose as he reared back and fell to the ground.

One of the other researchers drew a syringe from his pocket, the type with a long, titanium needle. It was filled with a sedative, Astra guessed as the physician tried to stab the instrument into Hammer's flesh. But the Marine saw it coming and caught the researcher's hand by the wrist. The physician screamed in pain and Hammer drove a powerful side kick into the chest of the third researcher, who went flying across the room and hit the cabinet close enough to Astra that she heard the man's bones snap. He dropped to the floor and didn't move.

Meanwhile, Hammer twisted the man with the syringe's arm so that the metal needle was pointed back at his chest. Then he pushed hard enough that the needle penetrated the researcher just below his collarbone, completely burying the metal injector.

"Wait!" the physician begged. "It's too much."

"Looking for a little mercy, pal? Too bad, we're fresh out!" Hammer said as he pressed the plunger down and injected the full syringe into the man's chest.

Astra felt a shiver of fear. She felt sorry for the patient, and yet, she knew he was a killer, the type of man who didn't hesitate to take a life. Maybe the Marines had trained him to be that way or maybe it was already his nature, but she felt herself trembling as he turned toward her.

"How do I get out?" he asked.

"You can't," she said.

"We'll see," he snapped.

Sergeant Hammer was what the researchers called him. Astra had never spoken to the man. Yet she felt compassion for him just the same. Had she been able to help him, she probably would have done it. Yet she knew enough about the facility to know there was no clear way out.

Hammer ran past her and through the glass doors into what looked like a small vestibule. In fact, there were lockers in that space, and one might assume the people working in the lab kept their personal belongings there. The lockers were filled with emergency equipment such as gas masks, iodine pills and hazmat suits.

Hammer tried to open the other door, but it was locked. Behind him, the glass door to the lab closed. He turned and Astra could see him. He realized at that moment that he had made a mistake. As the sleeping gas pumped into the room from a fixture in the ceiling, he looked at her and tried to open the glass door, but it was locked too.

"Help me," he said.

She didn't respond, didn't move, but inwardly she made a decision that she wasn't sure she could carry out. What she knew for certain was that it was the right decision. The patient, Sergeant Hammer, needed help. Somehow, someway, she determined to give it to him.

He looked down at his body as clouds of some chemical agent began to fill the small vestibule. There was blood running freely from his previous wounds. He turned with his back against the glass door and slid down to the floor. Only then did she notice that there were more lacerations on his back. Blood smeared down the glass.

The man with the broken nose groaned, then coughed up more blood. She went to him and helped him roll onto his side so that he didn't choke on the blood that still pulsed from his nose. Both of his eyes were already swollen down to mere slits, and she realized that Hammer's knee strike had broken more than the researcher's nose.

"Just breathe," she told him. "It's over. Help is on the way."

She moved over to where the second researcher lay with the needle still sticking out of his chest. She pulled it free and checked his pulse. It was weak, but there was a heartbeat. With nothing more she could do for him, she turned to the third man. He lay unmoving and, after a quick check, she realized he wasn't breathing either. Right above her on the cabinet was a manual breath pump. She rolled the researcher over and grabbed the pump. It had a mask that covered a person's mouth and nose. She set it in place, held it down, then pumped the plastic bag. She saw the man's chest rise and fall.

After two breaths with the pump, she checked for a pulse. Astra had no medical training, but she had seen people perform CPR on television. The man's heart wasn't beating. She stood up, pulled down a portable defibrillator, and ripped open the man's button-up shirt. He was soft and slightly overweight, with patches of brown hair on his chest and stomach. Astra was suddenly struck by the difference between the researcher and the patient. Hammer had been all muscle and strength; the researcher was soft, weak and probably wouldn't survive. She pressed the sticky tabs to his chest and let the device takeover. It took a reading, then shocked him. On the display screen, she saw that no heartbeat was recorded. A small needle came out of the automated device and injected adrenaline into the researcher, then it shocked him two more times. But it was all to no avail. He was dead and Astra felt herself trembling again.

A few minutes later, the outer door to the vestibule opened. The sedative gas had already been pumped out by the room's sophisticated ventilation system. The men who came into the room were military police with body armor and weapons. They didn't hesitate or take precautions because of the patient's wounds. They just put his hands into thick, plastic restraints. His ankles, too, then lifted him onto a gurney that used repulser lift technology instead of wheels. One man pressed a button and the device rose up into the air about waist high, then another MP pushed the patient out the main door.

A few seconds later, a doctor in a white coat came in. The name on his badge said Zeldin, Cal MD. He led a team of medical technicians in with more gurneys. They quickly put the sedated researcher on one and gave him a shot in the shoulder with something Astra guessed would counteract the drug he had been trying to inject into Sergeant Hammer.

Dr. Zeldin went to the man with the broken nose.

"Lie still, Conrad," he ordered, before activating a medical scanner which he held over the researcher's face.

"Hurths... hurths bad," the researcher cried.

"Not surprising," Zeldin said. "You've got broken bones across your face. Here," he told him as he gave the man a small injection, "this will help. You'll need surgery. Just hang on."

They put him on a gurney and Zeldin gave directions to have him moved to emergency trauma care. Only then did they turn to the corpse of the third researcher. Zeldin glanced down at the automated medical device. There was no need to ask if the man it was connected to was alive or dead. The device wouldn't have shut itself down had there been any chance to revive the researcher.

"This won't go over well," Zeldin said.

"That man... the patient..." Astra said.

"This is all highly classified," Zeldin said, but she could sense he felt almost as frustrated by it as she did. "I'm sorry you were caught up in it."

"What are they doing... to him?" Astra asked, her voice quivering along with the rest of her body.

"That's an excellent question," Dr. Zeldin said. "Why don't you come with me. We'll get you something to help calm you down."

"Tea," she said. "I just need a few minutes."

"I've got tea," Zeldin said.

He took her arm. It was a kind gesture, but she felt almost like he was laying claim to her. At first, she didn't understand. His possessiveness felt a bit frightening. Then she met Captain Kittle, and things became clearer.

5

“Wait!” a tall man with graying hair snapped. He wore a captain's uniform and spoke with authority. There weren't many starship commanders in the R&D division and Astra didn't know the man by sight, but he clearly had authority. The medical technicians moving the unconscious researcher stopped. The captain lifted the physician's wrist and looked at it.

"Broken," the captain said. "How do you like that?"

"I doubt he likes it at all," Dr. Zeldin said.

The captain turned his attention to Zeldin and Astra, giving the techs a wave of dismissal.

"He broke it with one hand," the captain remarked. "I want complete X-rays and let's make sure Dr. Hallard isn't suffering from some type of brittle bone disease. My money is on Hammer's sheer strength. Imagine being able to snap another man's arm just by squeezing it?"

"That's not something I would imagine doing, even if I were capable of it," Zeldin said.

"Where are you taking the help?"

"To my office," Zeldin said.

"She hurt?"

"She's traumatized."

"Hang on," the captain said, stepping in front of Zeldin. "Does she even have clearance?"

"She's a civilian contractor in charge of supplies. And yes, she's been vetted and has clearance. Everyone working in this building has it."

"I don't want loose lips letting word out about what Hammer can do," the captain said. "You know not to talk, but I don't even want to hear that you're gossiping with the other maids, you hear me? I'll have you drummed out of here if I catch even one hint that you told anyone what you saw back there."

"Captain, please," Zeldin said. "She's been through enough. Let us pass."

The tall officer stepped aside, but he wasn't finished. Astra felt that if Zeldin hadn't been with her, the captain might have hurt her. It was the first time she had ever felt endangered at work.

"This isn't just top secret research, here. We're talking major applications across the spectrum. It absolutely has to be classified. Make sure she understands that, Zeldin. She could be locked up for treason if she talks."

The doctor kept Astra moving and when they turned the corner, he sighed. "I'm sorry. I think everyone is losing their minds."

Doctor Cal Zeldin had been assigned an office in the medical research division. His deployment on the *Intrepid* was over and, until he was given a new assignment, he was allowed to observe and assist in the research with Sergeant Hammer. Captain Kittle was also part of the team as a field consultant, which Zeldin didn't think was necessary. He certainly hadn't been asked his opinion about anything, nor had he made any useful suggestions or observations since they had arrived on Titan. Instead, he was simply riding the wave of success that had fallen into his lap.

When they reached Zeldin's office, he unlocked the door with his keycard and helped Astra into a soft, leather chair. In one corner of the room was a drink dispenser. He opened a box with tea bags inside, put one into a cup, then filled it with hot water.

"I hope chamomile is alright," he said. "I drink it sometimes to help me sleep."

"It's fine," Astra said, taking the cup and wrapping both hands around the warm ceramic as she breathed in the aroma from the tea. "Thank you."

Zeldin fixed himself a cup of coffee, then sat in the guest chair beside Astra instead of behind his desk.

"I know I'm not supposed to talk about what I saw," she said. "And I won't, but..."

"But what you saw wasn't right," the doctor said. "It wasn't ethical, I know. I'm wrestling with all that as well."

"Why?" she asked.

"Something happened to him," Zeldin said, referring to Sergeant Hammer. "I can't say what because I don't know, but it is good. If we can figure out what it is and how it happened, we could do a lot of good, maybe even more good than anyone has ever done before. Eradicate disease, lengthen life spans, heal people who are suffering... but I don't agree with how that research is being done. I don't think most people would."

"They're torturing him," Astra said. "He had cuts all over his body!"

"That's right," Zeldin said. "The key is in his DNA, which we have in droves. Now, they're just seeing how much his body can take. It won't help the cause that he killed Emil Lowinstine ... and if Conrad or Sagan come back to the project, they'll no doubt want revenge. It's despicable."

"And there's nothing we can do about it?"

Zeldin looked up. The woman sitting across from him was a decade younger than he was, with no higher education, a civilian contract laborer. She had lived on Titan all her life. He was a medical doctor and had traveled across the galaxy. He had seen other worlds and other intelligent races. He had even visited space installations that were larger than many planets, some orbiting stars, others built completely around them. He knew there were secrets to the universe that the human race didn't even know existed and many that they would never be able to comprehend. He felt a connection to the woman in his office, and he also felt an obligation to his species, to do whatever it took to unlock the secrets that were contained in Sergeant Hammer's body.

"I didn't say that," he admitted. "But there isn't much we can do. A little groundwork, maybe. Ultimately, we could give Sergeant Hammer the tools to do something about his situation, but that's about all."

"I think we should," the woman replied. "My name is Astra."

"I'm Cal," he said. "We're talking about breaking the oath I took to serve Space Command to the best of my ability."

"I don't think this is the best," she said. "Hurting that man, for whatever reason, isn't right."

Cal agreed. If it were up to him, they would keep Sergeant Hammer for the rest of his enlistment and then give him whatever it would take for the man to re-up. They could do medical testing that wouldn't hurt him, but he also understood there were military applications that needed to be discovered as well. Zeldin felt there were better ways to discover what Sergeant Hammer was really capable of.

"They won't just let him go, you know," Zeldin said. "Even if he gets away, they'll go after him."

"He doesn't stand a chance if we do nothing," she said.

"It's not much of a chance either way," Zeldin said. "Getting him out of the building is just the first step. He would need a place to hide, and a way to get off Titan, probably out of the Sol system altogether."

"A new identity," Astra said. "Money, clothes, some way to change his appearance."

"It would be impossible without help," the doctor said, leaning back in his chair and twisting his mug in his hands. "And that means we'll be on the run too."

"What could they do to us?"

"We would fall into the military justice system. It's autonomous and doesn't have the same protections you're used to. They could lock us away forever with no opportunity to plead our case to an objective third party. And that would probably be the best outcome."

"They might do worse?"

"Oh, yes. Treason is a capital offense," Zeldin said. "And you've seen what the people here are capable of."

They sat in silence for a while, then Astra spoke up. "It still isn't right."

"You're determined then?"

"I can't live with myself as if I don't know what's happening to that man."

"You don't owe him anything," Zeldin pointed out.

"If I do nothing, I'm complicit with the people who are hurting him," she said. "I don't know what I can do, but... something has to be done. What if we leak the story to the press?"

"They'll just move him and deny everything," Zeldin said. "It would ruin your life and wouldn't help Sergeant Hammer."

"I don't have money," she said. "I don't know the kind of people who could give someone a new identity. But I do know Titan. I've lived in Prime City all my life. I could get him to the shipyard. There are vessels that would take him off-world. It happens occasionally."

"I can't let you take that risk," Zeldin said.

"I won't stand by and do nothing."

"No, and neither will I," he told her. "So, how about this? You show me. Show me where to hide, how to get him on a vessel bound for another system. Then, I'll take him. If we get caught, you had nothing to do with it."

Astra looked up. She studied the doctor's face, trying to decide what she thought of his plan. At last, she nodded in agreement.

"Alright, for now, just go back to your normal routine. We don't need to be seen together on campus. Where can we meet?"

"The Omega, it's a bar. Have you heard of it?"

"No," Zeldin admitted. He had been on Titan many times and spent some of his leave in the city, but he wasn't familiar with the establishment she was talking about.

"It's a local joint," Astra admitted. "On the low side, about eight blocks south of the Space Command complex. Don't do a search for it. We can't leave a trail they might find."

"Good thinking," Zeldin told her. "I'll find it. When? We need to wait a few days. This weekend, maybe? Saturday night?"

She nodded and stood up. "Saturday night, seven o'clock. Be careful."

"You too."

She set her teacup down on his desk and stood up.

"I'll go back to work now. Thank you, doctor."

"My pleasure," he said, opening the door for her.

She hurried out and Cal Zeldin went to his desk. He felt like an idiot. Had he really just agreed to help Sergeant Hammer escape from Space Command? It was insanity. He was talking about throwing away his entire future. Of course, he could go and report the conversation he had just had. That would relieve him of any wrongdoing. But he had been around the block enough to know that it would also make the people in charge nervous. He would find himself on a ship bound for a distant star system within days of reporting on Astra. While he might salvage his career, he would be ruining her life completely. They wouldn't just fire her; they would interrogate her and do who knew what until she talked. That thought alone filled him with dread. But he hadn't seen the crossroads he was approaching. His conscience had led him to a place he had never expected to go and, in doing so, he had crossed an invisible line in the sand. There was no going back. He could go forward, or he could choose something less risky and more destructive to Astra and Sergeant Hammer. But he didn't think he would live with himself knowing that he had sent a kind-hearted and courageous young woman into dire straits with no warning.

He leaned back in his chair and contemplated the realization that his life wouldn't be the easy, highly compensated, leisurely drift into his golden years that he had been expecting it to be. There would be no membership in elite clubs or vacations at exclusive resorts. In fact, the easy part of his life had already been lived. There would be no more long cruises with almost no responsibilities. He would be looking over his shoulder the rest of his life, and if he was caught... well... that was too dire to even contemplate.

6

Jack woke up with a start only to find that he was strapped down to his bed. The room he had occupied was gone. He was in a lab and all pretense of treating him like a human being was gone.

"Ah, you're awake," one of the researchers said as he rolled over on a stool with casters. "Let me just record the time."

Jack heard typing. No one used keyboards or writing utensils in the research lab. Everything was typed onto touchscreen devices. The sadistic pricks who were holding him against his will all seemed to have fingernails long enough that they made tiny tapping sounds on the glass touch screen. Jack didn't bother to learn their names. Every day was a different group of researchers. The only thing they had in common was their white lab coats and their sadistic idea of research.

As he lay on the table, which was some type of cold metal, they had abandoned any pretense of his comfort and he stared up at the ceiling. There was a large environmental unit right above him. Air was flowing through narrow vents and he could just make out industrial nozzles positioned just inside the vents. More gas, he figured, in case he found a way to escape, which was all that was on his mind.

Sergeant Jack Hammer had never veered too far out of bounds since joining the Space Command Marine Corps. He had entertained relationships with a few female Marines, but never let them get too serious. He had sampled contraband spirits, usually the kind distilled somewhere on the ship, while deployed between star systems. He was not a heavy drinker and certainly not a womanizer. He had never disobeyed a direct order and had never gone AWOL. That would change the first chance he got. He would have died in the line of duty, but he wasn't willing to let the Corps - or Space Command was perhaps the more responsible entity - continue torturing him. The one thing he felt certain of was that the researchers would eventually kill him. They seemed to think their job was to test his limits under all sorts of stressful and dangerous conditions. What could his unique ability to heal cope with? He didn't know and, unfortunately, the researchers were intent on finding out.

Without being able to move much, or even look down at his own body since they had his head strapped to the table, he was forced to judge his condition by how he felt. What he felt were the lacerations that had been inflicted on him over the last two days. There were deep cuts across his chest, back, abdomen, and thighs. They were healing, and he could admit that they were healing faster than anyone might expect. But his recent scuffle had torn them open. He could feel the all too familiar burning sensation across his right thigh, his stomach and his back in several places. The pain wasn't debilitating, but it was sharp. The researchers didn't bother with trying to mediate his pain. Nor did they do anything to help the lacerations they inflicted on him to heal. There was no stitching up the wounds or even bandaging them. He expected their instruments to be sterile, but he also feared that it was only a matter of time before they started using dirty blades on purpose.

"Alright, time for today's experiments," the researcher on the stool said. "My name is Osborn. If you have questions, Sergeant, don't hesitate to ask."

"You going to keep me trussed up like an animal?" Jack asked.

"Well, considering that you murdered Dr. Lowinstine, I think it's best if we take precautions. Just FYI: this lab has a variety of atmospheric gases, so even if you could get out of the straps, you wouldn't get far. There are a dozen people monitoring you at all times. So, try to relax. Struggling will only make things worse for you."

Jack silently cursed his luck. He wished he was dead. He wished that he had been killed when the big creature stepped on him. That would have been a mercy considering where he was. Perhaps, he mused, he really was in hell, just a very specialized hell destined to be tortured for all eternity.

Death is better had become his mantra. It was macabre, but he couldn't imagine any way out. He had no hope and that was, in a way, worse than what they were doing to his body.

"Today, we're going to be changing the test," the researcher said.

The man was still out of sight to Jack's right. But a blowtorch makes a unique sound when it is lit and burning. There was the tell-tale *~Fwuft!~* of the torch being ignited, followed by the soft roar as the expelled gas burned.

"Don't!" Jack said.

"Three-second exposure," the researcher said. They used audio and video recordings for the experiments, with the responsible party dictating their actions. "Torch is burning at two thousand, one hundred degrees Fahrenheit. We'll begin with the right shoulder."

"No!" Jack shouted. "Don't do it!"

The researcher ignored his protests. Three seconds felt like an eternity. Jack screamed in pain. He couldn't turn his head and look, but he could feel the skin blister, peel back, and blacken from the torch's flame. It burned deep into the thick muscle tissue, which puckered and blistered. Nor did the pain end when the three seconds were over. The pain was nearly as intense as it had been and it left Jack panting.

"You sick bastard!" Jack screamed.

But the torture continued as the researcher circled the exam table. "Next area will be the left hip."

The worst burn was on the sole of his right foot. The pain was so exquisite that Jack passed out. In the control room, researchers were monitoring the experiment along with a myriad of data collectors.

"His heart rate is one-seventy," one of the researchers said.

They went on, calling off blood pressure, brain activity, body temperature, blood oxygen levels, and a variety of medical information that was being collected. Dr. Cal Zeldin was part of the team, although he took no active role. Beside him was Captain Kittle, who, unlike Zeldin, found the experimentation to be exhilarating. Cameras recorded it all, some from wide angles, others zoomed in close on various parts of Jack's body.

"Spontaneous urination," someone called out.

"Patient is still unconscious," another researcher announced.

In the lab, Dr. Petros Igorivich began scraping tissue samples from the burns. Most of the researchers on the team had specialities. It was no surprise that Igorivich was in charge of the burn unit. And in the days to come, he had a variety of common military injuries that he planned to replicate, from laser blast wounds, to acid burns, contact with hot metal burns and plasma splatter burns. It was going to be a horrible week for Sergeant Hammer.

After the initial experiment, or torture, depending on their point of view, the researchers returned to their offices. Each one had a specific role on the team and all the data collected was available via the research cloud that their high-powered computer stations synced with. Dr. Zeldin was one of the lead researchers, as he had been the first to discover Sergeant Hammer with his advanced regenerative healing ability. But in reality, he was there as a courtesy. His job was to keep a record of the patient's recovery, but like most medical jobs, it was redundant. Everything, from the conditions of the experiments to the researchers thoughts on the patient, and all his vitals were constantly monitored and recorded by the R&D

computer system. Zeldin's real job was keeping tabs on Captain Kittle. The man had friends in the halls of power and had made a claim on Sergeant Hammer as if the patient was the Captain's own property. Kittle intended to ride the wave of discovery and historic importance into a position of great reward. He was in the research facility day after day, usually before anyone else arrived and staying until everyone else had left.

Kittle followed Zeldin back to his office, then helped himself to a cup of coffee, which he drank black and scalding hot.

"That was something," Kittle declared, sitting down with his coffee across from Zeldin's desk. "Hard to believe he didn't pass out until the third burn."

Zeldin nodded as he worked hard to keep a poker face. The truth was, he was repulsed by the experimentation. He was a physician, after all, and while he had been excited by the discovery of Sergeant Hammer's astounding regenerative ability, he had an instinct to help people. Seeing them hurt on purpose was repugnant to him.

"How long do you expect it to take to heal burns like that?" Kittle said after another sip of his coffee. "Third-degree burns damage nerve endings. I'm anxious to see if he regains sensation as the tissue heals, especially on the sole of his foot."

"Assuming it will regrow like the cuts and broken bones," Zeldin said.

"No reason to think it wouldn't," Kittle said. "It's fascinating. I had dinner with Commodore Ovander last night. The arrogant prick. He had no idea what we were working on. I do enjoy when people fawn all over me in the hopes that I'll let some juicy nugget of information slip."

"We shouldn't be talking about any of this," Zeldin said.

Kittle frowned. They weren't on a starship, which meant that technically Dr. Zeldin outranked the captain. On board a ship, the Captain was the ultimate authority, and Kittle was a tyrant. He didn't enjoy being told what he could do, or should do, by anyone.

"Don't forget that I'm the one who set all this in motion, Doctor.

Of course, I know what should be kept secret. I would never talk, even under extreme interrogation."

"I didn't mean to imply—"

"But you did," Kittle said, standing up suddenly. "I may not be a physician, but I put all of this together. It was my connections that afforded us this time and these resources. You serve at my discretion, Doctor. Never forget that."

He set his cup down and left Zeldin's office. It was in that moment that the doctor's decision solidified. He had still been weighing the pros and cons of helping Sergeant Hammer, but at that moment, Zeldin's delusions about life after his military service, burst like a bubble in a gust of wind. He suddenly realized that he would never have had the life he envisioned. No matter his credentials or post-military achievements, he would always be under someone's authority and therefore beholden to someone else's ideas and whims.

Two hours later, Admiral of the Fleet Evander Royce met with the heads of all Space Command departments. There was still lots of work being done across the galaxy. There were billions of planetary bodies that held fortunes in natural resources. Of the hundred or so known intelligent species, there was a race to lay claim to as much of the unexplored space as possible. The role of Space Command was to find, claim and defend as many resources as possible.

But with all the exciting developments across the galaxy, what the Admiral of the Fleet was most interested in was the Marine in R&D. As soon as the other Admirals completed their reports, he dismissed them. Keeping only Admiral Kathryn Ross behind. She was in charge of Command Logistics, which included the base they operated in on Titan. The Research & Development division wasn't her direct responsibility; that fell to Rear Admiral Duncan, a munitions engineer with a list of academic achievements and military inventions to his name. He was currently the director of Space Command's R&D division. Both Duncan and Ross were set to give reports, as well as the Captain, nominally in charge of the project, Frank Kittle.

"What developments do you have in the Hammer project?" Royce asked.

"I have suggestions for a new name," Ross joked.

"I rather like it," Duncan said

"Hammers have nothing to do with medical research," Ross pointed out.

"Which makes it ideal for security," Admiral Royce said. "Only a handful of people know of Project Hammer's existence. Anyone who comes across it won't guess what we're up to."

"Fair enough," Kathryn said. "I have Captain Kittle waiting outside. He'll give you an update on the experiments being carried out on the patient. What I can tell you is that we're making progress on isolating the DNA changes that Sergeant Hammer underwent during the gamma radiation surge."

"Is it something we'll be able to replicate?"

"In theory," Kathryn explained. "We're talking about cutting-edge genetic research here. How the Sergeant's body adapted is still a mystery. The research team is searching his genome for the answers. He must have some latent gene that left his DNA open to alteration without detriment to the entire chain of information. We've got Plato and Aristotle generative AI programs crunching the data. If there's an answer, we'll find it."

"Bring in the Captain," Royce said.

He was aware of Captain Frank Kittle. The man was old school, a hard-nosed space captain with a long history of getting things done. He had friends in Space Command and in government; many had served under him, only to go on and surpass his career achievements. By reputation, he had remained a captain because of his love of field command. But the rumors about his reckless use of the people under his command in order to achieve mission goals had foiled any chance of his moving up in rank.

The big door to the Star Command Cabinet opened. In walked

Kittle, shoulders back, head up, as if he were on inspection. He walked briskly to a spot behind Duncan and Ross and stood at attention.

"Captain, this is an informal report," Royce said. "Update us on what's taking place with Sergeant Hammer."

"Aye, Admiral," Kittle said, his eyes fixed on a point somewhere at the top of Evander Royce's head. "There are some things we were prepared for, but which still took us by surprise, sir."

"Someone died, is what I've heard," Admiral Royce said.

"That's correct, sir, Doctor Emil Lowinstine's back was broken when the patient lashed out in violence. Two other researchers were injured but survived the attack."

"He overcame three men?" the Admiral of the Fleet asked.

"Aye, Admiral, and he did it easily. We've been testing his regenerative ability, but all our tests show that Sergeant Hammer has gained impressive strength due to muscle density, more than mass, and also bone hardness. That's what we know for certain. I don't think he's aware of it yet, Admiral. So far, our methods of keeping him under control are working, but if he really wanted to break free, I'm told he probably could."

"What methods are being employed?" Royce asked.

"Cargo style straps," Kittle explained. "We have several around his body, arms, legs, and even his head."

"And you think he could break free of them?" Kathyrn Ross asked.

"If he was motivated. There's no way to really gauge his strength. But he showed incredible speed and strength during the altercation."

"What about the tests? Don't they weaken him?" Duncan asked.

"Temporarily," Kittle said. "He was in various stages of healing from previous tests across his body when the attack occurred. In fact, his violent actions resulted in several of the lacerations reopening slightly. But I was assured that any normal man in his state, even with weeks of time healing, wouldn't have the power to fight the way he did. Sergeant Hammer kicked Dr. Lowinstine so hard that he was sent flying across the room and into a countertop with enough force to snap his spine. He was killed instantly. All attempts to revive him failed."

"One kick?" Royce asked.

Kittle grinned. It made him look wicked, the Admiral thought, but his negative traits were being put to good use.

"Just one," Kittle replied. "Admiral, if we had a platoon of Marines like him, we could take any position on the battlefield. If we had an army like him?" Kittle shrugged his shoulders as if to say the possibilities were endless. "We would be unstoppable. Every species across the galaxy would fall at our feet."

"There's more to this research than creating super soldiers," Kathryn Ross said.

Royce wasn't surprised by her attitude. Her focus was on Star Command's assets, and perhaps the most important were the people who carried out the military's duties. Drones were useful and robotic fighting platforms had their place, but it was the people who made Humanity's fighting forces unique.

"We'll squeeze every last benefit from this opportunity that we can get," Royce said. "None of that is lost on me. I want to help sick children just as much as anyone else. I want to see our sailors and Marines healed in a timely manner and back in the field. But there are some unique aspects to this that we can't ignore. Thank you for the update, Captain Kittle. Carry on."

"Aye, Admiral," Kittle said loudly as he saluted, then turned on his heel and left.

"He's a piece of work," Kathryn said.

"But he's the right man for the job," Duncan said. "He demands results."

"Agreed," Royce said. "This is an exciting time. I want to be sure we figure this all out. An opportunity like this might not come around again."

"And what if it's just a freak accident that can't be replicated?" Kathryn said. "What do we do with Sergeant Hammer?"

"No matter the outcome of the research," Duncan said. "I doubt there will be anything left of Sergeant Hammer when the experimentation is complete."

Royce nodded. He didn't like to think about the Marine who was undergoing such trying experiments, but Evander Royce was paid to think about the greater good. And in this case, the ends far outweighed the means.

"Very good," he said. "That will be all for today. If anything changes, keep me informed."

7

Two days later, Dr. Zeldin left early. The Star Command headquarters was a sprawling complex and it took him almost twenty minutes before he got outside. Titan was still a cold planet and the average temperature was still below freezing. The temperature fluctuated between a warm, seven-day week when the moon was on the sun side of Saturn, and an eight-day, cold week. But the thickening atmosphere and regular combustion of fossil fuels contributed to a warming world.

It was a dark week, so Cal Zeldin put on his parka and gloves, then braced himself as he went outside. The cold air was piercing, but not so bad that he couldn't make the walk through town. There were heaters built into the cover over the sidewalks. Warm air wafted down over him in waves as he hurried toward The Omega.

The bar was on the bottom level of a wide building. It had an industrial theme and dark interior, with small metal tables between the large heating units that dominated the space and sent warm air up into the higher stories of the structure. Neon lights lit the bottom edge of the bar top, and a series of colored spots pointed down behind the bar to reflect off the mirrored shelves and crystal fixtures.

Music played from speakers lost in the darkness of the black ceiling, which also hid the rows of pipes and ducts that pumped heat higher up into the building.

On the tables were small lamps with dark shades that cast the light down toward the surface rather than up or out into the room. Cal went to the bar, pulling off his gloves and stuffing them into his pockets as he went. He leaned against the padded edge and caught the eye of the woman working. The sides and crown of her head was shaved smooth, but a thick plume of hair grew from the back. She had it braided and then coiled on her head like a serpent.

"Help you?" she asked, not bothering to hide the suspicion in her eyes.

"Got anything warm?"

"Irish coffee," she said. "But whiskey will do the trick faster, in my opinion."

Cal wasn't there to get drunk. "I'll take the coffee," he said.

She poured him a mug of drip coffee, added cream liquor, stirred it with a spoon, then slid it across the bar. He took it in both hands, letting the warmth radiate into his fingers. Then he turned and looked around. He took his time, letting his eyes adjust to the dim lighting. Eventually, he spotted Astra in the back corner. She was alone, nursing her own drink and watching him without being obvious.

He pushed off the bar and made his way back to where she was waiting.

"Anyone follow you?" she asked.

He hadn't thought of that. "I can't imagine any reason why they would," he told her. "Nothing's changed. Getting Sergeant Hammer out won't be easy."

"I never shirked a task," she said. "Ain't nothing on Titan easy, doctor."

"Call me, Cal," she said. "I won't be a doctor much longer."

"I have a friend. He knows the captain on a ship that's inbound with a cargo of Neodymium and Sarmarium," Astra said. "He gets here the day after tomorrow and leaves the following day for the Hilo system."

"That's not much time?"

"No, but that ship has room for working passengers," she said. "Hilo needs robotic engineers, chemists, laborers, and logistical specialists for the mines. There's other work there too, but the point is, we can get the Sergeant on board without any need for papers or payment. As long as he's willing to work."

"I'm sure he'd be willing to do anything to get away from this place," Cal said. "The problem is, he might not be able to for a few days. I had thought we could get him out and hide long enough for him to recover."

"So, get him out tonight," Astra said.

"That's impossible."

"Is it? Don't you have access to him?"

"Look, it isn't like he's a library book. I can't just check him out and never bring him back."

"He has to know there's a chance," she said.

"I can't see him without being seen," Cal explained. "He might have the strength to hobble out of the facility, but that's a big if. They burned the sole of his foot today."

"Dear God, we have to do something, or they'll kill him."

"I can deactivate the security system and help him out of the building. But we won't get far on foot."

"What alternative is there?"

"Can you drive?"

"Well... sure, but I don't have a vehicle."

"Nor do I, but I can get one," Cal said. "I'll get him out, then deliver the Sergeant to you in a public place."

"The depot on Axis Street. You know it?"

"Yes," Cal said, thinking of the hovertrain that ran in a circuit around Titan. There were actually dozens of trains that moved between the cities built on the moon's equator. They were free, allowing citizens to explore other communities and employment opportunities outside their own town. They all used the same magnetic rail and depots. He knew it was one of the busiest spots in town.

"Get him there, tonight at two in the morning. If you aren't there by three, I'll leave and assume you failed."

Cal was a bit surprised by the younger woman's take-charge attitude. Not that he had ever commanded troops in battle, but he was a military man and she was just a logistical specialist. It seemed a bit backward for her to be giving him orders, but they were both risking their freedom, maybe even their lives, so he didn't complain. Nor did he flash her a smile, even though something deep down inside wanted to. He wondered if he would have been plotting to rescue Sergeant Hammer if she had been a man. Her reaction to the sergeant's violence had broken through the shock he felt since delivering the sergeant to the Space Command R&D.

She stood up, gave Cal a hopeful last glance, then went straight for the door. He watched her leave, then looked around the bar. If anyone was watching them, they were out of sight. And no one followed her out. Cal waited until his coffee was cold. He had only sipped it, and there was over half a mug left when he got his phone out and ordered a rental vehicle. He took a rideshare to the automated auto rental garage where he found that his vehicle, a small two-seater with a combustion engine, was waiting for him. He got in, activated the unit's repulsers, and started back to Space Command.

As he drove, he considered the reality of his situation. The facts were undeniable. Even if there weren't cameras recording everything that happened in the lab and around the Space Command facility, the MPs would still discover the part he played in helping Sergeant Hammer escape. Staying behind was simply not an option. Which was why he stopped at a pawn store. He had over two hundred thousand credits in his banking account. And spent almost all of it on two gold watches, some diamond rings, collectable coins, and a gold medallion necklace.

He put on one of the watches and one of the men's rings. The rest went into his duffel bag. His next stop was the garage at Space Command. He had a small berth in the visiting officers' tower. He took an elevator up to his room and filled two duffel bags with clothes. One for him, the other for Sergeant Hammer, which included a gray hoodie and a black baseball cap.

Returning to the garage, he put his bag inside, then made his way back to the R&D division. There was a maintenance closet down the hall from the lab where Sergeant Hammer was being held. Cal stepped in, picked up a pair of door wedges used by the cleaning crew to keep doors open in labs and offices as they cleaned. By that point, it was past ten o'clock. He still had several hours to kill. After leaving the bag with clothes for the sergeant in the maintenance closet, he went to his office. It wasn't too late to change his mind, he told himself. What he had planned was lunacy. He didn't owe Sergeant Hammer anything. For all he knew, the effects of the gamma surge would catch up to him. He might die before they could even get him onto the mining ship, then he would have blown up his life for nothing. For almost three hours, he debated with himself. But on his computer screen was an image of the lab. There were no bandages over the burns Igorivich had inflicted. They still looked terrible. Raw, blackened skin that was oozing a gray liquid. All around them, the sergeant's skin was red and slightly puckered. He lay unmoving on the metal table. But the computer also had a readout of his vital signs. Dr. Zeldin was certain the patient was alive. For how long was anyone's guess, but if he was left under the sadistic experimentation of the researchers, it was bound to be short.

At one o'clock in the morning, 0100 military time, Cal Zeldin logged into the laboratory's controls. It was all run by computer and could be controlled remotely. Cal didn't think shutting down the security system would garner much attention, even though several of the researchers were bound to be logged into the system from their domiciles. That would probably change once he went into the lab. No one was scheduled to be in until 0800 at the earliest. But that was a chance he would have to take. If the facility went on lock-down, or he just got unlucky, they would be captured or killed. And to be honest, Cal was leaning toward the latter.

No alarms sounded when he shut down the security in the lab and unlocked the doors to the lab remotely. Cal picked up the pair of rubber wedges and set out to do something that would make him a wanted man for the rest of his life.

8

Jack was awake. Sleep was difficult. Every inch of his body hurt. His head was aching. His back and neck hurt from lying on the table, unable to move. At first, he had tried to flex the muscles in his back or shift his shoulder blades, but the straps holding him down were too tight. His rear and legs had gone numb, and any effort to move them or flex those muscles sent waves of pins and needles ripping down his lower body.

Then there were the cuts. It had been over twenty-four hours since the fight and the lacerations were sealed up. How his body was doing it, he had no idea. The researchers had put him back on a liquid diet, using a large, plastic syringe to pump a runny gruel into his mouth to feed him. Yet somehow his cuts were growing back together. They still hurt, narrow lines of fire that were beginning to itch. He thought he might go mad, not being able to scratch the newly forming skin.

Worst of all were the burns. They hurt constantly, a deep, terrible sensation that felt like he was still on fire. His foot was the worst. Three seconds with a blow torch had caused damage to all the soft tissue, bones, and thousands of nerve endings. Jack couldn't imagine anything making it hurt worse. He would have gladly had it amputated if someone had given him that option.

All he could do was linger in a daze of sorts, his mind slipping in and out of consciousness as the pain filled his brain like a toxic fog.

"Sergeant Hammer, can you hear me?"

The words were like a lifeline in the sea of pain and despair he was drowning in. Not just welcome words, but a voice that was familiar. With an effort, Jack opened his eyes. A man with a troubled expression leaned over him. He was older than Jack, with just a touch of gray at his temples.

"I'm here to help," the man said.

"Doctor Zeldin?" Jack managed as the man above him unfastened the strap over his head.

"Time to move, Marine. I'll answer your questions when we get out of here."

It was music to Jack's ears. All he wanted was to escape, and yet, moving wasn't easy.

Zeldin moved with feverish intensity. It took Jack a few seconds to realize the doctor wasn't there in an official capacity. Jack's wary nature took over.

"Is this some kind of test?" he asked.

"It's against orders," Zeldin said. "You okay with that, Sergeant?"

"Hell yes," he replied. "Ooohhhh."

"We have to move. The security could be triggered any moment."

It was easy for him to say. Jack's muscles were all stiff, and some were already cramping in his back just from the effort of sitting up. As the doctor's hands fumbled with the straps over his legs, Jack began to lift himself up with his hands.

"I'm going to need a minute," Jack said.

"I'll give you half that," Zeldin said as he rushed over to the counter that lined one side of the room. He ripped open a drawer and pulled out an analgesic spray. From an overhead bin, he retrieved a roll of gauze. He hurried over to where Jack was flexing his knees and ankles. The pain was intense. It felt like his entire body was on fire, but he understood the opportunity that had suddenly been afforded to him. A chance to escape was not something he would squander. Better to die trying than to continue being tortured day after day.

Zeldin didn't ask permission. He sprayed the bottom of Jack's burned foot. The chemical hit the tender flesh and felt like a fresh wave of fire. Jack started to pull away.

"Don't," Zeldin said. "This will help."

Even as he said the words, the pain that had raged in his brain since that morning when the sadistic researcher had burned him eased. It did not make the pain go away, but it went from a raging agony to a dull ache. Zeldin held the spray can out to him.

"Use it. We're running out of time, Sergeant."

While the doctor did a quick and sloppy wrap of his burned foot, Jack sprayed the burn on his left hip, then the burn on his right shoulder. In the few seconds it took to apply the analgesic spray, Zeldin had Jack's foot wrapped up.

"Here we go," the doctor said. "Hold onto me."

Jack turned, rotating on his bare bottom until his legs hung off the table. He groaned from the pain as the sudden change in posture sent blood surging through his legs.

"It's just the tissue getting the oxygen it needs," Zeldin said. "Fight through it, Sergeant."

"Yes, sir," he replied automatically.

Jack was used to following orders. Since his bootcamp days, he was accustomed to being told to push through pain, fatigue and weakness. He had always obeyed his superiors, and the escape from the lab was no different.

His feet hit the floor and fresh waves of agony swept through him. Zeldin pulled him off the table, wrapped Jack's arm across the doctor's narrow shoulders, and they started for the door. Pins and needles seemed to assault his flesh. And the pain in his foot was the worst he'd ever been in. But there was something empowering about being on his feet and moving again. Freedom beckoned and he would run toward it no matter what state he was in.

By the time they reached the first set of doors, Jack was breathing hard and sweating. He saw the rubber wedge under the door and marveled at how such a simple little instrument could thwart high-tech security. As they passed the outer door, Dr. Zeldin kicked the wedge out from under it. The door closed, and Jack listened for the locking mechanism to click into place, but it didn't. Security hadn't been alerted... yet.

"Here," Zeldin said. "Get in here, Sergeant."

They ducked into a maintenance closet. It was small, with shelves stocked with cleaning chemicals. In the back was a large sink with an extendable hose on the faucet above. Beside the sink was a mop bucket on wheels. Inside the bucket was a standard duffel bag.

"We don't have a lot of time," Zeldin said. "I'm sorry, I don't have better supplies."

He handed Jack a pair of sweatpants. Pulling them on was both painful and dignifying. Desperation was a powerful motivator and he would have run away completely naked if that was his only option. But it felt good to have clothes again. Zeldin ripped open a large bandage with adhesive strips around the edges. He placed it over Jack's burned hip.

"That might help a bit with the chafing," he said.

"Why are you doing this, doctor?"

"What else could I do? They would have killed you eventually. I never meant for any of this."

Jack realized Dr. Zeldin had been involved in having him placed in the research division. A sudden urge to kill the man rose up inside Jack and he grabbed Zeldin by the front of his shirt, twisting the collar until it choked him and pressing him back hard against the shelving. The bottles of cleaning products shook from the impact and a few fell over.

"You did this?" he demanded. "This was your idea?"

"You have a gift," Zeldin managed to squeak out. "I wanted to study your DNA. I never thought they would hurt you."

But they had hurt him. His body had an amazing ability to heal and overcome the tortures that had been inflicted on him, but his mind was permanently scarred by what he had endured.

"I ought to rip your throat out!"

It took all his mental fortitude not to hurt the doctor. Jack felt like he had been stripped bare again. In those few seconds, his mind replayed the awful experiments that had been performed on him. Rage burned in his heart hotter than the torch used on him less than twenty-four hours previous. And yet, he backed down.

"You can kill me if you want," Zeldin stammered. "I deserve it. But I had no idea what they were going to do to you. And I'm here now. At least let me get you out of here before you rip out my throat or whatever you're planning."

Jack turned away. His stomach was suddenly churning. He bent over the sink and heaved, but his stomach was empty.

"We need to get out of here," Zeldin said. "I have shoes for you."

They were actually boots, well-worn lace-up combat boots. Zeldin had them from his abbreviated orientation into Space Command. Why he kept them, he never knew. When he exercised, which he tried to do three days a week, he wore running shoes. But every time he packed his belongings, which fit into a standard military ruck sack, he always started with the boots. He went down on one knee, loosening the laces on the right boot.

"Careful getting your foot in here," he warned.

The doctor didn't need to waste his breath. Jack's foot was throbbing with pain. Just the thought of putting a boot on was like a nightmare, but he understood the need. He couldn't be seen in the facility naked and barefoot.

The boot was a size too big, and Dr. Zeldin didn't bother cinching up the laces. Jack pulled on an oversized hoodie, got both boots on his feet, and then put on a puffy jacket. There were more clothes in the bag, but they didn't have time to go through them. Zeldin snatched it up and rubbed his throat as he told Jack the plan.

"I'm taking you to the garage. I've got a car there, but we can't use it for long. I'm dropping you off at the train station. Astra will meet you there."

"Astra?"

"The woman in the lab when you fought the researchers," Zeldin said. "She's going to help you. We're both risking our lives to help you, Sergeant."

"Why?"

"Because it's the right thing to do. Because I owe you. Because I couldn't live with myself if I didn't."

"Lots of I's in those reasons, doc," Jack said.

"You asked, I answered. Maybe I am being selfish, but it sure doesn't feel that way. Astra will have her own reasons, but we're trying to help."

"Just get me out of this place," Jack said, swallowing his anger. "Do that and we're square."

For a moment, Zeldin looked up at Jack. There were tears in the physician's eyes, although he didn't say anything else. He just opened the door and led the way down the hall.

It was Captain Kittle who discovered the missing patient. Like several other researchers, he kept a live stream of the lab going on his computer in his berth. He had fallen asleep in the one recliner in the small space. The ship captain preferred a berth on a starship. Not any berth, but a captain's berth, with its sitting area and office space. He liked having the largest quarters on board and feeling like he was the most important person while they were deployed. Of course, every ship got orders, but it was up to him to carry them out, and the entire crew followed his every command.

Things were different at Space Command. It was one of the reasons he didn't like it and had never sought promotion. If he couldn't be the most important person in any group or gathering, he preferred not to get involved. At Space Command, there was always someone telling you what to do and sometimes even how to do it. And it was one thing to get orders from a superior officer within the military. But he didn't think he could stand taking orders from a slimy politician who had never put his own life on the line.

Nevertheless, Kittle was getting older. He was in his fifties and despite his mental and physical discipline, things were starting to change. Losing his hair was no problem. Buzz cuts and even complete scalp shaving was common in the military. But he was having to get up in the middle of the night to relieve himself. He was getting sharp stinging pains in his feet and toes for no reason that he could determine. Worst of all, a layer of fat had developed across his stomach, just above his waistline. No matter how much he exercised it wouldn't go away. There were deep lines in his forehead and around his eyes. Hair was growing in his ears like a wild forest and he got tired in the afternoons. Not just taxed from a hard day, but a strong urge to nap that he had never experienced before. There were times when he was forced to get up from his captain's chair on the Bridge of his ship and walk around to keep from falling asleep in the middle of his watch.

They say time waits for no man, and Kittle was no fool. He could see the end of his career approaching, and while he would have a nice retirement income to be comfortable for the rest of his life, he didn't know how he would cope with being just an ordinary person. It sounded like torture. He would be forced to cook his own meals and clean up after himself. If he wanted others to do it, he would have to pay them. It seemed outlandish to him. The very people he had worked tirelessly to serve as a starship officer would simply write him off and expect him to live like everyone else?

No, that wouldn't do. He had to find a way to get back the vigor he had lost and set himself up for the future so that even after his career, people would acknowledge his greatness. That's what was at stake with Project Hammer. If he was honest, he didn't care about curing diseases or helping wounded members of Space Command to heal. He didn't care if there were super soldiers or no soldiers at all. He was a naval captain, a spaceman, and it was the space-faring crews who were the most important to him. More specifically, it was his ability to lead such crews that he wanted to maintain. To get what he was chasing, he needed the researchers to unlock the secrets of aging in Sergeant Hammer's special DNA. With that knowledge, he could turn back the hands of time, regain his vigor and youth in order to continue serving (even though being served was what he really wanted).

Perhaps he could continue as a starship Captain, or maybe the breakthroughs with Hammer's DNA could elevate him to the very top in the halls of power. He wouldn't be opposed to that. He had commanded starships; he could lead all of Space Command, or even rule as Prime Minister. He had just awoken from a dream where he was scolding a subordinate, which was one facet of command that he enjoyed most, when he looked over at the computer screen. Sergeant Hammer was his golden goose and he took pride in seeing the progress of the Marine's healing ability. But what he saw made him leap to his feet. The golden goose was gone. The exam table was empty.

Kittle snatched up his comlink and slapped the activation button. "Alert! Alert! Alert! This is a security emergency. Patient Delta, Utah Lima Zero Zero One is missing. I repeat, patient Delta Utah Lima Zero Zero One is not in the laboratory. Lock down the facility and find him. This is Captain Kittle of Project Hammer requesting a facility lockdown and search!"

He dropped back down into his chair and snatched at the pair of boots beside it. There was immediate chatter on the comlink in response to his orders. But a spike of fear seemed to pierce his liver. The golden goose was gone and if it wasn't found, heads would roll. As leader of the project, he would be the first on the chopping block and he wasn't going to let that happen. No matter what, he would get Sergeant Hammer back in that lab. If the secrets to long life were hidden in the man's body, Captain Kittle would rip it apart until he found it.

9

They were halfway to the garage when orange lights began flashing from the ceiling and an alarm sounded. Fortunately for Jack, the pins and needles had stopped. He was still in pain, still unable to put much weight on his wounded foot, but he could hobble alone without assistance. And with each passing minute, he felt a little stronger.

"Knew it," Zeldin muttered. "Here."

He drew a wireless activation fob from his pocket and passed it to Jack.

"What's this?"

"You need that to start the car."

"Aren't you coming?"

"Yes, but if something happens to me, you can still get away."

"What if something happens to me?" Jack asked.

"Then we're both screwed, so don't let that happen."

Up until that point, Jack's understanding of the situation had been narrowly focused on getting away from the facility and the researchers who were conducting their atrocious experiments on him. He suddenly realized that Dr. Zeldin was committing a treasonous act by springing him from the lab and helping him escape the R&D facility.

But there was no time to discuss what the doctor was doing. Jack's anger at the man had dwindled. He had undoubtedly been following orders when he recognized that something had changed in Jack's body that allowed him to heal faster than normal. The doctor probably didn't know what the researchers were planning when he delivered Jack to them. He was following orders and that was something a grunt like Jack understood. They weren't given the reasons or even the desired results, oftentimes. The officers said go here, do that, kill this, protect that. He had obeyed his orders without question and Dr. Zeldin probably had, too. When he realized what was actually being done, he did something to stop it. Jack could respect that, but he hadn't realized until that moment that by helping him, the doctor was committing a crime. He would be in real trouble if they were caught, not just lose your job trouble, but probably the spend the rest of your life in jail kind of trouble.

Jack wasn't sure what to say. Then a pair of MPs came rushing around the corner ahead of them and there was no need to speak. Dr. Zeldin pressed himself against the wall. Jack tensed, his body coiling to strike, but the doctor took his arm and pulled him back.

The MPs ignored them and raced down the corridor.

"There will be a time for fighting, I'm sure," Zeldin said. "But let's see how far we can get without it."

Jack nodded and they continued on. He had to do his best to walk normally. He flipped up the hood on his sweatshirt and the pair of men trudged through the halls like people tired after a long day.

"How's your foot?"

"Killing me," Jack admitted. "I'd like to get my hands on the guy with the blow torch."

"Dr. Petros Igorivich," Zeldin said. "Head of the medical division's burn ward."

"That monster is in charge of helping burn victims?" Jack asked.

"Yes," Zeldin said. "All the researchers have specialities. I used to admire them."

"And now?"

"They've lost their way. Let's not lose ours."

They made it to the final stretch of hallway that led out to the garage. What they didn't realize was that the security office for the entire division was there too, housed in the offices just inside the building. Some of it was administrative, but most was practical use by the MPs. There was a big security room with over a hundred video monitors that showed the feeds from all the security cameras in the building. There was a break room, a locker room, a small training space and an armory for the military police in charge of securing the R&D division. While the alert was too fresh for every one of the MPs to know who they were supposed to be looking for, the lockdown required every exit to have armed guards that would keep people from leaving.

Jack clocked the two MPs by the doors. They had stun batons, HELP sidearms (High Energy Laser Pistol), and non-lethal pump action shotguns, probably loaded with bean bag rounds. As a veteran Marine, Jack was familiar with all the weapons the MPs were equipped with. He knew that any one of them was enough to put down an average man. He wasn't average, but he wasn't at full strength either.

"Let me do the talking," Zeldin said.

Jack didn't think talking would help them very much, but he didn't argue. Zeldin increased his pace, and Jack stayed a few steps behind him. As they approached the doors, the guards stepped in front of them and held up a hand.

"Can't let you leave," the shorter of the pair said.

"Whole facility's on lockdown," the taller man said in a strong Irish accent. "I'll need to scan your IDs."

"Lockdown?" Zeldin said. "What's going on?"

"No clue," the shorter guard said.

"Probably a drill," Zeldin said, holding out his ID card, which the Irishman scanned with a handheld device. "They always run these at night."

"Maybe," the Irishman said.

"Hey, listen, this is Dr. Crimini. He's only here for a short layover, and I was giving him a tour. I really need to get him back to his ship, otherwise we'll all be in trouble."

"ID?" the shorter guard asked.

"We skipped the visitor check-in," Zeldin said as he shook his head. "I'm an idiot, I know. But, you know how long that takes, and Dr. Crimini only had a short time. I didn't want to waste it getting a visitor's badge."

"So... you don't have an ID?" the shorter guard asked.

"No, but I've got this," Jack said, stepped closer, and drove his palm straight into the guard's chin. The MP's head snapped back, and his knees gave way.

"What the—"

The Irishman dropped the scanner and started to draw his pistol. It was a standard-issue weapon, probably set to stun, but Jack wasn't about to take any chances. He pivoted on his good foot and threw a fast left hook. The punch caught the guard on the chin. He hadn't meant to cause lasting damage, but he was much stronger than he had been before. The punch landed square. Jack knew a lot of Marines who worked constantly on their accuracy. Hitting a small target with a strong punch wasn't easy. The challenge increased exponentially in a moving target such as a human opponent. Normally, Jack was sloppy in a fight. He had always depended on strength and aggression to get him through. Normally, he didn't have the speed and finesse necessary to compete as a boxer or MMA fighter. But that had changed after the gamma surge. He saw where he wanted to hit the guard and did it almost effortlessly, even though the Irishman was moving back in an effort to avoid the punch.

There was a nasty crack as the Irishman's jaw broke, followed by blood and teeth, which flew out of his mouth and hit the light colored wall. The guard spun around, his head smacking the wall just after his teeth, and then falling to the ground.

"You didn't have to hit him so hard," Zeldin snapped.

"Didn't mean to," Jack said as he pressed his left hand against his hip, which was suddenly throbbing. "Damn, that hurts."

Zeldin checked the door, but it was locked.

"We'll have to unlock it from the control booth," Jack said. "Give me his ID badge."

Both of the MPs had laminated cards clipped to their shirts. Zeldin leaned down, jerked the shorter guard's ID from his chest pocket, and handed it up to Jack. Then the doctor began to check the MP's vitals. It was a kindness, Jack thought, that revealed the doctor's nature. He cared for people, maybe even more than for his own safety. That was admirable, but probably a weakness that might get them both into trouble.

He hobbled through a nearby door and found himself in the security department's break room. To his left was an open door. Inside the small, closet-sized room, were racks of weapons. There were standard H8 high-capacity assault rifles in a tall gun rack. Below that were trays with more laser pistols and magazines for the rifles. On the opposite side was a rack with a few shotguns. They had light blue folding stocks and sliding forward pistol grips that marked them as non-lethal weapons. Jack was glad to see the shotguns had been handed out and not the H8 rifles.

He picked up a High Energy Laser Pistol, checked the battery, then the power setting. It was on stun. Frankly, he wouldn't have thought twice about killing people who were trying to keep him in the clutches of the barbarous researchers. But Dr. Zeldin's example of caring for the guards had inspired Jack. He stepped out of the armory and went straight to the door marked **SECURITY PERSONNEL ONLY**.

The door was metal, with a sophisticated locking mechanism. Jack had never used one, yet he had seen the MPs on starships swiping their ID cards to get into their quarters. Master Sergeants who manned the armories used the same system. Jack was just a grunt. He had never earned the right to go into the restricted spaces. But he had the guard's ID, and when he swiped it through the electronic locked it gave a beep, and the door opened. Inside were four men, all seated and staring up at their monitors. Apparently, there were no cameras facing the hallway where Jack had just taken out two of the guards. Several of the MPs had on headsets and didn't even look up as he entered.

He shot the first one who did, a heavyset man with a thick handlebar mustache. He had Sergeant stripes on the shoulder of his uniform. The laser went off with a high-pitched whine, and that certainly got the attention of the other men. Jack shot the second and third before they could get out of their seats. The fourth MP made a valiant effort. They weren't armed. It wasn't their role to enforce anything while in the security room. Their job was to watch the monitors for trouble and coordinate the rest of the MP force. The fourth guard knew he didn't stand a chance of attacking and disarming Jack, not because he knew anything about Jack's extraordinary physical abilities, but because he had no defense against the laser pistol. Instead, he called out over an open mic, "Assault on HQ! Converge on this location."

Jack couldn't take the words the man had spoken back. He stunned him with the laser pistol, then stepped to the nearest console. He had never worked security, but the controls were clearly labeled. One read **Reset,** and it seemed like the fastest way to unlock the doors. He pushed the button, and all the lights on the security panel went off.

"That did something!" Zeldin shouted. "It's open, come on!"

Jack stuffed the pistol into the wide center pocket of his hoodie, then stepped back into the armory. He knew two things: first, taking a rifle would in all likelihood result in his death, and second, that he would rather be dead than go back to being cut and burned by the researchers. He snatched up an H8 rifle and two magazines of ammunition, then hurried back out of the security space and followed Dr. Zeldin into the parking garage.

10

Astra wasn't normally out and about at two o'clock in the morning. Not that there was a major difference between night and day on Titan. The moon rotated in such a way that the same side was always facing the planet, just like Luna and Earth. They were in the middle of a cold week, which meant they were on the far side of the planet from the sun, but it wasn't the sun that illuminated Titan. Rather, it was the reflection of sunlight off the gas atmosphere of Saturn that gave them light. The humans occupying Titan had installed their own twenty-four-hour cycle just the way the crew on an interstellar spaceship did.

Since becoming a Supply Supervisor at the R&D division of Space Command, she hadn't worked the night shift. Her job began each morning at 0800 by going over the requests for supplies that had been filed the day before. She then determined what could be fulfilled from their stock of supplies and what needed to be special-ordered. In the afternoons, she joined her team restocking supplies. They saw to everything from laboratories, to office supplies, on to toilet paper and paper towels in the restrooms.

Her day ended at five pm, or 1700 hours. She earned a salary which was enough for a modest apartment within walking distance of the Space Command facility, and after bills, she usually had enough extra money to keep a little spending cash on hand, even though cash was a relative term. She had an account for food, bills and necessities, a savings account and a flex spend account. Space Command put tight controls on what their digital currency could be spent on. The credits in her flex account could be spent on anything: a meal at a restaurant, a ticket to a movie theater, games on her entertainment devices, or donated to a registered charity.

She used ten credits to buy herself a coffee at the depot, which was busy even at two o'clock in the morning and had a variety of kiosks that sold all sorts of snacks and distractions for people traveling on the E-Train. Some said the E represented the equator, others that the train was electrically powered, and still others that it was an elevated train as opposed to one that ran along the ground or under the ground. Astra didn't know and didn't care. The truth was she had never been more frightened in all her life than she was tonight, as she sat down at the cafe amidst the throngs of people buying tickets, picking up their luggage or going up the escalators to the boarding platforms.

At any minute, she expected to see Dr. Zeldin with the patient the researchers were experimenting on. That man had seemed like a wild animal. She had seen a movie once about a circus on old Earth. In that film, the animal trainer was cruel, especially to a huge lion that was always kept in a filthy cage. Eventually, the lion got free and killed the trainer before it was shot and killed itself. Astra felt the patient she had seen in the laboratory was like the lion in that movie ... or maybe the lion was like the man.

She wasn't sure what made her more frightened, the consequence for helping the man escape or the man himself. Part of her looked anxiously for Dr. Zeldin and part of her hoped they wouldn't show. In a small part of her mind, she held out hope that they had been caught escaping, but no one would ever know about her role in the crime. Maybe she could just go on with her life. But in reality, that frightened her just as much as helping the patient escape.

Growing up on Titan hadn't been easy. There weren't a lot of opportunities for someone to expand and grow. She had been content getting a job. School on Titan had been rough, so getting out and earning money for the first time had been welcome. She managed to get her own apartment and create a life, but it was limited in scope. When she got the promotion to Supply Supervisor, she had expected things to change, but nothing had. Her bank account grew a little, and she had a steady schedule instead of a rotating one, but that was all. Happiness seemed elusive. She dated, but never got serious with anyone. It felt a bit meaningless just repeating the same tasks day after day, week after week.

When she was exposed to the man attacking the researchers, she felt both frightened and more alive than ever before. Afterward, helping him seemed like the courageous thing to do. Although since then, her courage had waned until it was nearly gone. She thought about running away. Dr. Zeldin would never find her. She didn't have to risk everything for the two men. They were strangers to her after all. But something held her in the seat. She sipped the coffee, letting the bittersweet liquid warm her from the inside while she waited to see what her future would hold.

Across the city, in a penthouse on the top floor of Space Command's personnel tower, Admiral of the Fleet Evander Royce was pacing the floor. He had been asleep in bed with his wife, Bremilda, when the call came in. Being the highest-ranking member of the Space Command Chiefs of Staff brought with it a grueling schedule. He worked sixteen hours on average every single day. There were constant reports coming in that needed his full attention. Some outlined what the fleet was achieving, others detailed what other space-faring species were involved in. Humanity was new to the scene and held only a handful of meaningful worlds. They had yet to be attacked by the more aggressive species, but Royce knew it was only a matter of time. They needed to build up their forces exponentially, but building a single spaceship was expensive. Building a ship of war was much more costly and just maintaining the fleet they had was a challenge, both in manpower and in financial resources. Space Command was a government-run military and, as such, dependent on that government to allocate the funding needed. If it were up to Royce, he would make Space Command autonomous, then raise money from the worlds they annexed by taxing the resources exported from those worlds. But it wasn't his decision and all he could do was try his best to lead Space Command in a positive direction. Hopefully, in doing so, it would raise the reputation of the fleet in the eyes of people on Earth, Mars, Europa and even Titan.

But the new project, the discovery of the fascinating abilities of a lowly Marine, had changed what Space Command could do. Once Sergeant Hammer's powers of regeneration were figured out and replicated, Space Command would share that biotech with humanity and, in exchange for the eradication of disease and longer life spans, Space Command would be given what it needed to elevate humanity to become a major stakeholder in the galaxy. At least, that was Admiral Royce's earnest desire. But then he had been awakened with the news that Sergeant Hammer was missing.

So, he paced and waited for news. He had already given the order for all Military Police to assist the guard unit in R&D in tracking down Hammer. But he had not gotten an update in nearly ten minutes. That fact alone made his blood run cold. He tried to tell himself he didn't need Hammer. They already had samples of his DNA, his blood, and even biopsies of all his major organs and systems. Bone, skin, and muscle, they had it all, yet not the man himself. And Admiral Royce had the sinking suspicion that without the man, they might end up with nothing at all.

Down in the R&D division, Captain Kittle had arrived and immediately taken charge. The MPs were locking down the facility, posting guards at every exit, and preparing to search every office, lab, workspace and storage compartment. Upon arriving at the lab, Kittle noticed two things. The first was the rubber wedges used to hold the doors open. He had suspected that someone had assisted Sergeant Hammer. The rubber wedges, one of which was still holding open the inner door, had certainly been brought in from the outside.

The second thing he discovered was that the straps hadn't been snapped. Kittle was under no illusions about Sergeant Hammer's strength, but that's not how he had escaped the lab.

"Captain, I'm Lieutenant Gomez. I'm the senior MP during the night shift," a tall officer with dark black hair and thick bushy eyebrows announced as he came into the lab with a pair of junior officers. "Can you tell me what happened?"

"The subject in this lab is a man named Hammer," Kittle explained. "Someone helped him to escape."

Kittle went to the computer console in the lab and brought up the security feed. The sight of Dr. Zeldin was a kick in the gut, but Kittle took it without complaint. He didn't know what would make an officer turn traitorous, probably greed. Zeldin wanted all the credit and all the reward for Hammer's abilities. He got screenshots of both men and sent them to Gomez's Network Interface Slate.

"That's who you're looking for, Lieutenant. Get those pictures to every one of your people A-SAP!"

"Aye, Captain, it's done. We'll search the facility top to bottom."

"Do that, and have your people ready for a fight. The subject is incredibly strong and fast. He'll turn violent when you try to apprehend him. Just keep in mind that we must bring him in alive. He is invaluable to Space Command. Is that understood, Lieutenant?"

"Aye, Captain, I understand."

"Make sure your people understand. Now move!"

The lieutenant, probably the low man on the totem pole in the security department, turned on his heel and hurried out of the lab. Kittle ignored him, reversed the video footage, then watched it all from the beginning. It only lasted a couple of minutes. Zeldin went in and began immediately unstrapping the patient. He then sprayed him with something, wrapped his foot with a bandage, and then helped him out.

"What the hell are you thinking, doctor? You have to know I'm going to catch your sorry ass. And when I do, I'll make you wish you'd never been born."

He slammed his hand down on the countertop with a loud slapping sound. Then he started for the door. He was almost out of the lab when a pair of MPs went running past him.

"Hold it there, corporal!" Kittle shouted, causing one of the MPs to stop and turn. "What's happening?"

"There was an emergency call," the corporal said, "at the MP station. We've all been ordered back there."

"Let's move then," Kittle said. "That's got to be the patient. Hurry!"

The captain and the corporal sprinted down the hall in hopes of catching Sergeant Hammer and Dr. Zeldin.

11

Jack was no stranger to security operations, but he didn't expect to be confronted by a guard in the garage. Titan had many of the trappings of life on Earth and Mars, including a large number of Space Command professionals with their own personal vehicles. Some lived off base, especially those who didn't see themselves as military per se, such as the highly educated researchers. But the garage was fairly empty at two o'clock in the morning. And Jack, with a bulky military rifle, was easy to spot.

"Freeze!" the MP shouted. "Drop that weapon! Do it! Put it on the ground!"

"Don't stop," Jack ordered Dr. Zeldin.

The physician had been helping Jack hobble toward their rental vehicle. But Jack's firm hand on the older man's shoulder kept him moving.

"I said stop!" the MP screamed.

"Okay, okay," Cal Zeldin said. "I'm stopping."

They were almost eight feet apart. Jack wanted more distance. The MP was alone, and keeping them both covered with his laser pistol wasn't easy. He shifted back and forth, pointing his pistol at each of them in turn.

Jack pretended to be compliant. He set the rifle's butt down on the ground, but held onto the barrel with his left hand.

"I said drop the weapon!" the MP said. "Do it, or I'll light you up!"

"You sure you want to do that?" Jack said, taking a chance that the MP wasn't aware of what had been done to him. "I'm a Marine, just like you."

"Shut your mouth!" the MP growled. "Put the gun on the ground."

"You take me in, and I'm a dead man," Jack said. "Do you have any idea what they're doing to me?"

"Don't know, don't care, now drop it."

Jack bent down, his body turned slightly away from the MP, who couldn't see that his right hand had gone into the pocket of his coat. He set the rifle on the ground and straightened back up, but pulled his shirt up at the same time.

"This is what they're doing to me," he said. "It's torture, corporal. They've gone from cutting to burning me with a torch."

The look on the MP's face was nothing short of horror. Jack knew the lacerations across his abdomen and chest were healing, but they were still dark red, with pale white skin around them. And they ran all the way across his torso from side to side. And in that second, when the shock set in on the MP, his pistol wavered off Jack. With lightning-fast speed, Jack drew his own laser pistol and fired. The MP fired too, squeezing off a blast just before Jack did, but his shot was wide of the mark. Jack was right on target. The MP stiffened and fell over.

"Tell me he isn't dead!" Zeldin said, rushing toward the MP.

"Stunned," Jack told him as he bent over and picked up the assault rifle. "But if I have to kill to get away from those monsters, you have to know I'll do it. And I'll die before I let them take me back."

"Then we better move," Zeldin said. "I'd prefer not to die."

Jack noticed the Dr. snatching up the MP's laser pistol. He nodded in silent approval and hobbled toward the rental car. It was small, a compact, almost flimsy machine. The body was made of fiberglass and plastic with a combustion engine that ran on liquid propane. Jack knew one bullet or laser blast into that tank would kill them both instantly. But it didn't seem like a bad way to go. He yanked open the passenger door and fell into the seat. It felt good to be off his feet.

Dr. Cal Zeldin settled into the seat next to him and shoved the laser pistol he had picked up into a storage nook in the door. He hit the start button, and the little engine purred to life. Inside the garage with its low ceiling, they had to use the car's four wheels. He put the gear shift into reverse and rolled out of the parking space while Jack rammed one of the magazines into the assault rifle and tugged the charging handle back. He held it that way and looked into the breech to make sure a bullet had been loaded. A finger-length round, black and red in its carbon nanotube jacket, pointed at one end, and loaded with compressed gas at the other, was pushed into the barrel and ready to fire. He released the handle and let it snap down into place.

"I hate those," Zeldin said as he steered the car around the unconscious MP. "Do you have any idea the kind of damage they can do to a human body?"

"Pretty sure I do, Doc," Jack said. "I don't plan to use it if I don't have to."

Zeldin made a turn around one of the massive support pillars, and another pair of MPs came into view at the top of the ramp that led out of the garage.

"Don't stop," Jack ordered. "No matter what."

"God help us!" Zeldin said, as Jack hit the button to lower his window.

They were far enough away from the guards that the pair of them could be seen moving to block the car. They were armed with short-barreled tactical shotguns, but they weren't pointing them at the vehicle. Jack, on the other hand, leaned out the window and fired his rifle in a steady series of short bursts. The report of the projectile weapon was loud, both in the car and echoing through the garage. The bullets ricocheted off the concrete walls, ceiling, and floor of the garage. Jack wasn't aiming directly at the guards, just in their direction. And, like any sane person would do, they both immediately ran for cover back into the little guard shack. The lower half of the structure was metal, but the upper half was glass. They were speeding toward it, and Jack shifted his aim. A single three-round burst managed to shatter all the glass and keep the guards pinned down as the rental car zoomed up the ramp and into the street.

At such an early hour, there was no traffic. Zeldin immediately activated the car's repulser lifts, elevating the vehicle nearly six feet off the ground and increasing speed. Behind them, they heard shooting as the guards returned fire. There were thumps against the car's tiny cargo space and rear window, but the beanbag rounds didn't penetrate. The rear window developed a crack.

"That's going to cost me," Zeldin groaned. "This is a rental!"

They both burst out laughing more from the release of their mounting fear and stress than from the bad joke. Jack pressed the release just above the trigger guard on the rifle's rear pistol grip. The nearly depleted magazine dropped to the floor of the car.

"They won't give up," he said.

"I know," Zeldin told him. "We've got a plan."

"We?" Jack said. "Why don't you fill me in?"

"Astra, that's her name, the Supply Supervisor who was restocking the lab when you tried to escape the first time, wanted to help."

"She knows the consequences?"

"She does," Zeldin said. "We both do."

Jack was grateful, but he felt guilty at the same time. Dr. Zeldin was no longer a physician; he was a fugitive, a deserter and, according to the Space Command Code of Conduct, a traitor.

He went on with his explanation. "This was her idea, really. I was struggling with what the researchers were doing to you, but she was the one who insisted that we help you. Believe me, I tried to think of an alternative. But there was no one to appeal to. Nothing going on in the R&D division is outside the scope of the Space Command Chiefs of Staff. And I know your project was being followed by the Admiral of the Fleet himself. Captain Kittle bragged often about how important the project was and how he was reporting directly to the top brass, including Admiral Royce.

"I could have turned to the press or the government, but my fear was that they wouldn't care what happened to you. Once they understood what was at stake, they probably would have handed the researchers whatever torture tool they wanted."

Jack rubbed a hand over his face. His body ached in a dozen different places, but his right foot was the worst. The burn on the sole of his foot was far from healed, and walking on it had been torture. He had endured because of fear and lots of adrenaline, but as they wound through the city streets, he felt the pain starting to overwhelm him. He groaned a little as he shifted in his seat, and Dr. Zeldin reached into a console between their seats. He pulled out a small pill bottle.

"I wouldn't normally prescribe these," he said. "They're addictive, so be careful."

"What is it?"

"Perc-20," he said. "A synthetic opioid. It'll take the edge off the pain, but it will also slow your reflexes."

"Thanks," Jack said, taking the bottle of pills.

"Usually they're hard to come by, but the R&D division has a closet full of restricted drugs. They won't miss them."

Jack looked at the bottle. He wasn't afraid of getting addicted to the painkillers, but he did fear what might happen if they had to fight their way out of another tight situation. As much as he was hurting, he decided to save the pills for later and stuck them in his pocket.

"Where are we going?" he asked.

"I'm under no illusions, Sergeant. I know that Space Command wants you back and they'll stop at nothing to get you. They will already know that I was the man who helped you escape. Soon, they'll put everything together. My guess is, we're only fifteen to thirty minutes ahead of them, but they might be listening to us already. These rentals could have any number of tracking devices built in. If the brass hasn't launched a drone to track us, I'd be surprised. So, I'm not going to tell you where we're going. I don't want any surprises waiting for us when we get there."

Jack hadn't thought of all that. His mind was still struggling to keep up and, while he was normally a clear thinker, his brain was mired in his physical symptoms. He hadn't slept well in over twenty-four hours and the shock of being burned just seventeen hours earlier was difficult to deal with. What he did know was that he had to trust Dr. Zeldin and his partner in crime from the maintenance department. Jack tried to remember the woman, but he couldn't. The fight with the researchers was foggy in memory, probably because of the gas they used on him. He remembered lashing out and getting trapped in the vestibule, but that was all that his mind had retained.

"Smart," he said. "Glad you've got it all figured out, Doc."

"I've written out a few things on paper," Zeldin said, "just in case we get separated. Hang onto that duffle bag, you'll need it."

He reached into his pocket and retrieved the note. He looked at Jack and put a finger to his lips, then handed him the folded paper. Jack took it and unfolded the single page with his rough hands. The writing was in clear, block letters.

Astra will meet you at the depot. The rental has GPS, so SC will know we've been there. I will attempt to lead them away, or at least buy you enough time to escape. If I can, I will meet up with you later.

We can't use our IDs or access our money anymore. I have converted my credits into trade goods. You'll find a watch, some rings, and a necklace that are of very good quality. Hopefully,

we'll be able to use them to barter for what we need, but first, we have to get off Titan. Astra has a plan for that in a few days. Find her. She'll take you somewhere safe where you can heal.

If I don't make it back to you, know that I am sorry for my part in this. I didn't know what they would do to you. I never would have turned you over to the researchers if I had. Maybe someday you'll be able to forgive me.

Jack folded the paper back up and Zeldin handed him a lighter.

"Better safe than sorry," he said.

"Yeah," Jack said. "I hate to ask, but I'm starving."

"Got it," Zeldin said.

He slowed down and steered the hovercar into a fast-food restaurant drive-through lane while Jack lit the note on fire and tossed it out the window, where it burned itself out on the parking lot.

12

Captain Kittle was in charge. He had set himself up in the security offices and was directing a task force. Space Command had powerful resources, but they weren't prepared for a fast recovery op. The big organization was slow and Kittle was frustrated with the reluctance of many people to get out of their beds and go to work.

It was zero two-thirty hours and Kittle still didn't have a strike team assembled. He was accustomed to commanding a ship of war that was filled with resources that were ready for use at a moment's notice. From powerful weapons systems to platoons of Marines, they were always ready for an order from the captain. But on Titan, things were different. The MPs were licking their wounds. Seven of their people had been hurt or stunned. The latter took several hours of recovery time for most people. Those who were left were angry, but not prepared to chase down the fugitives.

Lieutenant Hector Gomez was nominally in charge of the MPs, but he clearly wasn't comfortable doing what was necessary to apprehend Sergeant Hammer.

"Does no one here understand that Hammer is the most valuable asset on this moon?" Kittle demanded. "Stop dragging your feet, Gomez. Your career is on the chopping block, man. You were in charge when Sergeant Hammer escaped. You'll be the one blamed."

Gomez looked mortified. Security on Titan was really just an exercise. The Sol system had never been invaded. Space Command wasn't under threat. They utilized security because they were a military installation. While it was true that some of the weapons being developed on Titan were top secret, there had never been any espionage to root out. In fact, the MPs working in Space Command's R&D division had never had an active case file before Sergeant Hammer's first escape attempt and subsequent violence that led to the death of one researcher and two more being hospitalized. Most of the research being done was lab work, from munitions to biological advancement. They certainly hadn't considered the idea that perhaps the researchers might use human test subjects who objected to what was being done to them. They didn't see themselves as prison guards and had no contingency plans to track down an escapee.

"I'm coordinating with Captain Morris," Gomez said. "They want more information."

"They can have it," Kittle said. "Just as soon as they drag themselves out of bed and get down here. I'm not risking top secret information leaking out by talking to lazy commanders on unsecured lines of communication. What you need to do is get your team ready to roll out."

"Roll out where?"

"We're tracking them," Kittle said. "Dr. Zeldin is helping him. It took me less than five minutes to tap into his finances. He's cleared out his savings and rented a car."

The MP looked blank. The information didn't seem to be making it into his brain. Kittle didn't know if Gomez was stupid or just bewildered by the barrage of information.

"Think it through, lieutenant! They're running. If they get off-world, we might never catch them."

It wasn't true. Kittle knew that Sergeant Hammer was valuable enough to track him down wherever he ran to. And as long as Kittle was in charge, he wouldn't rest until his quarry was back in Space Command custody.

"But we don't know where they are," Gomez said.

Kittle felt a wave of revulsion at the lieutenant's ignorance. Hadn't he just said that Zeldin rented a car? And yet Gomez wasn't smart enough to understand the advantage that gave him. Kittle was seeing it all too often in Space Command. Perhaps it was a lack of proper candidates, but it seemed as if the officer corps was getting watered down with ineptitude.

"Lieutenant, they are in a rented vehicle. Those all have tracking devices and I've already gotten the code from the rental agency. Look!"

He held out a data slate with an active tracing dot moving and blinking in the parking lot of a restaurant. Gomez leaned forward and peered at the screen.

"That doesn't make any sense," he said. "Why would they stop to eat if they're running? Maybe you got the wrong information."

"Negative, lieutenant. I've already checked the backlog. That vehicle was in our garage from 0141 to 0228. That's Zeldin."

"But... why?"

"Two possibilities," Kittle said, frustrated that he had to spell everything out for the incompetent lieutenant. He had always heard that the least capable recruits were pushed into the Military Police division. He guessed that included the least intelligent. "First, it's possible they are switching vehicles. That would defeat our ability to keep tabs on them via the rental car's GPS. I'm still waiting for permission to gain access to the city's video surveillance, which will allow us to see what they're doing, perhaps in real time. The second possibility is they're getting food."

"That's ridiculous," Gomez said. "No one on the run stops for burgers."

"Actually, Lieutenant, what you don't know about Sergeant Hammer is that his condition has given him a voracious appetite. They could actually be getting food, which is why you need to mobilize your unit in pursuit. They've made a critical mistake. You could be on top of them before they leave the restaurant."

"Well, I… actually, no, we can't do that. We need to requisition a vehicle to get to that location. And I'm not sure we have the jurisdiction to—"

"Lieutenant!" Kittle shouted. "Get your head out of your ass, son! This is a project of the highest importance. It goes all the way up the food chain, and you better believe there will be hell to pay when Admiral of the Fleet Royce catches wind of this, and he absolutely will. I just met with him yesterday and he's anxious for updates. We are Space Command, Gomez, not some small-town constable. If we want to detain someone, we do it, and let the brass smooth any ruffled feathers along the way. Do you understand what I'm telling you, lieutenant? This is a major operation, and you are blowing it by hemming and hawing about jurisdiction. You need to move! Get your people to that restaurant. If they move, I will update you on their location. Gear up and move out before you are stripped of rank and sent back to whatever rock they found you on. Go! Now!"

He shoved Lieutenant Hector Gomez, who stumbled, caught himself, straightened his uniform shirt, then started barking commands to his MPs. Kittle shook his head in disgust. There was no chance Gomez could get the job done. Kittle should probably have gone with them, but he felt he was needed more at the R&D division facility. The one thing he felt certain of was that Dr. Zeldin wasn't acting alone.

It still took the team of MPs ten minutes to leave the Space Command campus. They took a police vehicle that looked older than Gomez. There were seven Marines, including the lieutenant, but none of them looked tough enough to take Sergeant Hammer down.

The video of Hammer beating the hell out of three researchers just a few days earlier replayed over and over in Kittle's head. There was a difference in what he did that day and what he was capable of still, because of the tests carried out on the man. Most people would be in so much pain they couldn't function after just one burn. Hammer had three burns and one of them was on the sole of his foot. How he was walking at all was a complete mystery to Kittle, but it was also more evidence of just what the man was capable of. Super Soldier wasn't a strong enough title for Sergeant Hammer. Even in his weakened condition, he knocked out two MPs guarding the garage exit. He hit one of them so hard that it shattered the man's jaw and knocked out half his teeth. After that, he stormed the guardroom and stunned all four MPs inside. It was a clinic on tactical operations, yet it was accomplished by just one man with major wounds across his entire body.

"Captain Kittle, tell me you have a handle on this situation," a weary-looking Rear Admiral Duncan exclaimed as he came lumbering down the hall. He was nearly bald, but the hair on the sides of his head that was normally slicked back against his scalp was standing out sideways. The head of Space Command's Research & Development division looked like a clown. His skin was pale, his shirt untucked, and his face was puffy from sleep.

"Admiral, we are working to contain things. As you know, Sergeant Hammer is not your average Marine."

"No, but I also know he's worth more than the others by a factor of ten. So, we better not let him get far. Tell me where we're at in bringing him, then I want a full account of what happened. Admiral Ross has alerted Admiral Royce."

Kittle wasn't surprised, and yet he felt a twinge of regret. He needed to spin the situation in his favor.

"Sir, we're tracking them," Kittle said. "And Lieutenant Gomez just left with his MPs in pursuit, but I don't have confidence they'll succeed."

"What's plan B?"

"That depends on the amount of resources Space Command is willing to put toward regaining custody of Sergeant Hammer, but my suggestion would be to activate a special forces recovery unit, sir. The sooner the better."

Admiral Duncan's chin worked sideways for a moment as if he was swallowing something bitter, then he nodded. "I'll make the call."

13

Food had never tasted so good. It was just fast food hamburgers and French fries. The burgers were made from vat-grown beef, with cheese made from hydrogenated palm oil, and rehydrated onions and tomatoes. The only thing that wasn't altered was the pickles, if you didn't count the pickling process.

Yet it tasted so good. His body was yearning for sustenance, and he was finally giving it what it wanted. Zeldin had ordered six double cheeseburgers and a large fries. Jack had already eaten three and was hurriedly unwrapping the fourth.

"Are you sure you don't want one?"

"I couldn't eat it even if I did," Zeldin said. "The tension has me wound too tight."

"I get that," Jack said. "I used to be that way too. Couldn't eat before an op or I would yack all over the floor of the drop ship."

"How many times were you deployed?"

"Sixteen deployments on interstellar runs, eleven drops onto unexplored planetary bodies. I stood guard on three runs to inter-species conferences. Two real combat operations, one on Vandy Prime, another on Luchen."

He took another bite of his burger and resisted the urge to groan with pleasure. During his time on Titan, he had been poked and prodded every single day. His needs got the minimum attention necessary and his wants were completely ignored. Nothing had been good about it after the first day. Since then, he hadn't had a moment of joy or a feeling of pleasure about anything. They may have been on the run, but the taste of a good old-fashioned cheeseburger was a pure joy to Jack.

It wasn't just the taste that thrilled him. Strangely enough, he could feel his body digesting the food. Theoretically, he understood that many of the highly processed foods available were designed for easy digestion and fast absorption of the vitamins and minerals that such common fare were fortified with. He was pretty sure he could feel his body making fast work of taking what it needed from the food. Not only that, but he could feel himself shifting into a recovery state that was much more effective than he had been in the lab. Even the pain lessened from the burns, which no doubt added to the feeling of euphoria the food was giving him.

"That's an admirable record," Zeldin said. "I'm sorry things have taken such a dishonorable turn."

"I don't guess that's your fault," Jack said. "You were following orders. And I know how that is, at least you did what you could to get me out of that place."

It was 0230 on the button and Zeldin pulled the little rental car into the parking lot of the train depot. Jack rolled up the sack with his last two burgers and stuffed it inside his duffel bag. He had already put on a ring and the designer wrist watch. They were maybe a bit out of place, but it gave him an ideal way of transporting his bartering tender. He might lose his bag, but unless someone took the watch from his wrist or pulled the ring from his finger, he wouldn't lose them ... and he knew he would have to be unconscious or dead for that to happen.

Jack stuck out his hand and Zeldin shook it. There was no need for goodbyes. They didn't know what the authorities could see and hear, so they said nothing. Instead, Jack got out. He had wanted to bring the assault rifle, but it was too big, and the metal would set off the detectors at the entrance to the depot. Likewise, he was forced to leave the laser pistol behind, too, but he had nearly used up its small power supply anyway.

He closed the door and moved away from the car. He heard it leave but didn't look back. His back tingled and he spotted several cameras in the parking lot alone. There were some on the light poles and others on the building. He had no way to hide if the authorities had access to the surveillance system. The best he could do was keep the hood up and his face down. It might be enough to defeat facial recognition programs, but he couldn't be sure. Space Command had all his information, from blood type to DNA. It had dozens of pictures of him, his finger and palm prints, voice pattern, retina maps and even his dental records. He knew that many law enforcement systems utilized gait recognition, but even if they had his, the limp from his wounded foot would probably throw that system off.

The depot wasn't crowded, but it was still busy at two-thirty in the morning. Dozens of people were coming and going. Jack tried to blend in. Like many of the travelers, he was dressed for comfort, not fashion, and his duffel bag didn't stand out either. Almost everyone had a bag or suitcase of some kind. Backpacks were the most common, but there were people with satchels and leather attache cases, too.

Jack entered the main building and moved slowly, glancing up from time to time, but trying not to show too much of his face. It was hard to walk with a limp and only look up occasionally without seeming strange, but there were some homeless people at the periphery of the long depot building, so Jack hoped he didn't look too out of place.

Astra saw him almost as soon as he came inside. Jack wasn't the only person to enter the building wearing a hoodie with the cowl up over his face. But she knew he had been through hell, and the way he moved, made it clear to her that he was in a lot of pain. She got up, threw her coffee away, then walked toward Jack. He was moving away from her, but she was moving faster. She pulled even with him but never looked at him.

"Follow me," she said, then pulled ahead and turned into a hallway that led to the public restrooms and the employee section of the building.

Jack didn't respond in any way. He didn't even look up to see who was talking to him. It was a woman's voice and that was enough for him. He watched her feet, then shuffled along after her. They went past the bathrooms to a heavy metal door with the words **Maintenance Personnel Only** painted on it. Astra was already through the door, and it had almost closed when Jack reached it. He pushed through and found Astra just inside, pulling on a janitor's coveralls.

"What are you doing?"

"Trying to erase our trail," she said as she zipped up the coveralls and pulled her hair into a ponytail. "Get in."

She pointed to a trash bin, the big kind on industrial casters. He glanced inside, the bin was empty, and he could easily fit in it, but it was dirty and smelled foul.

"How does this help us?" Jack asked. "Don't automated service bots do all the cleaning?"

"This is Titan, Sergeant," Astra said. "We have laws to protect the workforce. Robots do the dirty and dangerous jobs, but there are always half a dozen maintenance people on duty here. Now get in and stay low."

He hoisted himself up over the edge with his arms. He was plenty strong enough, but the burn on his shoulder made the operation painful, and the burn on his hip was agonizing whenever he utilized his core in any fashion. He took his time, favoring his wounded foot, and settling back into the smelly cart. When he looked up, Astra wasn't there. He was about to rise up and look for her when a bag of trash landed on top of him.

"Hey!"

"Gotta sell it," Astra said. "Just lie down and don't move."

He did as he was told and Astra added more trash bags. They clearly had trash in them, but they didn't leak, and nothing foul was getting on Jack.

"Can you believe we've colonized the system, built interstellar ships, and established cities on distant planets, but we're putting trash in bags?"

"You're lucky," Astra said. "At Space Command, we compact all the trash before sending it out."

Jack didn't feel lucky. Nor did he realize that the rolling trash bin had a little electric motor so that Astra didn't have to push it. She held down the lever on the handle it trundled forward on its own. There were paddles on each side of the push bar that turned the bin. She walked it out of the maintenance area and through a side door that led out to the trash collection area just as a tall, armored land vehicle charged into the parking lot with blue and red lights flashing.

"Don't move and stay quiet," Astra said. "MPs are here."

Jack felt helpless, but he knew a good hiding spot when he saw one. He could tell they were outside because he felt the cold penetrating the hard plastic sides of the bin he was propped against.

Certain things in life exacerbate one's troubles. The stress of the situation outside the depot did nothing to alleviate the pain Jack felt. Any relief he had experienced while eating with Dr. Zeldin in the rental car was gone. His burns ached horribly with periods of hot, piercing pains that shot from the wounds deeper into his body. To make matters worse, his lacerations began to itch. It took all his willpower not to scratch at them. He didn't want to draw attention by moving the trash in the bin, nor did he want to reopen the cuts in what he thought had to be the germiest place he could possibly be outside of an open sewer.

Astra busied herself inside the waste disposal area. There were delivery crates that needed stacking and lots of cardboard boxes to break down for recycling. While she worked, she kept tabs on the MP vehicle. Two officers stayed with the vehicle. Their voices carried, and they kept their radios turned up loud enough that even when she wasn't spying on them, she could hear the reports.

Nor did she need to see the MPs in the depot to know they would spread out and search the upper deck where people boarded the trains first. They took their time, which frustrated Astra, but she worked steadily and slowly herself. The insulated coveralls were a bit big. At one point, she went back inside and found a scarf, which she wrapped around her head and ears, then returned to her faux work in the waste disposal area just outside the maintenance section of the train depot. Occasionally, trains would come humming into the station overhead, but it was almost two whole hours before the MPs began to search the auxiliary rooms on the lower floor. Astra was nervous. It was almost six o'clock before the MPs reached her area. Two came out with their body armor, smart helmets and shotguns. Astra didn't have to pretend to be frightened.

"What are you doing out here?" one of the MPs demanded.

"Working," she said. "I'm on trash duty."

"Just stand aside," the man said. He stayed by the door and waved for the other MP to search the area.

"Really?" the second MP complained. "You're a real jerk, Jankowski!"

"Stuff it, Reilly, this ain't no drill."

"That's what you keep saying, but who died and made you king?"

The MP named Jankowski reached up and tapped the double stripes on the shoulder of his uniform. "Chain of command, smart guy."

Reilly was just a private first class while his companion was a corporal. Astra was reminded of the child who, after being scolded, kicked the dog to assert dominance over something in her life. At the Space Command facility, civilian contractors were seen as less than everyone else. Even the lowest new recruit outranked her despite the fact that she had been working at the facility for over a decade. When they gave her an order, they expected her to obey without question or complaint. Not that they often did. She was almost invisible. The researchers and occasional high-ranking naval commanders pretended not to see her. The Marine officers did the same, but occasionally a Marine enlisted man would make a comment in her direction. It was never wanted and almost always inappropriate. Her boss had warned her when she told him about the first incident that, should she take the complaint to the military personnel, it would accomplish nothing and cost her any chance she had at advancement. So, she ignored the Marines who occasionally made their juvenile comments and did her job. But in her decade at Space Command, she had come to dislike Marines. They were loud, rude and always seemed to leave a mess wherever they went.

"I'll tell you where you can shove that chain," Reilly said, "but you'd probably enjoy it."

"Very funny, private, now get to it. We haven't got all night."

Astra agreed. She stood back out of the way. Jankowski covered her with his shotgun, not that it was necessary, while his partner did a perfunctory search.

"You check the trash bin?" Jankowski said when Reilly declared the space free from fugitives.

"I looked."

"Gotta do better than that," Jankowski said. "Search it."

"You search it."

"Don't disobey me, private. That's a direct order. Search that trash bin."

Reilly went to the bin and drove the butt of his shotgun down inside. Astra felt certain they would be caught. She would spend the rest of her life in a tiny, dirty cell with no hope of freedom. Reilly thrashed around and pounded the trash bags. Then he shrugged.

"Nothing," he said.

"Very well," Jankowski said in a long, exaggerated complaint. "Let's call it." He keyed his smart helmet with his free hand. It covered his head and eyes, but left his mouth visible. Astra heard him radio in. "Lieutenant, we've finished in the maintenance bay. It's all clear."

"Just a goose chase," she heard from the radios across the parking lot. It was amazing how well the sound traveled. "Let's load up and make tracks."

"You can go back to work now, miss," Reilly said. "I gotta say though, it's a crime to make you work in the trash."

"Move it, private!" Jankowski snarled.

"What?" Reilly demanded.

The corporal shoved him back inside and then followed. When they were gone, Astra breathed a sigh of relief. It was a quarter till seven when the MPs left. Had they stayed around fifteen more minutes, Astra would have been discovered. She wasn't part of their work crew, and the day shift started at 0700.

When she got to the trash bin, she wasn't sure what she might find, but Jack wasn't hurt.

"That was close," he said.

"What would you have done if he had found you?" she asked.

"I don't know," Jack said. "But I'm not going back. I'd rather be dead than go back."

Astra looked at him with disbelief, but she didn't argue. She opened a side gate and led him out of the waste disposal area and away from the depot. They couldn't go back to her apartment. It was no longer safe. She had taken a room in a seedy motel under the name Mara Thawn and paid using a preloaded credit card, the kind with no name just numbers. It was two blocks from the depot, and they walked arm in arm like lovers. But it was really just to help Jack with his burned foot.

"Why were they doing that stuff to you?" Astra asked.

"I think the doc would know more than me," Jack said. He was trembling from the cold and simultaneously sweating from the pain. He smelled like a dirty trash can, and could barely stay on his feet; he was so tired.

"He said you were important."

"I'm not," Jack said. "I was in the wrong place at the wrong time."

"You killed that researcher," she pointed out.

"He had it coming," Jack said. "They all do."

Jack told her his story, finishing just as they reached the room she had rented. It was warm inside, and there were two beds. Jack peeled off his smelly clothes and sat on the edge of the bathtub while he sponged himself off as best as he could. He knew that getting the burns wet was a bad idea. There were more clothes in the duffle that Zeldin had given him. He put on a T-shirt and gym shorts, then he climbed into one of the beds and fell instantly asleep. It was dangerous to trust a stranger, but he had no other options. There was a good chance the MPs could show up again. If that happened, he would deal with it head-on. Until then, he knew his body needed rest to heal and recover his strength.

Astra paced, checking the curtains. They had three days to wait. Three days seemed like an eternity, but there was nothing she could do about it. When Jack fell asleep, she took his dirty clothes and washed them in the bathroom sink. It was far from a perfect situation, but she did her best, then hung them up to dry in the shower. Her own bags were already next to the bed she would sleep in. She had left almost everything she owned behind. It was all mostly second-hand to begin with; all her cookware and dishes were bought at a thrift store. Her furniture was used. The entertainment console in her apartment had come with the place and stayed when she left. Most of what she owned were actually digital copies of movies, television shows, books, and music that she accessed via subscription services. She had to leave that behind as well, along with her computer, phone, and tablet. Smart devices had eyes and ears that the authorities could tap into. Most criminals were caught because they ultimately couldn't stay off-line, but Astra had no intentions of getting caught.

There was a new life waiting for her out in deep space, on a planet outside the Sol system. She planned to grab it with both hands and make the most of it. It was that hope more than anything that motivated her. Not the man sleeping in the bed across from her own, or the doctor she didn't know if she would ever see again, or even the prospect of doing something rebellious. Those might motivate some people and Astra had certainly felt that she had to do something to help the man with the horrible scars across his body. But that motivation had been swallowed up by fear and it was the prospect of a fresh start that she focused on. Just three more days, and they could sail away into a life with options, a life where she could hope for more than just getting to retirement age with a few good years left to live. But three days seemed like a long, long time.

14

The mobile command post was a high-tech aircraft. Kittle was not the pilot, and the ship didn't have a crew, so he wasn't in complete control. In fact, he was forced to strap into a chair and wait for permission from the pilot to get up and get to work. Once they were in the air and stable, Kittle ordered the computer specialist to fire up the multiple consoles.

"Captain, there's an incoming message," the communication director said. "It's Admiral Ross."

"Put her through," Kittle said, moving to the communication platform. It was a circle in front of a tall video screen. Three small cameras around the platform allowed for a full hologram to be transmitted to Space Control. On the flat screen in front of Kittle, the picture of Kathryn Ross appeared. She looked tense.

"Give us an update, Captain," she ordered immediately.

He had no idea who us was, but he didn't need to know. Who he was speaking to didn't change the facts.

"We're tracking Dr. Zeldin," he said. "Once we have drones, we'll be able to see exactly who is in the car he rented. It's still our best lead at the moment. We got no hits on the AI search programs at the train depot. As you know, the doctor stopped there for approximately sixty seconds, but was in a dead space, and we couldn't see if anyone was with him. We did track an unknown figure that fit the description of Sergeant Hammer, but we got no hits on facial recognition. Which means it probably wasn't him."

"How is all this possible?" Kathryn Ross asked. "It seems much too complex for one man."

"He's not working alone; we've suspected as much," Kittle explained. "My suspicion is that he made contact with a civilian company, probably a pharmaceutical company with deep pockets. They have entire divisions devoted to corporate espionage. My guess is they're moving Sergeant Hammer, trying to get him to a clandestine site to do their own research and development. That would explain the doctor's resourcefulness."

"Why?" a forceful voice demanded.

Kittle realized that Kathryn Ross wasn't the senior officer on the call. Admiral of the Fleet Evander Royce was there too, but Kittle couldn't see him.

"Sir, it's my belief that Dr. Zeldin wanted all the credit for Sergeant Hammer's abilities. He didn't get what he wanted from us, so he sold the patient to the highest bidder."

"That makes for good fiction, Captain," Royce said. "But we deal in stark reality. If Zeldin wanted credit, he wouldn't have committed treason. He'll be a wanted man for the rest of his life. It makes no sense."

"Maybe it's all about the money," Ross said softly. "It usually is."

"He was set to get a share of any patents and resulting revenues," Royce continued. "I'm not sure I agree with this line of reasoning."

"Sir, if I might push back on that just a little," Kittle said. He was going out on a limb by disagreeing with the Admiral of the Fleet, but Kittle wasn't used to being told he was wrong. "Zeldin is a prideful man. I've served with him and spent time with him. I believe he felt that the best advances gained in the Hammer Project would be highly classified and used for the benefit of Space

Command alone. I don't think he wanted to share, sir, but that's just my opinion."

"If he was working with someone else, how do we find them?" Admiral Ross asked.

Kittle wasn't surprised that his superiors seemed just as clueless as Lieutenant Gomez had been. That was the curse of higher rank. In fact, there was almost no difference between the Space Force Chiefs of Staff and the politicians they were beholden to. Their focus was on their comforts. The pressure of being in actual command disappeared, and all too often was replaced with the cushion of simply reading reports about action in places so far removed that it became almost theoretical.

"Admiral, I have a team combing through Dr. Zeldin's life as we speak," Kittle said. "Captain Morris has a team searching Zeldin's berth in the visiting officers' tower. Computer experts are digging into his communications. I even have Commander Bingham going over everything Dr. Zeldin did on the *Intrepid* after discovering Sergeant Hammer's regenerative abilities. We will find the link. Dr. Zeldin was careful, but no one is perfect."

"I want updates, Captain Kittle." the Admiral of the Fleet's voice was forceful. "Admiral Ross will contact you as soon as we clear drone operations with Titan's air traffic control. Do you have people covering the space port?"

"I urged Captain Morris to do so, Admiral, but he claims not to have the manpower and that I don't have the authority to give him orders."

"I will see to it that he is brought up to speed. Major Hue has Marines at the space port on their way to deployment. We'll get them up to speed and make sure that Sergeant Hammer can't board a ship to get off-world."

"What else do you need, Captain Kittle?" Royce asked.

"Sir, if we're going to bring Sergeant Hammer in alive, then it's going to take more than a squad of MPs. He's dangerous, and the longer our search takes, the more dangerous he becomes. The research teams hadn't even gotten to the strength and physical prowess testing. We simply don't know what Sergeant Hammer is truly capable of. With your permission, Admiral, I'd like a special forces unit on standby."

"Makes sense," Royce said. "Admiral Ross will get a team from Colonel Beamer geared up and mobile. Shouldn't take long. I want you to find Hammer and bring him back to us. This project is the highest priority. Get it done, Kittle."

"You can count on me, Admiral."

Kathryn Ross gave a nod, then the video screen went dark. Kittle fought the urge to sag a little. He didn't want the team he hastily assembled to track down Zeldin and Hammer to see any weakness. He went back to his seat and took a gulp of his coffee. Caffeine didn't do what it used to, but he needed something. He had only gotten a few hours of sleep and the gentle hum of the aircraft was lulling him to sleep.

"Meyers, Ford, do you have drones ready to launch?"

"Aye, Captain," Lieutenant Meyers said. "High altitude drone is ready for launch."

"I'm checking the cameras now on the fast mover," Lieutenant Ford said. "Wireless connection is strong. We should be ready to go momentarily."

Kittle wished the bureaucratic chain of command on Titan was as responsive as his team. But he would have to make do with what they had. The aircraft he was in had drones ready to launch and a team of MPs that could be dropped into place ahead of Dr. Zeldin. Kittle's heart beat faster at the thought of bringing his friend in. Zeldin's treason felt like a personal betrayal to Kittle. The physician would answer for his crimes and, at some point, Kittle planned a little payback of his own. Once he got his hands on Dr. Zeldin, the traitor would rue the day.

He felt like a sniper with his target in his crosshairs. All he needed was the go order and his hunt would be complete.

15

Dr. Zeldin was no fool, which was why, after stopping on the outskirts of town to refuel his rental car, he plugged in an auto-driver unit. He had seen it in the pawn shop and managed to get it without leaving any record of having purchased it. He overpaid for one of the watches and the pawnbroker threw in the auto-driver as part of the purchase. It helped that auto-drivers were illegal on Titan; it gave them both an incentive to deny where the device came from. The blockchain on his digital currency account wouldn't show an itemized statement from the pawn shop. When the brass sent someone to question the pawnbroker, he wouldn't mention having included it. Not that it would matter for long. Space Command would track the vehicle down, stop it and discover he wasn't inside.

The auto-driver plugged into the car's computer diagnostics port. He input an address on the far side of Titan and let the car go, then he slipped into a seedy bar. There were plenty on the edge of town, most with patrons who didn't like the police and wouldn't be quick to answer questions. Throughout Prime City, there were cameras on lamp posts, traffic lights, building corners and rooftops.

Municipal Services operated and maintained them. The video from the cameras fed into a massive AI that could monitor them all in real time and still have enough computing power to allow for searches. Cal Zeldin knew how to throw off the computer search. He went to the bathroom and slipped a lift into his left shoe. It wasn't much, but it would change his gait just enough that the computer wouldn't recognize it. But the real issue was facial recognition. To make his way back through the city, he couldn't rely on a hat or hood. Head-wear made the AI pay more attention to a person. If he only needed to go a few blocks, it might work, which was why he sent Jack into the train depot with just a hoodie. But if he was going to traverse the city, he needed more, and he needed a disguise that would fool most people.

The Transcontinental was what most people referred to as a freak show ... and not a good one, either. Loud music pulsed, and red lights illuminated the various stages where performers in outlandish costumes danced or simply paraded themselves about. It was not Zeldin's habit to frequent such places, but he knew they existed, and so, as he thought about how to get back into the city unnoticed, it occurred to him that the workers in such a place might be able to help.

He waited until the performance ended, then moved to the edge of the stage where there were steps that led to a side door. A man with female breasts and a surgically attached, robotic tail saw him waiting and slowly made his way down the steps. The man wore a tight-fitting suit that had animal fur on the back that matched his tail. His hair was long and teased out so that it stood up around his neck and blended with his beard. Both had been artificially colored to look like a lion's mane. On his face were what appeared to be feline whiskers at the corners of his mouth, and when he smiled or spoke, or pretended to roar when he was performing, you could see enlarged fangs.

"I need your assistance, please," Zeldin said.

"I don't do kink, mister," the lion man said.

"Oh, no, that's not what I'm after," Zeldin said.

The man was big, over six feet tall, and muscular, even though when he spoke, it was with a high-pitched, effeminate voice. He pointed a finger at Zeldin. "I said no, and I meant it."

"I can pay," Zeldin said, following the lion man into the dark hallway that led backstage.

"You aren't allowed back here."

"I'm desperate," Zeldin said, which wasn't exactly true. The lion man was the first performer he had approached in the freak show. There was bound to be more, but Zeldin did feel the pressure to get what he needed so he could rendezvous with Astra and Sergeant Hammer. He felt responsible for them both, but especially for Astra, who was in danger. Maybe it wasn't strictly his fault, but he felt like it was.

"That's obvious," the lion man said. "Whatever you're into, ask someone else. This is my second job, and I'm exhausted."

"I just need a temporary facial alteration," Cal said. "Something that would get me past AI security."

The lion man was at the door to the dressing room, but he stopped and turned around.

"You are in trouble then," he said.

"It's not what you think," Zeldin said. "I'm not a criminal. But I helped someone get out of a bad situation and now powerful people want to find me."

"I've heard it all a thousand times, honey. You can come back with me, but if you're lying or if you try something, I'll break your neck. You've been warned."

Zeldin had no doubt the lion man could do it. But he followed the performer back into the dressing room. He passed a woman with fish scales across her body and another that looked alien. Up close, the costumes looked shabby and the surgical enhancements had obviously been done on the cheap. The lion man's tail came out of a hole in the back of his fur-covered bodysuit, but Zeldin noticed the enflamed skin that was puckering around it.

"It must take a great commitment to have a tail like that," Zeldin said.

"It takes too much alcohol and the mind of a young idiot," the lion man said in a weary voice. "But I've known performers who have gone the distance. One man I knew had his lower legs amputated so that he could go around on all fours like a real cat. I'm not that crazy. Sit," he said, pointing to a wooden chair against the wall in the tiny closet that was his dressing room.

He powered down the robotic tail, then, with a twist, removed it from the metal plate that was surgically attached to his back. Zeldin guessed it had screws in his sacrum. The man had no modesty. He peeled off the body suit and was completely nude underneath, but Zeldin had seen that much through the hose-like front of the suit. He pulled on a silky robe and picked up a vape pipe shaped like a delicate cigarette on a long, black filter. He took a deep draw, then exhaled slowly. Zeldin smelled the skunky odor of marijuana.

"It's for the pain," he said. "It never stops."

"I'm a doctor," Zeldin said. "I understand what you're going through. How is it connected to your sacrum?"

"Screws," the lion man said with a grimace. "I think they over-torqued them or something."

"The body doesn't like metal," Zeldin said. "Have you thought of having it removed?"

"Think about it every day," he said. "But the reversal costs three times as much, and the recovery time is months. I can't afford that."

"I'm sorry," Zeldin said. "I wish I could help."

He reached into his pocket and brought out a gold coin. It was in a little plastic case that had an official sticker along the outside that said **1/2 ounce 24 Karat Fine Gold.**

"Maybe this will," he said, holding it out to the lion man, who took the coin.

"What is it?"

"Gold," Zeldin said. "The real deal. Take it to any gold broker, a pawn shop, or coin store, and they'll pay you flex credits straight into your account."

"How much?"

"The price of gold goes up and down. The last time I checked it, which was when I bought that coin, it was a little over nine thousand credits an ounce."

The lion man glanced at the coin, then back up at Zeldin.

"You're saying this is worth forty-five hundred credits?"

"Yes, a bit more than actually. But, if you sell it the dealer will have a fee, that's how they make money. Don't let them charge you more than ten percent, though. That's not scrap gold or jewelry, it's certified, government-minted gold bullion. If someone tries to charge you more, threaten to walk. Trust me, there are a lot of gold buyers. But you should easily clear four thousand if you sold it today."

"This is a scam, right?"

"No, it's not. Look, you don't know my name. What I'm asking for is a few cosmetic tricks, nothing drastic or flashy. If you have something that will last a few days, that would be ideal. I need it to look natural."

"To fool the surveillance systems."

"That's right. I'm paying for a good job ... and for silence."

"Who might come asking?"

"Space Command," Zeldin said.

The lion man chuckled. "Seriously? I thought you were running from the bad guys. I thought you were like a snitch for the triads or street hustlers or something."

"There is a man in Space Command who is just as bad, trust me. If they come asking, you don't know me, never saw me. If they start pressing you, just refuse to talk. I need four days. After that, it won't matter. A thousand credits a day seems reasonable."

"Whatever," the lion man said with a smirk. "Let's get started."

The process took half an hour. The lion man used latex to thicken Zeldin's chin and jawline. The latex was flesh colored, but he used a bit of makeup to help it blend with his natural skin. And then he used more latex to alter the doctor's browline and forehead, adding more wrinkles.

"That should do it," the lion man said. "You look different, and that's all it takes."

Zeldin looked in the mirror and nodded. "You do good work."

"I've had a lot of practice," he said, waving a finger with a long fake nail at his own face. "This takes a lot of work, honey."

"Thank you," Zeldin said, standing up and shaking the lion man's hand. "Is there a back way out of here?"

The performer showed Zeldin the employee exit. And he began his long walk through the city. It was almost midday by that point. Zeldin hadn't slept in a long time. He hadn't had any food either. Unlike Astra, who had preloaded cards, the only money Zeldin had was trade goods. And he had spent too much on the cosmetic makeover. He would have to soldier on with no food and no rest. He couldn't risk using public transportation. Instead, with his duffle bag slung over his shoulder, he set out on a long trek through the city, staying in groups where he was less likely to be identified, and blending in with the throng. Prime City was a dynamic metropolis on a major moon near the hyperspace launch window beyond Saturn. It was large enough that he would have to travel over twenty miles to reach the city center. It would be a long, taxing hike. But the alternative was worse. If he was going to start his life over, it was better to do it with people he knew. Sergeant Hammer and Astra weren't exactly friends, but the truth was, as a physician in Space Command, he had never stayed in any place long enough to cultivate true friendships. Maybe fleeing for his life with a pair of like-minded people would turn out to be a good thing.

16

"Captain, I have a direct message from Admiral Ross," the communications director said. "She says that drone operations are a go."

"Outstanding," Kittle exclaimed. It's about damn time. Drone operators, launch your machines."

It was an exercise in futility. Kittle knew the outcome. The rental car hadn't slowed down. It hadn't taken any exits. He was too far out to see inside the vehicle, but the GPS signal showed that it stayed two miles an hour below the speed limit at all times. It was a classic design for automated vehicles. And Kittle had the sinking suspicion that he was chasing a ghost.

"High altitude drone is away," Meyers announced.

"Surveillance drone is away," Ford echoed.

Both of the remote pilots had headsets on that covered their eyes and showed them an augmented view from their drone's vantage point. It took less than half an hour for the drones to move into position. The HA or overwatch drone moved in first. It took position directly over the moving car, matching its speed and direction, but high enough to give the faster drone with surveillance cameras the information it needed to move in close. The rental car was cheap, a flimsy vehicle built for economy. It had no overhead window, and it was so small that the heat from the engine made it impossible to tell anything on thermal imaging.

Kittle wondered if Dr. Zeldin was really smart enough to thwart his efforts or if the traitor had just gotten lucky. Eventually, the fast drone got low enough and close enough to point its cameras inside the vehicle. It might have been faster to approach from the rear, but there was something in the back that obstructed their view. Kittle was forced to wait while the drone made a wide, sweeping turn as it raced ahead of the rental car, then waited for it directly in the car's path.

"Hovering at fifteen feet, captain," Ford said.

Vehicle is approaching the drone position," one of his computer experts called out.

"Get me a visual," Kittle said.

"Aye, Captain, bringing the vehicle into focus now," Ford said. "There, I've got it."

He did. The view from the drone was displayed on one of the big view screens in the flying command center. Kittle sighed with frustration.

"Looks like the car is empty," Ford said.

"Must be a driverless vehicle, Captain," the computer analyst said.

"Stay with it," Kittle ordered. "We need absolute confirmation. Pilot, get us ahead of that rental car. I'm putting the MP squad into play."

"Roger that," the pilot responded from the cockpit.

Kittle dropped into a chair and ran a hand over his tired face. His quarry had slipped out of his trap. It made no sense. How had the doctor outsmarted his captain?

"Get me a direct line to the Admiral's office," Kittle ordered. "Let me know when it's established."

"Aye, Captain," the communication officer said. "Initiating a tight beam, high data laser stream to Space Command HQ. It's locked! You can begin your transmission, sir."

Kittle got to his feet and straightened his uniform. It wouldn't be in his favor if Sergeant Hammer slipped off-world. He had taken charge when the patient had escaped. And he had led the charge in pursuing the car. A good commander needed to know three things: the capabilities of his army, the terrain, and the tendencies of his opposing general. The first two factors were essential for success in battle. History was replete with examples of commanders who lost battles because they didn't know their army's capabilities. In most of those examples, it was fear that the opposing force was too large, and one's own forces too small, to ensure victory. And yet, very often, it was the smaller force that won the day. Terrain was also a major factor. For as long as there had been armies and warfare, there had been battlefields. Usually, Kittle's terrain was outer space, where incredible distances played a role in engaging an enemy. But on Titan, he had been mistaken.

It was a hard pill to swallow. And he knew, without a doubt, that Admiral Kathryn Ross was going to make it even more difficult. All because he had assumed that he knew Dr. Zeldin. They had served together on two deployments, totaling over a year spent together on a starship. In that time, the two men had many conversations. They had dined together, although not frequently. Kittle's assessment of the doctor was of a good physician and a competent administrator. Zeldin had never directly diagnosed or treated anyone while under Kittle's command, other than Sergeant Hammer. Kittle had assumed that Zeldin would be sloppy and frightened. Yet, somehow, the man had been daring enough to free Sergeant Hammer and help him flee from Space Command. And, at some point in the process, he had managed to fool even Kittle himself.

When the image of Admiral Ross blinked to life on the view screen, Captain Kittle saluted, then launched into an explanation.

"We've made contact with the rental vehicle utilized by Dr. Zeldin," he said.

"Is the escapee in custody?" Admiral Ross asked.

"Negative, Admiral. It seems that both Dr. Zeldin and Sergeant Hammer have slipped past us."

"How?"

"I can't be certain, but my guess is they utilized an auto-driver."

"They can't," she said. "Auto-drivers are illegal on Titan."

"True, but they can be obtained and utilized. I'm ordering my team to go back over the car's every move. At some point, they got out and sent the car on without them."

"Why didn't we stop the car sooner?"

"We didn't have our resources in place yet, Admiral."

"And so we've wasted countless hours," she snapped.

"Dr. Zeldin clearly has help. I can't imagine he would be so resourceful on his own."

"I don't give a damn about the doctor, or whoever he's in league with, Captain. Get me that Sergeant. He's the only thing that matters, do you understand? He is the future of Space Force. I don't care what it takes, you find him and you bring him back alive. That's an order."

"Understood, Admiral. I'm on it. You can count on me."

"Yes, well, Admiral Royce knows you are leading the hunt, so, for your own sake, captain, you'd better deliver. The Admiral of the Fleet is not a patient man."

Her image froze for a moment, then disappeared. Kittle wanted to scream, but he couldn't let his people see him lose control. Somehow, someway, he would make Kathryn Ross pay for doubting his abilities. But that was a fight for another day.

"Get me the MP team leader."

"Aye, activating intercom to passenger cabin Alpha," the Comms Officer said.

"This is Sergeant Drucker. How may we be of assistance, Captain?"

"We're putting you on the ground to stop a car that's using an auto-driver," Kittle said. "Once you have it, tear the thing apart. I want to know everything that was left inside and anything that might shed some light on the people who set it in motion."

"Aye, Captain. We'll stop the car and do a thorough search, no doubt about that."

"Very good. Kittle out."

He stepped away from the communication platform and slumped into his chair. He suddenly felt old. He was fifty-one, after all. He had been in Space Command for twenty-nine years. Twenty of those were as an independent commander of interstellar vessels. He had earned the right to retire. But thirty years of service was the maximum for anyone not in a high command position. He would have to make a decision soon: to retire when he was forced out or to start climbing the ladder while he still had time. Of course, there was always the chance that even if he tried to gain position and rank that he might be held back. His record was impeccable, but that didn't automatically guarantee promotion. Space Command was not a merit-based service. It was more important who you knew, rather than what you accomplished. Which was why it was so important that Sergeant Hammer's secrets were obtained. One way or another, they had to get as much from him as possible. It was not only for Kittle's physical future, but for his stock in Space Command as well.

He would return to Prime City. Instinct told him that was where Zeldin was hiding. It was maybe brilliant or, more likely, simple fortuitousness. The doctor had gotten lucky. He had benefited from the ineptitude of the MPs on duty at Space Command and the sluggish response from their superiors. Kittle knew that having to wait hours for permission from the civil authorities just to launch their drones was a major strike against him. But he was a man accustomed to hardships and finding ways to get things done.

Dr. Zeldin's luck would run out. There had been no reported sightings of either Zeldin or Sergeant Hammer at the space port. Nor had the municipal AI programs picked them up on facial recognition. That together led Kittle to believe that his quarry had gone to ground. They were hiding, probably within striking distance of Space Command. He would search everywhere, even go house to house if that was what it took. One way or another, Captain Kittle would have his prize. No one would deprive him of it. He would succeed or die trying; there was no other way.

17

The smell of something savory woke Jack. He didn't move at first. Wrapped in a cocoon of warm blankets and lying on a soft bed, he searched his mind for pain. Lying still, he didn't feel any. That was a surprise and a welcome one. It also made him not want to move, but his stomach growled sharply.

Rolling onto his back, he reassessed his physical situation. The skin on his shoulder, hip, and foot was tight. When he tried to move them, he could feel that the burns weren't healed, but they did seem greatly improved. He opened his eyes and saw the low ceiling of the motel room.

"You're awake," Astra said from across the room. "Hungry?"

"Starving," he said.

"Good. You can eat and then I better see what I can do about those bandages," she said.

Jack used his good arm to push himself up to a sitting position on the bed. Astra handed him a burrito wrapped in a metallic wrapper and a bottle of water. His hand actually trembled as he forced himself to set the food down and get a drink first.

"Where'd you get this?"

"There's a food truck around the corner," she said. "How are you feeling?"

"What did Dr. Zeldin tell you about me?" he asked.

"That you heal fast," she admitted. "It must be true, I saw you fight those men with cuts across your body. He said they didn't know how it worked or what happened to make you different."

"Just a freak accident, I guess," Jack said, tearing open his burrito and taking a bite.

Astra walked over and sat on the edge of the bed. "Do you mind?" she asked.

Jack wasn't modest. In the Marines, he was used to sharing bathroom facilities with an entire platoon. But he felt a bit embarrassed being alone in the motel room with Astra. She was attractive, but not flashy. He couldn't see any makeup on her face, but her caramel colored skin didn't need any. She had black hair and dark brown eyes that he had trouble looking away from.

"Go ahead," he told her.

She lifted the edge of his T-shirt. Underneath his skin seemed flawless. There was no sign of the cuts on his stomach or chest.

"The cuts..." she said, still holding his shirt up. "They're gone. They didn't even leave a scar."

"I'd say lucky me, but I know Space Command wants me back in that lab. The last thing they did was use a blowtorch on me."

She rocked back in shock. "No!"

He nodded. She lowered his shirt back down.

"Take a look at my shoulder," he told her.

She rolled up the short sleeve to reveal the wide bandage underneath. It had been white and sterile, she knew, because she had stocked several labs with that exact bandage. Dark liquid had stained it. She was almost afraid to peel it off, but she did anyway. Underneath the skin was black and cracked.

"Oh," she said, putting a hand over her mouth. Jack saw tears in her eyes.

"It's okay," he told her.

"Nothing about this is okay," she said.

"It's healing," he told her. "I can feel it. All I need is this," he held up the burrito, "and sleep. I'll be right as rain in no time."

"Don't you need medicine?" she asked. "I don't think that can heal without skin grafts and stuff."

"I suppose we'll find out," Jack said. "Any word from Doc Zeldin?"

"Not yet," Astra said.

"Did he tell you his plan?"

"Just that he would meet us at the ship."

"What ship?"

"The *Rosa Marie* is a cargo ship. It runs ore from Veta Madre in the Ocho system. They take on passengers to work the vessel back to Ocho. No papers, no questions, just work in exchange for a new world."

"Veta Madre's no paradise," Jack said.

"We aren't looking for paradise, just opportunity," Astra said. "From there, you can figure out your next move. But the ship arrives tomorrow and will leave the next day. Will you be well enough to work by then?"

"I don't know," Jack admitted. "The cuts on my chest were done three days ago, I think. It's hard to know for certain."

"How long since they burned you?"

"Thirty hours, maybe," he guessed. "I don't really know."

She went back to the window. There was a small chair there, and after she looked outside, she sat down. On a small, round table beside her was a pillowcase. She picked up and used her teeth to make a tear in the thin fabric. Jack ate his burrito and watched as she tore the pillowcase into long strips.

"What are you doing that for?" he asked after he swallowed the last bite of his meal.

"Bandages," she said. "I could buy some, but—"

"That would attract attention," Jack cut in. "I'm glad you didn't."

"We have to lay low for two more days," she said. "Tomorrow, I'll make contact with the *Rosa Maria's* people and make sure we can get passage out of the system."

"Space Command won't stop looking for me," Jack said. "Not here, not in the Ocho system, not ever."

"My Abuela used to say, *worry about today, tomorrow has enough trouble of its own.*"

"Sounds like she was a smart lady," Jack said.

"We lay low, keep you out of sight until Tuesday morning. Then we make our move and hope for the best."

"Why are you doing this?" Jack asked. "I know Zeldin feels guilty for handing me over to the monsters at Space Command R&D. But why are you blowing up your life for me?"

"I'm not doing it for you, not entirely," she said as she glanced out between the heavy curtains again. "The truth is, I don't have much of a life to blow up."

"What do you mean? You could do anything?"

"I'm second-generation Titan," she said. "My father was a sanitation worker, my mother worked in child care. They were both dead before I turned twenty years old."

"There's nothing wrong with honest work," Jack said.

"You don't live here, Sergeant," she said. "You visit. You look around and see a thriving world. But the truth is, most of the native-born people on Titan have very few prospects. Every boy I knew growing up either got work on interstellar freighters or at the poles collecting methane. We can work in general labor jobs, but the good careers always go to people from off-world. Titan is a stepping stone for most people, but it's a millstone around the neck of people born and raised here.

"That's why I'm leaving," she continued. "Seeing you and what the researchers were doing to you, made me realize I couldn't stay. I couldn't just leave you there to be tortured and killed, either. The doctor felt the same way."

"I'm grateful," Jack said, although he felt guilty too. He had needed help, but by helping him, Zeldin and Astra had condemned themselves.

She stood up and crossed back to his bed.

"Show me where else they hurt you," she said. "I'll get you cleaned up and you can get some more sleep."

"Don't you need to sleep?"

"Can't," she said. "I'm too nervous."

"I can stand watch," he told her.

"Maybe later," she said. "Come on, show me."

He did. Twenty minutes later, he was asleep again. Astra had never seen anyone like Jack. He wasn't handsome so much as rugged. His face was almost square and there was dark stubble on his cheeks, chin and scalp. His body was all compact muscle. He didn't seem big and strong, but there didn't appear to be an ounce of fat on the man. And though he wasn't bulky, every muscle was visible and appeared to be powerful.

The burn wounds were terrible and a bit strange. She had seen burns before, but nothing like what she saw on Jack. His burns looked like the charred ends of a tight roll of paper or a cigar that has been half-smoked and allowed to burn out. There was a crater in his foot with blackened edges. Inside, she could see muscle, tendon, and even bone. How he had stood on that foot, much less walked on it, was a total mystery. His hip was bad, too. There was only a thin layer of muscle between the skin and the wide hip bone. That muscle had burned up, but it almost looked like she could see it growing back.

Astra was no doctor, but she had known plenty of people who had gotten hurt. That was simply part of life for the working class on Titan. From broken bones to severed limbs, nearly everyone had scars. But not Jack. Astra had known methane miners. They worked in large, industrial collectors that were essentially pods on the sides of massive vacuums. Titan's surface was covered with lakes and streams of pure, liquid methane. It was collected and refined, mostly by people born and raised on Saturn's largest moon. There were dangers involved, of course. The most common was severe frostbite, as liquid methane was an extremely cold substance. She had seen people with missing fingers, toes and even places on their faces and ears where the flesh was frozen. There was no way to repair it short of cosmetic surgery, but while the scars could be covered, there was no way to restore feeling or sensation in the lost digit or area.

Yet somehow, it seemed that Jack's body was regenerating new skin, bone, tendons and muscles. She didn't understand it, but couldn't help but be fascinated by the man. He ate like a horse and slept like a dead man. Yet despite his injuries and his rugged appearance, he seemed so peaceful. Watching him sleep, she could almost forget that the most powerful government agency in the system was looking for them. Yet it was that thought, and the fear that accompanied it, that kept her awake.

Astra glanced out the window again. There were only a couple of other rooms being used and the tiny lot outside her room remained empty. No one was watching the motel that she could see. Little did she know that sixty miles above her head, a satellite was looking down on Prime City. At Space Command, there were powerful AI programs scouring the video feed for any sign of them. The three fugitives were hiding in the lion's den and, sooner or later, the sleeping beasts would wake up. The lions would be hungry.

18

Prime City was like any metropolis on Earth, Mars or Europa. Among the millions of people who called it home, there were unruly elements. Some were people down on their luck who were angry and frustrated with what they perceived as systematic discrimination against them. There were others who, through no fault of their own, usually due to life-altering injuries sustained in the workplace, became addicted to pain medication. Even though a variety of *recreational* drugs, from marijuana to heroin, to mescaline and magic mushrooms, were available legally, they were also expensive. And so people naturally turned to cheaper ways to get what they needed, even though they did significant damage to the human body and often made the users violent after a time.

Then there were hustlers who felt that money conned was sweeter than money earned, worked their way through the masses, sometimes stealing wallets, other times running long cons that bilked people out of billions of credits. Digital Currency was supposed to be the answer to crime. It was highly regulated. Every credit issued carried with it markers that allowed it to be spent on specific things. For instance, if a person's yearly medical scan showed them to be pre-diabetic, the government could restrict their use of credits to just fruits and vegetables. Big Brother was constantly watching out for the little guy, whether the populace liked it or not.

Of course, serious criminals simply found new ways around the digital currency limitations. If all money was digital, then it could be hacked, counterfeited, redirected and abused in ways the bankers never imagined. In Prime City, the Cronus Crew was the most visible organized crime group. They called themselves a gang, and they were certainly involved in those types of crimes, from cooking street drugs to human trafficking; they were also involved in government scams and computer-based crimes.

Dr. Cal Zeldin knew nothing about the CC on Titan. He didn't recognize the young watchers on the street corners he passed who wore black baseball caps with no logo, and silver clips on the bottom of their oversized jackets. He would have been better off to hide the expensive watch he had invested in and the two gold rings with diamonds he was wearing. It made sense to him to keep the valuables close, but as he made his way through the city on foot, those things stood out to the criminals who were trained to spot such valuables.

Word was passed among the Cronus Crew, and three enforcers were sent to collect from the obviously wealthy man passing through their territory. At times, Cal Zeldin moved along with the flow of traffic, but in other places the crowds thinned. He turned onto a narrow street with only a handful of people on it when the enforcers following him moved in.

Perhaps it was fatigue, or maybe he was too focused on reaching his goal, but he never heard the three criminals who came up behind him. He was just passing a dirty alley lined with dumpsters and littered with trash when they grabbed him and flung him into the alley.

One of the gangsters turned and stood at the entrance to the alley, watching for trouble. If anyone saw them attack Dr. Zeldin, they pretended not to have and moved steadily on their way. The other two men grabbed Cal, pushing him into the alley, forcing him into the shadows between the buildings. His feet barely touched the ground as they assaulted him.

"Hey! Wait... what are you doing? Let go of me!"

They did, with a shove that sent him tumbling to the ground and slamming into the side of a dumpster. He was on his knees looking up at the two men. One was black, the other white. They looked like bodybuilders. The white man had tattoos on his neck and face. The black man pulled back his coat to reveal a knife the size of a machete.

"Stop talking," the knifeman said. "Give us the bag."

"And that watch," the man with tattoos said. "Rings too."

"Okay, okay, yes," Zeldin said, holding up his hands in front of him as if he could ward off the ire of the two criminals. "I'll give you whatever you want. Anything at all, just, don't hurt me."

The two men didn't reply or make any kind of gesture in response to Dr. Zeldin's plea, but he could see the violent intent in their eyes. They would take what they wanted from him, beat him, maybe kill him and leave his body in the alley.

"Give us the bag," the first man repeated. "Wallet too."

"Yeah, alright. My wallet's in my coat," Zeldin said. It wasn't true. His wallet was in the back pocket of the wool slacks he was wearing. But inside his coat, stuffed into the breast pocket, was the laser pistol he had taken from the MP at Space Command. Being a medical doctor on a spaceship left a person with a lot of time on their hands. Dr. Zeldin did his job and spent a good majority of his free time reading medical journals and the user manuals for the automated medical equipment used on the ships he traveled in. But even that didn't keep him busy all the time. On military ships, there were combat simulators that were used to keep the Marine units sharp and prepared for action. But often a few of those simulators were set up for individual use. And Dr. Zeldin had spent his fair share of time shooting virtual aliens and perfecting his aim with a wide variety of simulated firearms.

He pulled out the pistol in a quick jerk. The two gangsters were over six paces from where Cal Zeldin knelt on the filthy ground. They saw the quick motion and started toward him. They were fast for men of their size and weight, but they weren't faster than the laser weapon. Cal shot the knifeman first. The blast caught him just above his belt and set a million volts of electric energy through his body. A split second later, Cal's second shot hit the tattooed man in the chest. Both of the enforcers stiffened as the energy raced through their bodies, causing their muscles to spasm. Their eyes rolled back into their heads so that only the whites showed. The man with the tattoos bit his tongue as his jaw clamped down and blood oozed between his lips, before he fell straight backward. The knifeman, also stiff, toppled sideways and hit his head against the side of an air circulation unit. Both men would recover from the stun blast, but both of them had taken hard blows to the head during their fall. The tattooed man's head smacked against the pavement with a crunch.

Despite the non-lethal setting on the High Energy Laser Pistol, it was still a dangerous device. Both of the enforcers would need medical treatment, but Cal didn't feel bad for them. He was a doctor, but he felt no compulsion to help the men who had intended to rob and beat him. When he stood up, his legs felt weak. The third man had seen the enforcers go down and decided it was time to disappear. The laser pistol didn't have a loud recoil, but it did make a unique sound. And even if he couldn't see them, Cal knew there were witnesses everywhere. He was surrounded by apartment houses. There were undoubtedly people looking down at him at that very moment. It would only take one to have him questioned by the authorities, and there was no doubt in the doctor's mind that Space Command would be monitoring local law enforcement activity. They may even be working hand in hand to find him. Cal knew he had to get as far away from the scene of the attack as possible.

Every person on Titan was issued an ID card. It was a plain white, hard plastic card with a digital chip that connected to the municipal networks where a person's identity, health records, legal standing and banking information were held. Cal took the wallets of both his attackers, removed their ID cards, and tossed the wallets back onto the men. He hurried to the edge of the alley, looked up and down the connecting street, then rushed on his way. At the corner was a private transport unit. He scanned the knifeman's ID card. The vehicle, a boxy-looking hovercar with a sliding door on the passenger side that gave access to a pair of middle row captain seats and a bench seat in back. There was a safety screen behind the driver's seat, and a computer console in the front passenger spot. It had a screen that showed a photo of the person whose ID had been used to open the door, but the driver paid it no attention.

"Where to?"

"The train depot on Axis street," Dr. Zeldin said, his heart racing.

The computer's voice command function picked up Cal's words, entered the location into the interactive map, and calculated the route, distance, and resulting fee. Simultaneously, another app checked the fee against the money in the knifeman's flex account. There was enough to cover the fee, and a green light on the vehicle's dashboard lit in green.

"You got it," the driver said, putting the vehicle into drive mode and activating the repulser lift. The doors locked and the boxy vehicle rose smoothly into the air.

Dr. Zeldin breathed a sigh of relief. No one had come running and shooting at him. Not that he had necessarily expected that. There was no doubt the gangs had guns. But they were selective in using them, both because finding ammunition for the weapons was difficult and because they attracted law enforcement. In fact, it was possible that if one of the two thugs was seriously hurt that law enforcement would look into the matter. The HELP weapon left a unique mark on a person's body that didn't immediately go away. Sometimes it lasted for hours, sometimes for days, depending on the target's physical make-up. Dr. Zeldin had to assume that the weapons he and Sergeant Hammer had taken from the MPs would point the recovery team to any incident where a HELP was fired. Even if they had seized his rental car and found the other pistol and the assault rifle that Sergeant Hammer had used, they would know that one weapon was still missing. The report that someone had used one against the gang members would point them in the right direction. In fact, if they had the identity of the gang members he had shot, they would be able to track the transaction he had just made with the private transport unit.

"I have a question," he said.

"Go ahead," the driver said. He had a mirror mounted on his dashboard that allowed him to look back at the passengers without turning around. But he didn't even bother to glance down at it.

"Could I pay the fee for you to drive back to where you picked me up?"

"I suppose," the driver said. "Not sure why you would do that. The depot's a good place to get a fare."

"I'm sure that's the case," Zeldin said. "But I have my reasons."

"No skin off my back, mister. You pay, I go. That's all that I care about."

Zeldin nodded. He didn't know if the transport unit would transmit video or images of him to the authorities. If so, his disguise would be worthless. But he didn't feel like he had any options. He needed to disappear and there just wasn't a good place to do it. The best he could manage was to try and lead whoever might be looking for him off track and hope they could get off-world before the clues came together and he was caught. The latter wasn't an enjoyable thought. It made him shudder to think of it. He sat back in his seat and closed his eyes. He might only get ten minutes of rest, but that was better than nothing. He had no idea when he might feel safe enough to rest again. It felt like he was in a long passageway that seemed to have no end. And the walls were closing in on him.

19

Admiral of the Fleet Evander Royce was accustomed to getting his way. He told one battle group to move and they moved. He told another to stay and they stayed. He set the overarching strategy and gave orders to battleships with thousands of crew members on board, sometimes sending them into grave danger. He expected that in every case he would be obeyed without hesitation, which was almost always the case.

But the Admiral had not gotten his way with the Hammer Project. In fact, the news was negative on multiple fronts.

"Explain it to me again, Vice Admiral," Royce said. "With less technical jargon, please."

"Sir, the teams looking into Sergeant Hammer's DNA are stumped," VA Duncan said. He had been called in to give a report, which he was prepared to do, but didn't enjoy doing. No one wanted to give their boss bad news.

"Why?" Royce snapped.

"There doesn't seem to be a significant change in Sergeant Hammer's DNA. The code, as you well know, is some three billion base pairs. That's the equivalent of roughly nine thousand, five hundred books, sir. It's essentially a small library of information contained in each cell of the human body. We know that radiation can essentially scramble that information. Gamma radiation is particularly nasty when it comes to disruption and mutation. But in Sergeant Hammer's case, the change, at least the change we expect to find, is beneficial."

"So what's the problem, Vice Admiral?"

"Sir, the problem is that when we compare Sergeant Hammer's DNA pre and post exposure to the gamma radiation, there does not appear to be a change."

"There doesn't appear to be any difference whatsoever?"

"Well, sir, that's what we're looking at now. The DNA is information and that information hasn't changed. What's different is how his cells are reacting to that DNA. It's like a computer with an upgraded processing unit. It's doing the work faster and better, with less waste and more competency."

"Maybe my command staff needs exposure to this gamma radiation," Royce grumbled.

"Yes, sir, well... keep in mind that the same gamma surge killed all the rest of Sergeant Hammer's platoon, along with the flight crew of the drop ship they were in."

"Of course, it was a joke, Vice Admiral."

"A funny one, sir. Thank you for sharing it."

"Duncan, you know I hate brown-nosing."

"Aye, Admiral, my mistake. Won't happen again, sir."

"The question remains, can we replicate the process that Sergeant Hammer underwent?"

"Yes, we're still trying to answer that question."

"Do you have any actual answers, Vice Admiral?"

"We have a working theory on why Sergeant Hammer survived the gamma radiation, Admiral."

Royce was in his office. On his desk was a hologram of Vice Admiral Duncan. It was one foot tall, with a blue tint. Across the room, built into either side of the office doors, were large display screens. They showed the status of Space Command ships and entire battle groups, along with their location. In another window, news broadcasts ran with the volume muted and headlines played on a ticker at the bottom of that screen.

The Admiral of the Fleet had a tuxedo hanging on the back of the door leading into his private lavatory. A heavy crystal tumbler sat within reach on the desk, not far from the holograph of Vice Admiral Duncan, who was giving Royce a lecture. The Admiral of the Fleet had to suppress the urge to pick it up and let the forty-year-old whiskey race down his already pickled tongue and flood his blood supply with 100 proof alcohol.

"The body reacts to distress, whether that be from a germ or injury," Duncan said. "For instance, we don't have to tell the body what to do when we break our arm. No, the body goes to work, flooding the area with enzymes and blood cells that aid the healing process. Sergeant Hammer was gravely injured when exposed to the gamma radiation. I believe his entire body was in a state of urgent repair. Think of it like a battleship. Most of the time, it functions under normal status, but when in danger, it goes into Red Alert status. The alert tells every crew member across every deck and discipline where to be and what to do, without the need for officers to make constant commands. Likewise, our bodies, when in danger or need, reacts of it's own accord. Sergeant Hammer, due to his pre-radiation injuries, was in a bodily state of Red Alert, which allowed it to use the gamma radiation like a stimulant. I think his body's healing systems got smarter. Hence, his ability, not simply to heal, but to regenerate and upgrade. Before he escaped, we had recorded increases in his bone density, heart strength, circulatory volume, oxygen transmission and even brain function."

"Are you saying that to replicate his... abilities, we'll have to crush each person the way he was injured?" Royce asked. "Because I don't think that's advisable. If we're wrong, a lot of people could die."

"No, sir, I don't think that will be necessary. We just need more time to crack the code. The gamma burst didn't add anything, as much as it enabled his body to function at a much higher level. But we still don't know how the change was initiated at a cellular level. Once we discover that, we can formulate a plan that will create the same changes in anyone. But there are many possible combinations. There are over fifty bodily hormones alone that could have affected Sergeant Hammer. Then there are the frequencies of the gamma radiation, which are unknown. Likewise, we don't know the exact duration of the radiation surge that passed through his body. That's why it's so important that we get him back, Admiral. For all we know, the amazing rejuvenating effects have mutated. He could be dead, or highly susceptible to bacteria, or suffering from diminished mental capacity. His increased metabolism could be speeding the aging process. The regeneration factor could result in additional limbs. What I'm getting at is that we just don't know. We need Sergeant Hammer back in the lab."

"We have a team working on that," Royce said. "But they appear no closer to achieving their goals than your research teams."

"How hard can it be to find someone?" Duncan complained. "Sergeant Hammer is a phenomenal specimen, but he was not in full health when he ran away. I would start by checking with the hospitals and medical clinics."

Admiral of the Fleet Evander Royce thought checking the hospitals was a waste of time. And yet even as that thought passed through his mind, he realized he hadn't asked Captain Kittle to check such obvious options. It couldn't be that easy, he reasoned, could it? He would have to ask Kittle, but first, he had a gala to attend. He disliked most formal functions, but part of being Admiral of the Fleet was courting the politicians, both local and system-wide, to ensure Space Command had the resources necessary to fulfill its charter.

"Thank you for the update, Vice Admiral," he said, giving in to the urge to take a gulp of the whiskey in his glass. "I have obligations to attend to. The next time we speak, I expect progress and answers, not more lectures."

"Aye, Admiral. We are doing our best."

"And if your best isn't good enough, then I'll have to find someone who can get the job done."

The hologram looked shocked, and Royce ended the transmission before Duncan could come up with another excuse. He leaned back in his chair and sighed, hoping that someone wouldn't decide that it was Royce who couldn't get the job done. No one was irreplaceable. Results were what counted and Evander Royce was the type of man who would accept nothing less.

20

The Marine was hungry again. Astra would have preferred to stay in the motel, but she had taken him in, so that meant it was her responsibility to provide him with the basic essentials of life, such as food. It didn't matter that she hadn't expected him to be ravenous.

As Astra left the motel room, she did her best to act casual, but she scanned her surroundings for any sign of danger. She knew how to watch out for criminals, but watching out for the authorities was new.

There were so many things about her life that had completely changed in a matter of days. Had she been unhappy before seeing the sergeant fighting the researchers? Yes, she knew she had been. But she had also been complacent, letting life happen to her. It had taken the shock of seeing a man with gruesome wounds being prepped for more barbarous tests. His actions, maybe crazy or maybe valiant, had given her the courage to act.

She hadn't expected the changes to happen so fast, but so slow at the same time. She had left home, left her job, not even bothering to pay her rent. Never in her entire life had she acted so brazenly impulsive. And yet, so much of her time had been spent in the motel, watching the parking lot, letting the stranger sleep. It made her feel uneasy or, maybe, just unprepared. She was nagged by a growing sense of vulnerability. Unlike Dr. Zeldin, she had no trade goods. The credits on her prepaid flex cards were quickly running out ... and she had to feed the sergeant again.

Not that she blamed him for his ravenous appetite. She was amazed at his body's ability to heal. It was supernatural, if not outright miraculous. People didn't just heal from the wounds he had endured at the hands of the researchers. Her mind almost refused to believe it, but she had seen the deep cuts across his body in the lab just days before. She remembered after his struggle with the researchers how they had broken open and oozed blood. But just a few hours earlier, she had checked his entire body, re-bandaging the burns with strips from the torn pillow case, and the cuts were gone. Not only healed, but gone as if they had never been there. He didn't even have scars. She couldn't imagine what kind of metabolism was necessary to perform such regenerative growth and healing.

She wondered if she had been fooled. Had the cuts been real in the first place? She thought so, but it was hard to believe they could heal so completely. It was less of her distrust in the man and more of a feeling that she had made a mistake. It was easy to think that she hadn't really seen what she thought she had seen. Perhaps her mind was playing tricks on her or she had projected something that wasn't really there. It left her feeling uneasy.

Not that the man had done anything to cause her to distrust him, but he was a stranger. And everything about him was odd. The way he looked, old and young at the same time, no blemishes or wrinkles, but still he seemed craggy and rugged. And his eyes... she couldn't think about them. They made her feel that she wanted to open up and tell him everything she was feeling. But they were dangerous, too, and soulful somehow.

Then, there was his name. Jack Hammer... who names a child Jack when his last name is Hammer. It was as if they wanted him to be famous or a serial killer. And the truth was, he could be a psycho. She didn't know the man and, yet, she had blown up her life for him. Leaving Titan and starting over was one thing but, in helping Jack, she had made an enemy for life. Why would she do that? It didn't make rational sense, even though she knew her compassion for his plight had played a role in her decision-making process; it still felt like she had become a passenger in her own life.

Around the corner from the motel was a series of food trucks. They were in an empty lot across the narrow street from a series of bars. Astra had always wondered how establishments that were so similar could thrive in such close proximity. Above them were cheap apartments, mostly tiny studios. The food trucks made a brisk business with midnight customers coming out of the bars and the people living in the tiny apartments who were too tired to cook anything for themselves.

She felt eyes on her before she even got to the lot. It was probably just paranoia, but she felt as though someone was lingering behind her, watching her every move. When she turned around, she couldn't see anyone, but the feeling persisted.

The Asian inspired truck called *Stir the Pot* offered a family meal. It was mostly noodles, but for the amount of food, it was cheap, and that's what Astra needed. A big meal for as few credits as possible. The family meal came in a disposable tray, which she carried with two hands. She was almost back at the motel when someone in the shadows whispered her name.

"Astra," the voice said. "Don't turn around."

"Who's there?"

"Cal... Dr. Cal Zeldin."

Astra set the tray on the sidewalk and bent down, pretending to tie her shoe.

"Are you being followed?"

"No," Cal said. "What room are you in?"

"Nine," she said, "on the street side."

"I'll keep an eye out and follow you in about fifteen minutes," he said. "Save me something to eat, I'm starving."

Astra nearly rolled her eyes. The last thing she needed was another ravenous man expecting her to feed them. But she felt a sense of relief just hearing the doctor's voice. He had taken a big chance rescuing Sergeant Hammer and the fact that he hadn't been caught was encouraging.

She stood up with the tray of food and moved on without another word. If they were being watched, she didn't want to be seen talking to the shadows. Maybe her feeling of being watched came from Zeldin ... or maybe it was more. She wanted the doctor around. He was her partner in crime and he had resources that she didn't have. But she felt like he was increasing their risk factor, too.

When she got back to the room, nothing had changed. Jack was sitting up on the edge of his bed with his burned foot crossed over his knee. The man reminded Astra of a pit bull. He seemed like he was all muscle and bone, not big, but powerfully built just the same. After his nap, he was full of energy. She was glad to see him sitting down, but it was obvious that sitting still was hard for him.

"Oh, Chinese," he said, referring to the food. "That smells so good."

"It's mostly noodles," she said.

"Fine by me," he replied. "I'm in your debt."

She thought that was true but, of course, she wouldn't hold it over him. There was no way to know it, but she felt intuitively that he would be important in her future. She had learned to trust her intuition.

"The doctor's back," she said as she used the cheap, plastic utensils to dish out two plates of food. "He's watching for any sign of Space Command, but he'll be here in a few minutes."

"He made it then," Hammer said. "That's good. He wouldn't tell me his plan."

Astra set one plate aside, then kept one for herself before

handing the tray to Jack. It was enough food for three people, and he practically cooed for joy.

"Are you seeing anyone out there or just looking because you're nervous?" Jack asked between bites.

Astra, who hadn't touched her food yet, let go of the edge of the heavy curtain. "Aren't you nervous?"

Jack shrugged. "My mind is made up," he explained. "Should they come for us, I'll fight until we escape or…"

"Or they kill us?"

"Me," he said. "I'm not going back to Space Command."

There was a note of bitterness in his voice. "I'm just a grunt; I own that. I've seen Marines get thrown into a meat grinder on alien worlds. The revolt on Tanan IV, fighting the Kellish Raiders on Sistine Six, those were bad situations. A lot of good people died. But that's what we signed up for and what we were trained to do. Sending us into battle is dangerous, but we had a fighting chance to make it out. I did in both instances while my friends and platoon mates died. But never, in over nine years with the Corps, have I ever heard of anything as sadistic as what was done to me at Space Command. They didn't treat me like a human being. It was more like a contest to see who could be the cruelest among the so-called researchers."

"I'm sorry. No one deserves to be treated like that."

Jack shrugged. "It's not your fault."

"I wasn't directly involved, but I worked there. I supported those researchers by cleaning and providing them with the supplies they needed."

"You're making up for it now, I suppose. They won't like that I deserted, but they took all kinds of samples from me. For all I know, they've already got what they want."

"They won't want you around telling stories about what they did to you," she said.

"Probably not, but I'm not a fool and I'm not helpless anymore. If they come for me, they better come with an army because I'll make them pay dearly for what they've done."

Astra wished she felt the same way, but she didn't want to die. She didn't want to get caught. In fact, she didn't want to spend the rest of her life running. There were big decisions looming ahead for her. Maybe staying with Dr. Zeldin and the remarkable Sergeant Hammer wasn't a good idea. If Space Command wanted them, they might not bother with her.

A knock at the door made her jump. But she got to her feet and looked through the peephole. It was Dr. Zeldin. She rotated the bolt lock and pulled open the door. It was a plain, metal door, painted brown, but heavy-duty, which she was thankful for.

"Thank you," Zeldin said, his voice strained. "I'm not cut out for this."

Astra was shocked. She put her hand to her mouth as Zeldin stepped aside and let her close the door.

"What happened to your face?" She asked.

"Cosmetic alteration," he said. "What do you think?"

"I think you look ..."

"Like a caveman," Hammer said. "That's a respectable brow ridge, doc."

"I had to throw off the AI facial trackers," Zeldin said.

"It's a change," Astra said, "but it seems like it's well done."

"It should be," he told her. "I paid through the nose. It's supposed to last a few days. Hopefully long enough to get us off this world."

Astra sat back down, wondering how her life had altered so much that she found herself hiding in a tiny motel room with two men she barely knew.

After eating his food, Dr. Zeldin fell asleep on the side of Jack's bed. Astra was a little surprised that he hadn't insisted on sleeping on her bed. It was still made up, while Jack's bed was a tangled mess. But maybe the doctor didn't want to make her feel as if there was no place for her or maybe he was just so tired he didn't care. He kept his coat on, kicked off his shoes, and laid down on the edge of the unmade bed. He was snoring softly within half a minute.

"Why don't you let me take over?" Jack said. "I've been sleeping all day."

Astra was tired. She didn't want to sleep, but she knew she had to.

"Are you sure?" She asked.

"Positive," he assured her. "I've stood watch many times and in lots of places much worse than this."

"Okay... thanks," Astra said.

She had a full suitcase of clothes, but she stayed in what she had been wearing the day before and got into the unoccupied bed. Jack turned out the lights and hobbled over to the window. He stood on his good leg and propped the knee of his bad leg on the seat that Astra had been using.

Lying in the dark, hearing the doctor snoring softly, she stared up at the ceiling. It was lost in the darkness of the motel room. The only light was from a small clock on the table between the two beds. It showed the time in a dim, red light that didn't illuminate anything around it.

"How's it look out there?" Astra asked.

"Empty," Jack said. "You picked a good spot."

"Thanks," she told him. "If they find out there are three of us in this room, they'll want more money."

"I guess that shouldn't be surprising," Jack said. "If it comes to that, I'll deal with it."

"How?" Astra asked.

"I can be very persuasive when I need to be," he told her.

"What's it feel like?"

"Come again?"

"The way your body is healing," she said. "What's that feel like?"

"It's strangely familiar," Jack said. "Do you drink coffee?"

"Sure," she said.

"It feels like I've had too much coffee. I kind of feel my body buzzing, only it seems deeper somehow. Like maybe I'm feeling the activity of my cells, but that's impossible."

She considered his explanation. It made sense. But when she tried to feel her cells, all she could feel was the scratchy sheets of the motel bed and lumps in the mattress. She started to ask him more about his abilities, but before she could, sleep swept her away. It was the only peace she had felt since she met Dr. Zeldin at the bar. Life had gotten hectic and scary, but that's what adventure really was. No one ever felt safe in an adventure, she told herself as the darkness lifted her up and she drifted away.

21

"Sir, I've got something!" Midshipman Summers declared.

He was just one of the young people working the computers. Little had been found in Dr. Zeldin's office in the R&D facility, or in his berth in the visiting officers' tower on the Space Command campus. Nor had there been much of use in the rental car, which the team of MPs finally corralled. It was empty, just as Kittle had expected. They did find the assault rifle and one of the laser pistols taken from the MPs at Space Command. There was still one weapon unaccounted for and no clues as to where the pair of traitors were hiding.

"What?" Kittle said. He was running on caffeine pills and bad coffee, which aggravated him as much as it helped him stay awake.

"There was an assault in Lowtown," the computer specialist called out. "One of our High Energy Laser Pistols was used in the altercation."

That was interesting, but the use of a HELP weapon alone wasn't enough to go on. Guns of all types were still bought and sold on the black market, including those procured for Space Command. Kittle walked over to the midshipman's console.

"Two known gang members were injured with head wounds consistent with falling after a stun blast," Summers continued. "They also had bruising at the impact site in concentric circles. It's exactly what we see with the High Energy blasters."

"What else?" Kittle said.

"That's where it gets interesting, sir. According to the police report, they were brought to the emergency medical kiosk on one hundred and twenty-first street at 1400 hours. The automated medical units did the usual scans before rendering aid. They were identified as Marcus Fanning and James Selvy. That's not what's interesting, though. I was curious, so I ran a search on their banking records. Get this, Marcus Fanning took a private transport unit from one hundred and nineteenth street at 1342 hours."

"You're saying these two men with head wounds took a vehicle to the med center?"

"No, sir, that's the thing. The private transport took whoever was using Marcus Fanning's ID all the way to the train depot on Axis Street, sir. It was there four minutes before taking that person all the way back to one hundred and nineteenth street in Lowtown."

"Interesting," Kittle said. "Do we have video of this person?"

"I checked municipal law enforcement. No one pinged facial recognition AI at either location. I'm getting ready to check the pods in that area, sir."

"Do it," Kittle ordered.

He had no idea why someone on the run would go from the outer section of Prime City, back into the heart of town. Better to keep running rather than get caught in the maze of Midtown, but he couldn't ignore the coincidence that the mystery passenger most likely gunned down the gangbangers with a pistol stolen from Space Command Military Police, then took a transport to the same depot that Dr. Zeldin had stopped at not long after absconding with Sergeant Hammer. In his mind, it was enough to get his team of spec-ops commandos on the move.

Captain Kittle tapped the transmit button on a nearby console's communication controls.

"Lieutenant Caffrey, your unit is up. Urban combat – high-level operative retrieval operation. Non-lethal rules of engagement. Have your people ready to roll in ten. Over."

"Copy that, Oscar Team is gearing up. Non-lethal munitions approved. Ten minutes on the clock. We'll be ready, sir. Oscar Team standing by."

Kittle had never wanted to be a Marine. They were handy to have around, though, and he admired their lack of pretension. He didn't need to video conference with the commando team. A simple audio transmission was enough to get them geared up and on the case.

"Captain, I have a visual," Midshipman Summers announced. "It's not a perfect angle, but enough to run facial recognition."

"You won't get anything," Kittle said, moving back behind the young computer specialist. He studied the video for a moment. The man certainly had Dr. Zeldin's build, at least as much as could be seen in the video, which was from the train depot and at least two hundred feet away. The perp was in a parka. He pulled the hood up, which made recognition even more difficult.

"He walks away from the vehicle and doesn't return," Summers said.

"But the same ID was used to send the transport back to Lowtown?"

"Aye, Captain. He must have paid the fare before he left."

"And we're certain that's not Marcus Fanning?"

"Affirmative, Captain. Fanning is confirmed in the medical center at the same time. He had a wide laceration in his scalp that required one hundred and fourteen stitches. His blood volume was low, and he was suffering from a concussion. That's not him."

"Why didn't the driver report it?"

Summer shrugged. "Maybe the return fare was enough of a bribe to keep him from it."

"Have the MPs bring that man in for questioning. And if there is video surveillance inside that transport, I want it."

"Aye, Captain, I'll make the call. I have a contact in Metro PD. We'll find the driver and get him in for questioning ASAP."

Captain Kittle had a love-hate relationship with young officers. Some were hardworking and eager to please their superiors. But many were also too dumb to be of much use. Midshipman Summers seemed to be one of the good ones.

Across the Space Command campus was a Marine Corps staging area. Marines were generally on Titan for leave or when gathering for deployment on a Space Command battle cruiser. There were several docking stations in orbit for those merely passing through. And while the Space Command Marines didn't have a permanent presence on Titan, each Marine division had facilities on the main campus. It was more of a hedge against threats than anything else. If the Sol system were ever attacked, Titan would obviously be a prime target. And Space Command would need an entire company of battle-ready Marines at the least. Therefore, it had been decided that the SCMC would have facilities of their own, each stocked with weapons, ammunition, and gear that could be used in the event of an attack on Titan.

Lieutenant Todd Caffrey was an experienced special forces commando. He had risen through the enlisted ranks and, after exemplary service in battle, had been recommended to the officer corps. He went through a condensed training course, then served as a second lieutenant for three years before completing the Spec-Ops training school, where he graduated at the top of his class. He was promoted to first lieutenant and given his own squad. They were primarily a special operations team utilized in high-value extractions and the occasional hit job. But they were trained and ready for combat operations on land, sea, air, and even in space.

"Staff Sergeant, we are a go," Caffrey declared.

"It's about damn time," Staff Sergeant Riggs said. "We been sitting on our thumbs all day, sir. What are we doing?"

"Snatch and grab by the sounds of it," the lieutenant said. "I don't have all the details yet. Get the squad geared up. Light armor, full comms, and non-lethal munitions."

"Ahh, hell! Another training sim, sir?"

"I don't know, Staff Sergeant. But the call came in from a deck captain running a special assignment. Truth is, it could be anything."

"Not trouble though," Riggs countered. "We aren't fighting on Titan."

Caffrey shrugged. "I haven't heard anything that would warrant us being called up. No other units have been tapped. Whatever it is, it must be out of the ordinary. Let's get in full battle-rattle with the team in the transport. We'll get our answers soon enough."

"Roger that, sir," Riggs said, before turning and shouting at the men lounging in the Spec-Ops prep room. "Alright, time to move. Light armor, full comms, non-lethals, you know the drill. Chandler, load up the grab bag. We're going full electric, but all weapons dialed back. We're bringing in our target alive. No mistakes, people, let's move, move, move!"

Light armor consisted of Kevlar-lined cargo pants and the old school flack jackets with loops for ammunition, which weren't used when operating laser weapons. Everyone took a Light Assault Laser Rifle and a HELP sidearm. Tear gas, flash bangs and sedative gas grenades were loaded into their utility belts. On their heads went full combat smart helmets with neck seals and O2 intakes. Small oxygen canisters were stuffed into the loops on their flack jackets in case they were forced into areas flooded by the chemical weapons they were carrying, or worse.

With their armor and weapons secure, they hurried out to a fast-moving combat transport. They were built for operations in gravity and atmosphere. The transports had a stealth mode that allowed them to fly in, land and take off again without making noise, which was perfect for urban combat operations.

"Now what?" Corporal Haskins asked.

"We go from sitting in there to sitting out here," Corporal Armena declared. "That's some real progress."

"Better than wading through sewage or crawling up the side of a mountain on an alien world where everything is trying to kill you," Sergeant Lasko grumbled.

"Says you," Haskins replied. "My ass is getting sore."

"Haskins, stop your whining," the Staff Sergeant ordered as the transport's turbines began to whine. "We're lifting off."

"What is this? Another training op?" Specialist Olinski asked.

"Negative," Lieutenant Caffrey declared. "We've got a live one this time. A high-value operative has gone rogue. Our job is to bring him back in... alive."

"Dead is more fun," Armena declared.

"Alive is more of a challenge," Olinski said. "Right, sir?"

"Whatever it is, it beats sitting around twiddling our thumbs," Lieutenant Caffrey said. "Details are coming in now. Everyone, bring up your operational parameters on your smart helmets. This one's called Project Hammer."

"They can run, but they can't hide," Haskins said.

"Oh, they can hide alright," Lasko said. "But not for long."

"Heads up, Oscar Team," Lieutenant Caffrey said. "You see that red marker."

Staff Sergeant Riggs gave a low whistle.

"Is that what I think it is, Lieutenant?" Lasko asked. "That marker means armed and extremely dangerous, right?"

"Correct, Sergeant. This is no drill."

"Why the hell are we operating with non-lethal ROE?" Staff Sergeant Riggs complained. "This guy murdered a researcher?"

"Looks like another Franken-soldier gone wrong to humans, Staff Sergeant," Lieutenant Caffrey said. "We won't take any chances. Check your weapons and comms. We're not sure where the asset is yet. Sergeant Riggs and I will be touch point for teams moving east and west from the Axis Street Depot. Stay frosty, people, this is the real deal."

22

Jack's body was changing; he could feel it. The wounds were healing, which was good, and he felt stronger than ever. In fact, he felt like he could tear a steel bar in two. It was hard to be still. Strength seemed to be flowing through his body, almost like he was a fire hydrant and the gamma radiation had released the high-pressure flow of strength through his muscles and bones.

But it wasn't just his physical body getting stronger that made him antsy. He was changing in other ways, too. His hearing, for instance, was becoming more acute. He could hear Dr. Zeldin snoring and Astra's soft breathing. There was also the hum of the air unit and the buzz from the lights in the awning just outside the room. Oddly enough, he could hear the television that was on in a room four doors down, and the strange, ethnic chatter coming from the motel office where the proprietor was listening to a foreign language podcast.

And it wasn't just his hearing that had increased. Jack found it odd, and even a little hard to believe, but he could actually feel the radio waves and cellular signals passing through the walls and roof of the motel. It was a bit like being in the ocean. He had gone once as a child and stood in the surf. The cold water had rushed toward him, pushing him backward for a moment, then returned, surging back out to sea. The radio and cell signals weren't as strong, but he could feel the currents of their flow. He could also sense the invisible beam from the motion-activated lights on the building across the street. It was like the light was already on, although instead of illuminating the sidewalk, it was visible to Jack like the red glow of lights on the bedside clock.

The burns were healing, too. He knew that; he could feel the tissue growing. It made him worry that perhaps he was losing his mind. There were a lot of strange new sensations to take in all at once. While he found them to be strange, he didn't feel manic or out of control. He wanted to move. In fact, he wanted to run, to jump, to lift things and throw them. It sounded a bit manic when he thought about it, but he also felt strong just standing still and taking it all in. He was more aware of the world and his surroundings than he had ever been.

For hours, he stood by the window in the dark room, the heavy curtain pulled open just a half inch. It was enough for him to see through, but he was looking with new eyes. And they were sharper without any visual aids. He could see in the dark, not that the parking lot was dark, but beyond it, outside the cones of yellow light from the poles in the motel parking lot, the street and alley between the far buildings should have been lost in darkness. But Jack could see them ... and it was a better night vision than any technology he had used in the past. The world wasn't bathed in green, but just a little less colorful. He could see the glint in the eyes of rats that were sneaking through the alley in search of food. That shouldn't have been possible.

Yet he couldn't deny the changes. They were exciting and scary. Questions rose in his mind, prompted by the changes. What did they mean? How were they possible? Was he no longer a man? Was he no longer human? It was hard to understand and Jack wasn't the type of man who spent a lot of time in deep introspection.

He had been standing for a few hours, but he wasn't tired when he caught sight of a pair of commandos at the far end of the alley across from the motel parking lot. That was perhaps the biggest change for him. Not just stamina, but the ability to stay still without feeling like he needed to move. He felt like he was buzzing with energy and could have run ten miles if given the chance, but somehow he didn't need to shift his weight or change his posture. Nothing itched and the ache from his burns was down to a tolerable level. He could even walk on his burned foot without too much pain. He stood like a sentinel staring out the window into the darkness, taking in what little changes there were in the area near the hotel. And, when he caught sight of the spooks in the alley, Jack recognized them for what they were.

He had known plenty of the Spec Op commandos. Some were arrogant, others were quiet killers. But they all had a way of moving, a sort of confidence that most people never gained. Whether they were walking into a meeting or advancing on an enemy position on the battlefield, they carried themselves with purpose and a level of competency that was visible. The commandos were mere shadows and easily five or six hundred feet distant. He shouldn't have been able to see them at all in the darkness, but he did. Two of them, in light armor, carrying short-barreled tactical rifles. He was trying to see what type of weapon they were, when his eyes seemed to focus in with incredible accuracy. It was a bit like zooming in a camera with a telephoto lens. The ability shocked him, but he could suddenly make out the laser LALR weapon with its thin barrel and thick power core built into the stock. They advanced through the alley and took a position near the street where they had a good view of the surrounding real estate.

The window of his room didn't open, and there were a lot of competing sounds, but as Jack focused on the two commandos, he suddenly found he could hear them when they spoke.

"Haskins and Lasko in position," one of the men said. "We've got a good view of this quadrant. Over."

There was a pause. Jack couldn't hear the response of their team leader via the comlink inside their helmet. But it was obvious they were on the hunt for him.

"Roger that, beginning thermal sweep now," the command responded.

One of the Marines pulled a device from the pack he was wearing on his back. It looked like a box with a cable running from it that led to a small device that extruded from a curved parabolic dish. It was the size of a small pistol, and Jack recognized it as a thermal imaging laser. It gave the commandos an idea of who was inside a room, even one with no windows. It had an adjustable power level so that it could penetrate through thick walls, even stone. What it revealed were blobs of color that represented heat differences. In the hands of a skilled operator without too much interference, it could reveal how many people were in a room, where they were in relation to each other and even what position they were in. There was no doubt they would catch him standing by the window. The time for hiding, at least in the seedy little motel room, was over.

Maybe he should have been scared, or at least nervous, about what was to come, but instead he felt relieved. Jack went first to Dr. Zeldin. He gave the man a gentle shake. The doctor's eyes fluttered open.

"Who is it?" He whispered.

"It's Jack. Time to get up, doc. Space Command has commandos in the alley across the street."

"What? I can't see... what are you doing?"

"I can see," Jack said. "I can see you right now."

"What? That's impossible."

"Test me."

Zeldin held up three fingers. "How many fingers am I holding up?"

"Three."

"Lucky guess," the doctor said. "Try again."

He lowered his ring finger, leaving up two fingers on his right hand, then added four more fingers with his left.

"Six," Jack said. "Two on your right, four on your left. Do I need to tell you which fingers you're holding up?"

"You can see in the dark."

"Oh, yeah, I can see, I can hear, things are changing. But you can't stay here. You need to get Astra and leave."

"What?"

"They're looking for me, possibly me and you."

"But if we stay inside, they won't know we're here."

"They've got thermal imaging equipment," Jack said. "They probably already know we're here."

"How do you know that?"

"I can see them."

"They're across the street? That's got to be what, a hundred yards or something?"

"Something like that," Jack said. "But I can see them, I can hear them. They're giving steady reports. I think you and Astra should leave. You'll be seen, but a couple leaving their hotel room won't be suspicious. You don't need to be here when they come to get me."

"What's happening?" Astra asked, her voice thick from sleep.

"You have to get up," Jack said. "This location is no longer secure."

To his credit, Zeldin got to his feet, stretched and made his way around the bed he had been sleeping on. His bag was on the floor, and he picked it up along the way.

"Come on," Zeldin said. "Let's go find some coffee."

He helped Astra to her feet. Jack could see her face even in the darkness. She looked frightened and distressed.

"Are we in trouble?" She asked.

"Space Command is checking this location," Jack said. "I think you and the doctor should go. I'll stay and draw them in. If I survive, I'll meet you at the space port in two days, just after sunrise, near the *Rosa Maria.*"

"If you survive?" Astra asked in shock.

"Come on," Dr. Zeldin said. "We need to move on."

None of them had bothered unpacking. Astra picked up her bags and nodded. "I'm ready," she said.

Zeldin pulled the High Energy Laser Pistol from his pocket and handed it to Jack.

"Maybe this will help. I'm sorry for everything, Sergeant."

"Don't be sorry. You did everything in your power to help when you saw how bad things were. I'll be forever grateful for that."

"Good luck, Jack," Astra said. "Don't be a hero."

"She's right," Zeldin said. "There is no such thing as a hopeless situation."

"I'll remember that," Jack told him.

As they made their way to the door, Jack sat down on the edge of the bed. He put on two pairs of socks, then stuffed his feet into the boots that Zeldin had shared with him. It was a tight fit, but the pressure felt good to Jack, especially when he stood up.

"Do you have a plan?" Zeldin asked as he and Astra reached the door in the darkness.

Jack nodded. "Draw them in, then give them hell."

23

Sergeant Lasko was a ten year vet in the Spec Op teams. He had seen combat on eight separate occasions and had participated in over twenty missions. They had huddled in the stinking alley across the street from a dive motel, a row of dirty food trucks, and within sight of a municipal building that included a medical station, emergency services depot and the midtown city maintenance garage.

It was just like a dozen other places within a few blocks of the train depot. Nothing about it was special. The rest of their Spec Op team was spread out in similar alleys doing the same work. Lasko hated urban fighting. There were too many civilians and too many places for an enemy to hide. It amounted to a lot of knocking on doors and dealing with angry people. Lasko didn't like people very much. Even his teammates could be aggravating at times, especially when he was paired with young guys who couldn't seem to stop talking.

"Man, it's cold out here," Haskins said. "And it smells like... I don't know, man, like a public toilet for wild animals or something."

Lasko didn't disagree, but he didn't need to say it. He was comfortable focusing on the job.

"Hey, I got a couple coming out of the motel," Haskins said. "Probably a hooker and her John. Their hour's probably up. Can't imagine staying in a place like that. There's just no telling what kind of nasty stuff people get up to in a joint like that."

Again, Lasko didn't disagree. The Midtown Motel was old, worn down and out of touch. No one built motels anymore. The building was a two-story structure built in a U shape around a parking lot, where the concrete was cracked and crumbling in places. It didn't appear that any maintenance had been carried out on the property in decades.

"Why do you think the city allows a place like that?" Haskins said. "It's such a dump. I mean, it's like a roach motel, it just attracts vermin."

"There are people who are down on their luck, Corporal," Lasko said, breaking his silence for the first time since they had arrived in the alley. "Not everyone can afford to stay in a resort or fancy hotel."

"I'm just saying that a place like that draws people who are up to no good. Why give them a place? I say knock it down, build a carwash or storage facility if you can't have a nice shopping complex. And those food trucks look like they have no regulations. I wouldn't put crap from a place like that in my body, no way, man. You might as well just eat out of a garbage can."

It was hard not to get angry with Haskins. The kid saw life through a strange lens and he never considered anyone else's point of view. Even when it was pointed out to him, he always failed to grasp that not everyone was like him. But it wasn't Lasko's job to educate the corporal in anything other than combat operations. And they weren't exactly on dangerous ground. There was no need for silence. Overhead, hover cars passed with their repulsers humming. A few blocks away, the E-Train rumbled into the station. Somewhere music was playing. No one was going to hear the corporal asking his inane questions and pointing out the obvious.

"Did you get a record of that couple?" Lasko asked.

"Got 'em, but it's too dark to run facial recognition," Haskins said.

Lasko didn't agree. The couple had come out of their room quickly and moved straight out into the dark parking lot. Had they stayed under the awning where the yellow lights shone, it would have been better, but there was a second, maybe two, where he could have captured their faces. But it didn't really matter to the veteran Sergeant. He couldn't care less about the success of the mission. He had no skin in the game other than his time and his discomfort. Haskins was right; it was cold and dreary. Titan had slipped around to the dark side of Saturn. The moon was only in complete darkness for a day and a half, then the glow from the planet's edges would illuminate everything again. It wasn't surprising that they were called to work in the darkest time of the cold week, but that was life.

He pulled his flack jacket tighter around his body and continued his sweep with the thermal imager. The tiny screen on the boxy device was shielded so as not to cast light up on the user's face. Most of the readings were dark red, with no heat signatures to pick up. The municipal building was empty, as was most of the hotel. He was about halfway through the sweep when something lit up the device.

"Wait," Lasko said. "What the..."

"What?" Haskins asked.

Lasko didn't respond to his teammate, but toggled his comlink and spoke in a steady voice.

"LT, I've got something," the veteran sergeant said. "It's just on thermal, but it's different. Over."

"Different, how, Sergeant? Over."

"Sir, it's bright orange. Looks like a man."

"Holy smokes! That's him!" Haskins said. "Look!"

He pointed in the same direction that Lasko was aiming the thermal imager. Jack Hammer had thrown back the curtains of the room he was in and was standing on display behind the glass.

"Sir, we have visual confirmation. I repeat, we have visual confirmation of the target. Over.'

"What's your position, Lasko?"

"We're in the alley off Kilmore Avenue, across from the Midtown
Motel, Lieutenant. The subject is in the motel. Room number nine, in
plain view. And sir, there's something unique about him. He's got the
thermal lit up like a Christmas tree. Awaiting instructions. Over."

"Hold your position, Sergeant," Lieutenant Caffrey said. "Can
you get a hit on facial recognition? Over."

"Affirmative," Haskins jumped into the conversation. "Sending
you the video feed now, sir. It's him. No doubt about it, Lieutenant.
We've got him. Over."

"Copy that, stand by," Lieutenant Caffrey ordered.

"We should go get him," Haskins said.

"That's not our orders," Lasko responded.

"I'm just saying we could," Haskins insisted, "so easy."

"He knows we're here, you bonehead. Why do you think he's
standing at the window?"

"I don't know. Besides, it's too dark for him to see us. You're
getting skittish in your old age, Sarge. And even if he could see us, so
what? What's one guy gonna do?"

That was the question that lingered in Lasko's mind. Why had a
Special Forces team been sent to retrieve one guy? It was overkill.
Any MP squad could handle picking up a high-level operative. There
was no need to bring out a Spec Ops team in full battle-rattle.
Sergeant Von Lasko was not someone who got nervous, but he was
naturally suspicious, and something about their mission didn't seem
right to him.

Lieutenant Caffrey was still in the drop ship, which was circling
at fifteen hundred feet up in stealth mode. They were well above all
civilian traffic, including hovercraft. Below them, the city was lit
with electric light that made it seem strangely less appealing. The
video he was sent played silently on the console he was tucked
behind. He preferred to lead from the front and would rather have

been on the ground with his team, but the mission was a simple retrieval. The briefing package he'd received from Captain Kittle listed the target as a Marine Sergeant who was part of a special development detail and had gone AWOL. He was listed as dangerous, but Caffrey knew that a threat was relative. What one person found to be dangerous wasn't always the case. For instance, a man with a knife wasn't all that dangerous to a man with a gun. And, more to the point, a single, violent man wasn't really dangerous to a team of highly skilled and experienced military commandos.

After double-checking that the man standing in the motel room was in fact the target via computer confirmation, the lieutenant called in the report.

"Captain, we have your man under observation," Caffrey said.

"You're certain it's Sergeant Hammer?"

"Yes, sir, we've got facial recognition confirmation and a strange reading on thermal imaging."

"Strange how?"

"Strange as in a bright orange halo," Caffrey said, glancing over the still image that Lasko had sent him from the thermal unit. "He's not just running hot, sir. This guy's internals are different."

"That's due to the circumstances that led to his being in the R&D division. We have to bring him in. What's the location?"

"Midtown, just off Kilmore Avenue. The Midtown Motel."

"Alright, I'll be your eye in the sky, Lieutenant. Go get our man. Remember, he has to be brought in alive. That's of the utmost importance."

Caffrey thought it odd to send a team whose training was to kill after a target that needed to be alive at all costs. Surely, he imagined, the MPs were better equipped for such an assignment, but he didn't voice his concerns. He had a well-trained team and they would get the job done.

"Yes, sir, I understand. We'll bring him. Is there anything else I should know?"

"I can't give you specifics because we don't have them yet," Kittle said. "But he is physically enhanced. Expect greater than normal strength, speed and stamina. It might take more than a single stun blast to incapacitate him. But don't take that to mean I want you to light him up either. The value of this asset cannot be stressed highly enough."

"Roger that. I'll be in touch shortly, captain. Caffrey out."

He pulled off his headset and made a downward hand motion that told the pilots he wanted them to land. Caffrey had a bad feeling in his gut. Enhanced physical traits, he thought, surely meant they had been using some new version of a super soldier serum. Space Command called for volunteers for experimental programs on a regular basis. The men in the trenches knew better than to volunteer. In Caffrey's mind, there was a reason why the super soldier programs always failed. Mankind, at least in Caffrey's mind, was already at its peak physically and mentally. Trying to change that always resulted in disastrous consequences. Violence and unbridled aggression were the usual side effects. Most of the Marines who underwent the experiments either got sick and had to be discharged from the Corps or went crazy. How could he blame the Marine for going AWOL if they were pumping him full of some crazy serum?

Empathy wasn't his duty and it especially wasn't the job at the moment. No matter what they had done to the target, his task was the same. No matter how he felt about what they were doing, it didn't give him the freedom to change his orders. Bringing the man in alive was what he was commanded to do and it was what he would do, even if he disagreed. His feelings didn't weigh in on the matter, not one bit.

"Staff Sergeant, do you read? Over."

"Five by five, Lieutenant. We are taking up position on the north side of the motel now, sir. Over."

"Very good. I want Sergeant Preston's team to converge on the east side. Corporal Armena, you take position on the west. Wait on my order. We will converge on the target in concert. I want this guy to see us coming and know he has no place to run. Over."

"Roger that," Riggs replied. "We will wait on your orders. Over."

"Sergeant Lasko, do you still have eyes on the target? Over."

"Roger that, LT. Over," Lasko said.

Haskins couldn't contain himself, "The crazy bastard is just standing in the window with the lights on like it's on display in a department store during the holidays. Over."

Caffrey sighed. The young Corporal Josh Haskins was still green and eager to prove himself. That wasn't an altogether bad thing but, the entire team agreed, he talked too much.

"Stand by," Caffrey ordered. "I will meet you at your position, Sergeant Lasko."

The drop ship landed on a pad inside the train depot grounds. Caffrey hurried out, sucking in the ship's exhaust and the cold night air as he ran to join his team. He was ready to wrap things up and get himself a beer. The sooner he forgot about the human experimentation Space Command was mixed up in, the better.

24

Jack never liked the wait before a fight. He was not a patient man to begin with and the emotional strain of knowing that deadly action was soon to be upon him, was a difficult burden to bear. Every Marine he had ever known dealt with the stress in their own way. Some talked before a battle, some prayed, others joked, some looked inward and others went stark raving mad. He didn't look down on any of the ways in which people handled their emotions because he always knew he couldn't put himself in someone else's shoes. Nor did he want to. Fighting had always been a straightforward task for Jack. Starting at a young age, when he was challenged, Jack went to business, letting his opponent know he wasn't to be trifled with.

In combat, things were different. A man in a gun fight couldn't just stand in the middle of the street. Nor could a platoon mate turn his back on the Marines fighting beside him. He had learned to work as a team, to pull his weight and help the next guy in line the same way those who went before him had helped Jack.

But in the motel, things were different. He wasn't scared, even though he knew the odds were high that he would be killed.

Getting captured was an even worse outcome. Still, there was also the chance that he would be victorious. It was one against many. Jack knew most Spec Op teams were made up of twelve Marines. There weren't even twelve shots left in the power pack of the pistol that Dr. Zeldin had left with him. But he just didn't care. The opportunity to let loose the beast inside of him was a heady thought. In a fight, he didn't have to hold back. He could hit and move, rip and run, without the need to check himself or pretend he wasn't a violent monster. Not that Jack felt himself losing control. He didn't want to kill the Marines. They were just doing their job. In fact, he still considered himself one of them and thought that he always would. But they were men of war, dressed for battle and armed for a fight. They just didn't know who they were up against or what he was capable of. In fact, no one knew what he was capable of, not even Jack. He thought it was time to find out.

Eventually, a third man joined the two Marines across the street. He was the commanding officer. Even in the darkness, Jack could see the lieutenant's insignia on his fatigues. And that meant there were probably three Marines on either side of the Motel. They were expecting him to run. He was going to disappoint them.

He reached over and turned out the light. The room went dark. It was slightly less dark outside, with the light glowing above the motel walkway that led to the rooms. That alone should have blinded him, just as that pale light from dirty, overhead sconces reflected off the window without penetrating into the room. To the Marines outside, it was like trying to look through a mirror.

Jack moved back and lifted the mattress off the bed nearest to the door. It was set on a wooden platform that was built into the floor. The platform wouldn't move, but the mattress did. He lifted the five foot wide, six and half foot long mattress the way one might pick up a sheet of cardboard. It helped that the mattress was firm, almost stiff, but Jack knew it shouldn't seem so light. He propped it against the window, then laid the table on its side, so that the top pressed into the mattress and the foot was wedged against the frame of the bed.

It wasn't enough to keep someone from breaking through. It wouldn't even stop a bullet or a laser blast, but it would bleed off some of the kinetic energy. The motel walls were thin and made of flimsy materials. Jack propped the other mattress against the wall of the bathroom directly in line with the window. If the Marines planned to fire at him blind or just gun him down, the layers would hopefully be enough to give Jack a fighting chance. He was protected on each side by the other rooms of the establishment and the back wall of the motel was made of concrete blocks. A high-caliber bullet at close range would still punch through the masonry, but there was nothing Jack could do about that.

He waited in the bathroom with the lights off. He didn't need light to see. Nor did he have to wait long. He heard the boots of the approaching Marines. Just outside the door, the commander gave orders.

"Alpha Team, Bravo Team, hold your positions. "Charlie, is there an exit on the back side of that motel?" A moment of silence passed, then the lieutenant said, "Lasko, you're free to proceed."

They had a master key, or maybe they just hacked into the motel's security. It probably wasn't hard to do. Either way, the door handle lock clicked open. But the room had a thick bolt lock, as well as a metal folding bar that was high up on the frame. The knob turned, but the door was still secure. Jack counted three seconds before the blow came. Someone hit the door with a heavy object that pounded the bolt lock through the wooden door jamb and ripped the folding bar off the wall. The metal motel door slammed back against the interior wall, and two Marines came in fast, pointing their rifles around in search of the target. Jack reached a hand out of the bathroom and toggled on the room lights. Both Marines grunted in pain. Jack had assumed they were using night vision and the sudden increase in light was blinding. At the same moment, he leaned out of the bathroom and fired two fast shots. The surge of energy ripped through their light armor and knocked both Marines unconscious.

Jack knew he had one shot left in his pistol. After that, the power cell would be run too low to be of much use. It might fire a time or two, but not with enough power to put a grown man down. He needed to get to the closest Marine and retrieve their weapons. But the commanding officer was outside, some fifteen feet from the door, ready to open fire if Jack showed himself.

"All units, all units, converge on my position," the officer said. Jack had no difficulty hearing him. "Lasko and Haskins are down. Let's get this bastard!"

Jack was careful not to let himself be seen. He slipped his hand around the bathroom doorframe and across the wall. Laser blasts sizzled through the air and ricocheted off the big mirror above the vanity that was part of the motel room. Only the shower and toilet were in a separate space. Jack guessed the laser blasts could probably rip right through the walls between the sleeping area and the shower. But he managed to toggle off the lights and then get low. His body was buzzing with adrenaline. For the first time since arriving on Titan, his body didn't hurt, or maybe he just wasn't paying attention, but he felt ready for what was coming.

Another laser blast flashed in the dark room like a bolt of lightning. It hit the mattress propped against the bathroom wall, burned through it, and then through the cheap sheetrock and into the shower stall. Jack knew his chances of fighting back were running out. One man couldn't fend off an attack by an overwhelming force. For all he knew, the Marines would break into the rooms on either side and fire all at once from three directions.

With his heart racing in his chest, he bent low and then flung himself out the door of the bathroom. With one powerful leap, he flew across the small motel room and managed to flip the metal door closed. Hitting the floor hurt. He had used his left arm to reach the door because the skin around the burn on his right shoulder was still tight. But that caused him to hit the floor, which was thin carpet over concrete, hard on his left hip where the researchers had burned him. The pain shooting through his hip and into his abdomen and leg was so powerful he yelped in pain, but he kept moving.

With one hand, he held the door shut against the busted frame. And with the other, he reached over and unfastened the tactical laser rifle from one of the fallen Marines. Laser fire pounded the door. It wasn't as kinetically strong as a projectile, but Jack felt the metal door getting hot. He rolled onto his back and put his good foot against the door.

The laser fire intensified. The door was bucking and the paint in the center of the door, a little over halfway up, began to bubble. Jack checked the laser rifle. It had a full battery and was set at semi-auto fire. The power range was dialed all the way down to stun level. They weren't there to kill him. They wanted to take him back to the researchers for more torture and tests. That fact only hardened his resolve. He pointed his rifle toward the door and removed his foot from the door.

The very next blast, a split second later, knocked the metal door open, and Jack fired through the open door. There were four Marines visible. He squeezed off three shots before the return fire forced him to roll over. Pain ripped through his bad shoulder as he flopped to the side. Lasers popped and sizzled against the carpet. It wasn't powerful enough to burn the material, but the carpet was made of acrylic strands and they melted together under the sudden barrage. Outside, there was shouting.

"Riggs, get those men back!" The commanding officer barked an order. "Preston, keep up that cover fire. Don't bunch up. Aremena, Orlinski, break through that window."

Laser fire smashed the glass. It shattered and fell to the concrete outside as the mattress jerked, then sagged through the opening the broken glass made. Jack used his good foot to shove himself back between the wooden bed frames that were bolted to the floor. Smoke was starting to collect at the ceiling of the motel room. The mattress by the window had caught on fire.

Jack sat up and fired through the open door, but the angle was wrong; his shots went wide. Then a strange object came bouncing across the floor. It stopped by the bathroom and started venting a gray cloud of chemical gas. Jack pulled himself to his feet and ran out the door.

The first blast hit his good shoulder. It felt like he had been thumped, the way his father had flicked his shoulder in church to make him be quiet, even though he was on the other side of Jack's mother. But the stun beam didn't stop him. He raised his own weapon and fired. The staff sergeant went down, along with a specialist and a corporal. But then another blast hit Jack in the stomach, and a third hit his throat. He felt a wave of intense heat, almost as if fire was rushing through his body. His knees buckled, and Jack fell, but he caught himself, squeezed off another shot that went wide of the mark, and was hit by a stun blast in the middle of his back. The world went quiet and dark. The last thought that went through Jack's mind was that the cold concrete felt good on his face.

25

"What the bloody hell just happened?" Lieutenant Todd Caffrey shouted.

"He's down, Lieutenant," Sergeant Mike Preston said, bending over Jack's body and pressing his fingers to their target's neck. "Still alive though. His pulse is strong."

"How is that possible?" Specialist Olinski asked. "I hit him as soon as he got through the door, I know I did."

"Is he wearing some kind of armor?" Lieutenant Caffrey asked.

Preston rolled the body over. Their target's face was drawn, the skin pulled tight over his cheekbones and forehead. When he reached down to look under the tee-shirt the man was wearing, he found nothing but hard-packed muscle.

"Negative, sir," Preston said. "He's clean."

"On the outside," Corporal Armena said. "Had to be high on something. Some kind of PCP, maybe."

"He's a guinea pig," Caffrey said. "But I never imagined anything like this."

"We better call it in," Preston said. "We're going to need medical."

"And fire," Olinski said.

"Prime City won't cry over losing this dump," Caffrey said. "Armena, Olinski, get Lasko and Haskins out of there. But keep in mind that room's full of sedative gas."

"Copy that," Corporal Armena said. "Let's go, Otto."

The two Marines lowered the bottom portion of their helmets and attached the little hoses that connected to the oxygen canisters before going into the motel room.

Sergeant Mike Preston looped a pair of plastic restraints over Jack's wrists, then put another set over his ankles.

Meanwhile, Lieutenant Caffrey made the call to his superiors.

"Captain, we have the target," he said via his comlink.

"Alive?"

"Yes, sir. He's been stunned. It wasn't easy, but he went down and we've got him."

"I want you to keep tabs on his vitals, Lieutenant. How many stun blasts did it take?"

"Sir, you knew it would take more than one?"

"I told you he was enhanced," Kittle said. "But I didn't know how he would respond. That sort of testing hadn't been done."

"A little more warning would have been helpful."

"Would it have changed the outcome?"

"We could have been more careful."

"Did you lose people, lieutenant?"

"Half my team suffered stun blasts, but they'll all survive."

"Then I'd call this the best possible scenario," Kittle snapped. "You don't like the way things turned out and I understand that. But Sergeant Hammer is the most valuable asset Space Command has ever possessed. All that really mattered was getting him back. I'd say that getting over a stun blast is nothing compared to what could have happened had he been firing kill shots."

Caffrey felt a shudder of fear run down his spine. He didn't like to think about losing Marines under his command. But the captain was right, theirs was a favorable outcome. It could have been much worse and, had it been, Caffrey wasn't sure he could have kept from taking his rage out on the arrogant Captain Kittle.

A variety of municipal services arrived at the Midtown Motel. Despite being right next door to a hub of EMS, it still took a medical team twelve minutes after Caffrey's call to Captain Kittle to arrive at the scene. By that point, the Marines had moved the unconscious teammates away from the hotel, which was embroiled in flames. The fire department arrived even later than the medical unit. Neither seemed especially interested in actually helping. The fire swept through the building in both directions and soon was burning from the office on one end to the maintenance area on the other.

Caffrey wanted to get his team back to Space Command HQ, but a call from Captain Kittle informed him that the higher priority was getting Sergeant Hammer back. They were to treat him as dangerous, even though he was clearly unconscious from the stun blasts. By the time a transport arrived for them, the Prime City police were on the scene. It was not surprising that the officials on the street had not been informed of anything involving Space Command soldiers operating in the civilian quarters.

"You the man in charge?" a detective with dark scruff on his chin and a wrinkled sport coat over his police issue body armor asked.

"I was," Caffrey said.

"Mind telling me what the hell Space Command is doing running roughshod over my city?"

"Our action was approved," Caffrey said.

"Not by me," the detective snapped. "And I doubt anyone on my side of the aisle approved you burning down a major structure."

"Sir, I'm just following orders," Caffrey said. "If you have a problem, you'll need to contact my superiors."

"But they ain't here, are they?" the detective growled. "And should I take the time to get on the horn with Space Command, I'll waste half a day being shuffled from department to department with no one taking a damn bit of responsibility for the suffering and damage you caused."

"I'm sorry, that's the way it is," Caffrey said.

"And I've got half a mind to run you in," the detective said. "I put you and your thugs in a steel cage and that'll get someone's attention."

"You don't want to do that," Caffrey told the man.

"The hell I don't."

"Think it through, sir. If you arrest us, you'll be on the hook for whatever your superiors and mine are fighting about. Eventually, me and my team will walk, but you'll be left as the scapegoat. Don't give them that opportunity, sir. It's not worth it."

The detective turned away, cursing Caffrey, Space Command, and his own superiors, but he didn't arrest Caffrey or cause problems when a hovercraft arrived to take the Commandos and Sergeant Hammer back to Space Command.

"Sergeant Preston, you and Specialist Orlinski stay with our people here," Caffrey said. It made him sick to see his teammates laid out on the ground. They weren't dead, just stunned, but his superiors were forcing him to leave them for municipal services to deal with. "Make sure they get taken to a med center and not split up all over the city."

"Roger that, LT," Preston said. "You can count on us."

"I am," Caffrey said. "Armena, Sil, Farmer, get this bastard loaded up."

Sergeant Hammer was lying on his back in the hovercraft, which was shaped like an ambulance, but was dull gray, with no markings on the body or lights mounted on top. He was placed on a simple, uncushioned gurney with mini-repulsers on the bottom. There were seat height metal platforms with tops that opened on hinges to either side of where the sergeant was laid out. Lieutenant Caffrey joined Corporal Ibu Armena. On the other side sat Specialist Tina Sil and Amy Farmer. They were the only two female commandos on the team.

"What's the play, LT?" Armena asked.

"Escort this guy back to HQ, then we round up our people," Caffrey said. "The sooner we're off this rock, the better."

"Never seen a guy need more than one stun blast before," Amy Farmer said.

"There's a lot you haven't seen," Armena pointed out.

"Don't be a prick, Ibu," Tina Sil remarked.

"We're all testy," Caffrey said. "You've got every right to be frustrated, or even angry. Let's just make sure it's pointed in the right direction."

"Not sure where that is," Armena said. "Should I be mad at the Sergeant or at the people playing god?"

"Yeah, Lieutenant, what did they do to this guy?" Farmer asked. "He didn't seem crazy."

"No, he was effective," Caffrey said. "We should have had more intel on this guy up front. But, the word I got is that Space Command doesn't even know what he's capable of."

"They let the rat out of the cage too soon," Armena said. "I hope they lock him in a box until he dies."

Caffrey knew how his subordinate felt, but he wasn't sure he agreed. None of them liked what was happening and it was difficult to stay mission-focused when the people giving orders weren't worthy of respect. Still, Caffrey couldn't encourage insubordination or they would all end up locked away. It was his job to protect his people, and so, he kept his mouth shut and waited for the nightmare to end.

26

Zeldin and Astra ended up in a diner six blocks away from the Midtown Motel. They sat in the back next to a dark hallway that led to the bathrooms and the rear exit. They sat side by side, facing the front of the dinner as they drank coffee and whispered about what they should do.

It was too dark to see the smoke from the motel, but they saw the glow as the flames consumed the building.

"Do you think he's alright?" Astra asked.

"I don't know," Zeldin said. "I feel responsible, but I'm sure he's more capable of taking care of himself than I ever could."

"He didn't have enough time to heal," she said, turning the thick mug of coffee in her hands on the tabletop.

Neither of them was hungry, but they ordered a plate of biscuits and coffee so that they wouldn't attract undue attention. The dinner was a simple place, long and narrow, with a counter that ran from front to back. Parallel to that was a row of booths. The front of the diner was glass, and above the waitress station were video displays. One was showing a sports recap show with games on Earth and

Mars being reported on. Another had a late-night political show on, with politicians and pundits arguing about something or other.

Zeldin was pretending to butter a biscuit while he watched the third display, which was set to a local station. A frazzled-looking field reporter was standing in front of a row of barriers that had been set up in the street and connected with yellow police tape. Behind the reporter was the Midtown Motel. The fire had been contained, but it was slowly destroying the structure. The parking lot was full of official vehicles with flashing lights and people in uniforms going back and forth. Zeldin couldn't hear the reporter. There was no volume on any of the displays, but his words were being captioned at the bottom of the screen.

"... we're being told there was some kind of military activity in the area, but no one is willing to confirm or deny that Space Command was involved. Thankfully, all the guests and employees of the motel were able to get out safely. But the building, which was constructed almost sixty years ago, was unable to be saved. At this time, there's no official response from PCFD or the business owners. I'm told a conglomerate owned the motel, but we haven't confirmed that yet, either, I'm afraid. Back to you, Grant."

"No word on what happened," Zeldin said. "Not what really happened."

"Which was what?" Astra asked. "Do you think Jack set the fire?"

"That reporter said no one was hurt," Zeldin said. "Maybe he escaped."

"Or maybe they caught him and hauled him back to Space Command. I could probably go in. I only missed one day of work."

"They won't let you anywhere near him," Zeldin said. "Besides, if they haven't figured out that you were involved, they will soon. If you go back, they'll lock you up and throw away the key."

"So, we just keep going?"

"I don't think we have much choice," Zeldin said. "Space Command knows I'm involved. They'll bring me in if I'm not careful. But if I can get off world, they probably won't bother coming to collect me. Sergeant Hammer is really all they care about."

"Now that they have him, we're expendable?" Astra asked.

Zeldin didn't want to answer that question. Instead, he made a pivot.

"We don't know that they have him," he said.

"But we have to assume that, don't we? And we have to assume they still want to arrest us as well."

The waitress, a thin woman about Astra's age, but with a long face and hooked nose, lumbered over and refilled their coffee mugs.

"Get you anything else?" she asked with zero enthusiasm or interest.

"No, we're fine, thank you," Cal said.

Astra plucked up an old fashioned sugar container. It was made of glass with a stainless steel top that was well polished. She turned it up and dumped sugar into her coffee.

"I'm so tired," she said.

"We'll find a safe place to rest," Zeldin said. "But I think we should stay here for a while. It'll be easier to blend into morning traffic."

"Where can we go? I've got almost no money left."

"The ship is set to arrive today, right?"

"Yes," Astra said.

"Maybe they'll let us on early," he proposed.

Astra didn't like to think of the alternative. Space Command might post a reward for them. If that happened, the spacers would happily turn them over to the authorities. She couldn't help but wonder if getting caught would be so bad. After all, she hadn't done much. There was no way to know what the penalty for aiding and abetting someone who ran away from Space Command, but that was all she was guilty of. It would be worse for Dr. Zeldin, and she didn't want him to suffer, but she had gone from a mundane life that was so predictable she felt like she was sleepwalking the months away. But as she sat in the dinner, sipping coffee and picking at the biscuit on her plate, she missed the security of her old life. As boring as it was, with no real chance to improve her lot on Titan, she had known what to do and how to avoid trouble. But that knowledge was gone. She felt untethered and while there was a sense of adventure in the idea of leaving the moon that had been her home all her life, she had never expected it to be so hard. Or so frightening, but she tensed up every time someone walked past the dinner. Were they with Space Command? Where they looking for her? What would they do when they caught her? She had believed them to be a reputable organization, but after seeing what they did to Jack, she was absolutely terrified of what Space Command might do to her.

"We need a backup plan," she urged him. "Your facial cosmetics are starting to fail."

"We'll find something," he told her.

He reached over and put his hand on her forearm. She didn't pull away. In that moment he realized how desperately he needed human contact. He had always been a loner, and that had gotten him through med school and many long deployments on Space Command vessels. But getting to know Astra had changed him. He didn't know if she felt the same way about him. He knew he was no catch. Not any more with Space Command on his heels and his career in shambles. But she didn't pull away or give him the look he had seen so often as a young man by attractive girls. They could send the message that they weren't interested with just a haughty glance. He knew how piercing rejection felt. But for the moment they were in a jam together and he was glad that he wasn't alone.

27

Jack had heard the Marine commander call him a rat. It made him mad, but he didn't move. There were Marines on either side of him, and his hands were bound with plastic restraints.

He could also hear the radio in the cab of the hovercraft.

Special Transport, what's your ETA?

The driver of the vehicle responded. "We're three miles out. Traffic's light. I'd say three minutes to HQ."

Roger that, three minutes Special Transport. Security team will be waiting.

A security team, Jack realized, would make escape especially difficult. And once he was back in their hands, he would probably be hurt so badly by the so-called researchers, that he wouldn't have the strength to flee, even if there was an opportunity. If he was going to act, it needed to be before they reached Space Command.

He took the chance of opening his eyes just a tiny bit. Through his eyelashes he could see the Marines, two on each side. They were still in armor, but their rifles were hanging loose on straps across their chests and pointing in opposite directions. Every second counted, and so, he launched himself into action.

Corporal Ibu Armena had been in plenty of fights. He was a tough guy, with a reputation that went all the way back to the Arab neighborhood on Mars where he had grown up. He had served two years in the Marines before volunteering for Special Forces training. Those three months had been the hardest of his life, and yet, not once in all that time did he consider giving up. He had served as a Spec Op commando for two years, with three deployments in that time, one with combat. He was on track for a promotion and would have been a sergeant already, if not for a fistfight in his first platoon that had besmirched his personnel file.

When he saw their target spring up, he was surprised. Most people who get stunned are out for hours. Armena had been stunned once in a training exercise. When he woke up it was with the worst hangover of his life. But Sergeant Hammer seemed unfazed, despite being hit with multiple stun blasts. He moved faster than Armena thought possible. In one fluid motion he sat up and drove both hands into the bottom of Armena's chin. His head was pushed back and smashed into the metal frame of the hovercraft so hard, it knocked him out clean.

Lieutenant Caffrey saw the attack and reacted without hesitation. With one hand he slapped the comlink transmit button on the side of his helmet, and with the other he swung the butt of his tactical rifle toward Sergeant Hammer's head.

"Target is awake!" he shouted as Jack raised his shoulder to block the blow from Caffrey's rifle.

Across the vehicle, Farmer raised both her feet at Jack, but to everyone's surprise he caught her boots, one in each hand, stopped the kick halfway. For a split second that seemed much longer, everyone froze in shock. Lieutenant Caffrey had never seen anyone move as fast as Sergeant Hammer or stop a kick with their bare hands. He felt a stab of fear as he drew back his rifle to swing at the target again.

But Jack let out a bellow of rage. He didn't hate the Marines, but he was furious that they were taking him back to Space Command.

They had no idea what he had been through, but there was no time to talk about it. He jerked Amy Farmer's legs back across his body. She flew off the bench she was sitting on and practically into his lap. At the same time the lieutenant struck at Jack with the butt of his rifle again, but his own squad mate was in the way. The metal stock was meant to be light and strong enough to protect the weapon's battery. It bashed Farmer in the side of her helmet and she flopped to the floor.

Tina Sil had been in her share of fights as a child. Her mother was a prostitute and she never knew her father. She was in and out of foster care where she learned to defend herself from bullies and even abusive adults. With a scream of her own, she leaped at Jack. Her body pressed him down, onto his back. She was astride his chest, her hands pushing under his jaw. It should have pinned him down, but despite using all her strength, his head didn't move. It was like pushing against a statue.

Meanwhile, Jack brought his legs up and kicked at Lieutenant Caffrey. His boots hit the officer, who managed to get his arms up to protect his face. But the kick sent him sprawling toward the cab. Jack's feet were still bound together, but he put them down on the gurney and bucked his torso upward. The move sent Tina Sil flying into the rear door of the hovercraft hard enough that they swung open. She started to fall out, but Jack grabbed her. The vehicle was traveling at nearly sixty miles per hour and at least thirty feet off the ground in what was considered the emergency vehicle altitude. Had she fallen out her light armor would not have saved her from major injury, maybe even death.

She was flailing as Jack pulled her back and tossed her onto the seat where she had been sitting before the fight. It took her a moment to gain her bearings, but then she just stared at Sergeant Hammer. He wasn't huge, in fact, he looked average in size, but he was incredibly strong. With a twist of his arms he snapped the plastic restraints. Tina Sil could have taken another pass at Jack, but instead she grabbed her friend, Specialist Amy Farmer who was unconscious on the floor beside him and pulled Farmer deeper into the vehicle.

Lieutenant Caffrey had seen Jack's reaction when the doors opened. He had saved Specialist Sil, but that didn't mean that Caffrey could let him go.

"I gotta bring you in, Sergeant," the lieutenant declared.

"You have to try," Jack said, reaching down with one hand and ripping the restraints from his legs. "I don't want to hurt you. You're just following orders, but I'm not going back."

"Sorry," Caffrey said, aiming his rifle at Jack.

What happened next was so fast that Lieutenant Caffrey couldn't believe his eyes. In the time it took him to squeeze the trigger on his rifle, the man he was targeting shot forward and pushed the barrel of the weapon toward the ceiling. The stun blast hit the metal roof and ricocheted out the open rear doors. Jack drove a fist into Caffrey's stomach. The breath in the officer's lungs burst out of his mouth and for a moment he couldn't suck back hard enough to re-inflate his lungs.

"Next time they send you after me, refuse the operation, lieutenant," Jack said, before slapping his hand across the side of Caffrey's helmet. The blow snapped his head sideways and caused two disks in his neck to bulge. He was knocked senseless, and his smart helmet lost power.

Jack let the officer fall to the floor and then he turned. Tina Sil was the only Marine left to stop him, but she did nothing. He stepped past her, hesitated at the rear of the vehicle for a moment, then jumped out of the hovercraft.

Tina reached up with a trembling hand and activated her comlink. "Space Command HQ this is Oscar team. The target has escaped. I repeat, the target has escaped. We request emergency medical assistance. We need help!"

28

The command center was returning to Space Command headquarters. Captain Kittle was basking in his victory. There were still a few loose ends, but the main facet of the mission had been completed. Sergeant Hammer was on his way back to the R&D division, and Captain Kittle was on his way to a meeting with Admiral of the Fleet Evander Royce.

"Sir, there is a communication from Lieutenant Caffrey," the communication officer said.

All the officers in the command center had been on board and at their stations for almost twenty-four hours straight. Most sat staring at their screens, bleary eyed and silent. They were strapped in for the landing as the airship returned to its port on top of the main administration building.

"Put it through," Kittle said.

The target is awake! the lieutenant shouted and from then on there was only the sound of struggle. The transmission lasted twelve seconds and left Captain Kittle's blood cold.

"That's it?"

"The connection was lost," the communications officer said. "I've tried to get it back, but Lieutenant Caffrey isn't responding."

The entire aircraft shook for a moment as it settled onto the struts on top of the admin building. Kittle didn't wait for the okay from the pilots. He jumped to his feet and rushed over to the communications console. "Get me the pilot of that hovercraft!"

"Aye, Captain, connecting you with the pilot now."

A warning sound was going off in the background. "Special Transport, this is Captain Kittle! What's your status? Over."

"Sir, I'm unsure what is happening," the pilot said. "I'm pulling into HQ now. I've had an audio warning for about half a minute now and none of the Marines are responding."

Kittle stood up straight. He was tired. His joints ached and his eyes felt dry. But there was a sudden, sick feeling in his gut as he realized what the lieutenant's call had meant. Sergeant Hammer wasn't just awake, he had somehow overcome the Marines in the transport.

"Alert the MPs," Kittle said. "If Hammer's still on that hovercraft the Marines are probably all dead."

He turned and ran for the exit. The command center had an extendable staircase that was resting on the landing pad. Kittle, despite his age and lack of sleep, vaulted himself down the stairs with the hand rails, and hit the tarmac at a run. He sprinted to the edge of the building and looked down toward the receiving center. The ambulatory hovercraft was there, a squarish, gray vehicle. It had settled in the loading area with it's rear to the building where an overhead door was rolled back. A squad of MPs came running with shotguns in hand. Their black uniforms made them appear to be proficient, but Kittle knew they didn't stand a chance against Sergeant Hammer.

They stood at the rear of the hovercraft, weapons held ready and pointing into the passenger area, but then a female commando appeared at the door. She had her helmet off and was saying something to the MPs. One of whom turned and shouted, "Medic!"

The MPs lowered their weapons and moved aside. The lone commando stepped down and then said something to the medical team who came out of the receiving center. Soon, three bodies were removed on gurneys. Even from a distance Kittle could see that none of them were Sergeant Hammer.

There was no longer a need to run. The rest of the officers were lumbering off the command center. Kittle wanted to get back onboard and order the aircraft to take off again. Not that it was necessary. Space Command wasn't under attack and Sergeant Hammer wasn't out of the city like they had suspected when they were tracking Dr. Zeldin's rental. Besides all of that, no one from the command center was in shape to continue with the mission. Kittle needed new pilots and fresh officers. He doubted he would get either one.

Worst of all, he had an obligation. Getting a meeting with the Admiral of Fleet was no small thing. Rear Admiral Duncan and Admiral Ross were waiting for him. It should have been a triumphant moment, yet somehow Sergeant Hammer had slipped his bonds and escaped from Star Command custody once more. Kittle had no hand in what had happened, it was the Spec Op team that had let Hammer overwhelm them and escape. But he knew he would bear the blame. That was the way of things in the military. Someone had to be at fault. He had stepped up and taken command of the emergency team tracking the rogue sergeant and, under his leadership, that team had failed. It didn't matter that they succeeded before they failed or that no one could really say what Sergeant Hammer was capable of. Captain Kittle would have to face the music, come what may.

He followed the other officers into the building, but avoided the elevator and took the stairwell down to the top floor of the admin center. He slipped into a bathroom, splashed water on his face, smoothed his hair, and straightened his uniform. It didn't matter that he was the bearer of bad news, if he was going to see the Admiral of the Fleet, he wanted to look his best.

"Here he is," Admiral Kathryn Ross said when he reached the outer portion of Admiral Royce's office. "The man of the hour."

"Yes," Kittle said. "I think I'm exactly the man the Admiral will want to see."

Ross gave Kittle a strange look, then turned to Duncan, who was clearly surprised by Kittle's words. The captain's usual swagger was gone and there was none of the arrogance either of them expected from him.

"The admiral will see you now," a woman at a tiny desk that seemed almost like a decoration rather than a workspace, said.

Kittle led the way into the Admiral of the Fleet's inner sanctum. Evander Royce had a large office. It was where he spent the lion share of his time. Like most executive offices it was part work space, part shrine. There were photos on the walls, most were in expensive frames, of the Admiral of the Fleet with various other officers and a host of politicians. There were even some celebrities on his wall of fame. Opposite from the wall of pictures were floor to ceiling windows that overlooked a fountain that was in the campus quad. Around it were ornate looking buildings, above them a sweeping view of Saturn. In the middle of the walkway was a holographic table. The trio had to go around to reach Royce, who was settled behind his massive desk. He waved them close.

"Tell me this fiasco is over," he said, clearly expecting good news.

Kittle knew instantly that word had reached the Admiral of the Fleet that Hammer was in custody. Royce had a wide grin on his face.

"Sir, I regret to inform you that while Sergeant Hammer was taken into custody earlier this morning, he overcame four armed commandos while in restraints and escaped before reaching the Space Command campus."

The room was silent. Kittle could see the emotions working through Evander Royce's mind playing out on his face. He was surprised, then shocked, maybe even a little frightened, and eventually, it was all replaced by anger. He stood up slowly.

"Captain Kittle," he said, as Admiral Ross and Duncan stepped back from him. "Are you telling me that the most valuable asset, not just of Space Command, just escaped your custody for a second time?"

"Yes, sir," Kittle said, nearly choking on the words. It made him angry that he was being blamed, but that was how things worked. Kittle hadn't captured Sergeant Hammer, but he had been ready to take credit for that. Neither had he been directly responsible for Hammer's escape, but he would take the blame just the same. "Sir, he was stunned. His hands and feet were bound with plastic restraints. We didn't expect him to come to for hours and, as you know, most people are groggy and sick after being stunned."

"But Hammer's not like most people," Royce said. "You, of all people, understand that, Captain. And just four guards?"

"Highly trained Spec Op commandos," Kittle said. "The same team responsible for finding and apprehending him."

"Why just four?"

Kittle balked. To tell the truth, that Hammer had taken out most of the commando squad would be akin to an admission of guilt.

"That's all that would fit in the hovercraft, sir," Kittle said. "I left that decision to Lieutenant Caffrey."

Royce shook his head. "This is a failure of leadership," he snapped. "I should have known that you weren't ready for an assignment of this magnitude."

It was Kittle's turn to get angry.

"Excuse me, Admiral, but with all due respect, none of your people here were volunteering for the job. In fact, if it wasn't for my actions, you would still be forming committees to see who should be in charge of finding Sergeant Hammer."

"It seems like we still need someone capable of doing it."

"I found him once, Admiral. I can do it again."

"You found him once, but you lost him twice."

"That is true, sir, but Sergeant Hammer is a unique individual, with strengths we haven't yet been able to really discover. My people say it took four stun blasts to incapacitate him and he came to in less than an hour. I haven't had the time to get a full debriefing from the one conscious Marine on the transport when he escaped, but he is alone, on foot, without resources. Instead of arguing over who is to blame, we should be finishing the job."

Royce looked hard at Kittle. He wasn't used to someone arguing with him. And while he didn't like it, he found it oddly refreshing. Sergeant Hammer was becoming an embarrassment. Getting too involved in the fiasco concerning him was career suicide. It was better, Royce thought, to pin it all on Kittle.

"Then what are you doing in my office, captain?" Royce said. "Go find him. We'll discuss your career when this is over. But captain, if you hope to retire with a Space Command pension and benefits, I suggest you don't let Hammer escape again."

"Aye, Admiral," Kittle said, snapping to attention and saluting. He didn't wait for Royce to return the salute. Instead, he turned on his heel and hurried out of the big office. He hadn't slept in over two days, but any thoughts of rest were banished from his mind. He had a job to do, and every second it took for Kittle to get his assets in play, the harder it would be to capture Hammer. But if that's what it took to save Kittle's career, that's exactly what Kittle would do.

29

The drop hurt. The burn on his foot wasn't fully healed, and pain shot up his leg upon impact, but his knees didn't buckle and he maintained his balance. Hover traffic followed the roads initially laid down by the city planners. The asphalt did not make for a soft place to land, but Jack hit the road and rolled forward over his good shoulder. Still, his burned foot and hip ached so bad that he stayed on his knees for several seconds, just trying to breathe through the pain. Then he looked over his shoulder. The unmarked Space Command transport hadn't turned or made an emergency descent. He had time. Not much, but enough to get moving.

He was only a half mile from the Space Command campus, in a part of Prime City known as Institution Row. Titan's government buildings were close to the Space Command facilities, and the Deep Space Science Laboratory, one of the most prestigious universities in the system, sprawled for several miles with a mix of classrooms, labs and dormitories. Looking around, Jack realized he was between a private computer processing farm and a small shopping center. He hurried off the street and toward the buildings that housed thousands of computer processors, towering racks of servers and AI-powered robotic factories. Robots had been capable of carrying out almost any task people could think of. After a wave of humanoid robotics had changed life on Earth, the movement for organic prosperity had led to a ban on most robotics in the Sol system. The only exceptions were for dangerous jobs, such as metal manufacturing plants, deep mining and refinery work. Gone were the days of walking and talking robots, at least in the Sol system. They were, however, widely used on colony worlds, with Titan and Europa the only two places in the Sol system where robotic manufacturing was allowed.

Jack didn't know much about Titan. He had been there between deployments, but mostly just on the Space Command campus, which had its own entertainment district that included bars, clubs, theaters and even a recreational drug dispensary. Space Command believed in keeping its enlisted forces happy or, at the least, very well distracted. Plus, it kept the money that many enlisted service members wasted while on liberty between deployments in Space Command's coffers. Jack hadn't spent much time off campus, but he knew a bit about the moon, including the fact that it was a major exporter of goods off planet. That necessitated transportation between the manufacturers and the spaceport, which was where Jack hoped to hide out until he could get off-world.

He couldn't run well, although he was fast enough. His burned foot was a major impediment. One more day, he thought, and the burn would be healed enough that he could function at close to one hundred percent. But Space Command hadn't given him another day. Despite Dr. Zeldin's best efforts and Astra's sacrifice on his behalf, they hadn't lasted more than twenty-four hours before Space Command closed in on them. Jack didn't know that it was dawn. They were in the dark window of a cold week on Titan, which meant there was no dawn. Time was just a social agreement on a moon so far from the system star. It was also very cold, but Jack didn't mind that too much. He was on the move, his body warmed from the inside out. He found that a lot of things that he used to be very aware of simply didn't affect him as much anymore. Pain, cold and even hunger were not as noticeable. He still felt pain, sometimes great pain, but it didn't cripple him. What would have left him laid up for weeks, he could push through and still function. He was always hungry, but going without food didn't make him feel weak or shaky. The cold didn't stop him from jogging along between the nondescript server buildings. They were thick-walled and stout buildings with complex liquid cooling systems. The doors were locked and had key card readers. Jack needed to get inside and out of sight, but the processing facility was proving to be less accommodating than he had hoped.

There weren't a lot of people at the server facility. He did spot one man in thick coveralls going into one of the smaller buildings. Jack followed. The door wasn't locked, which was a relief. He might have been able to break into one of the buildings, which would almost certainly set off alarms. The last thing Jack wanted was to attract attention. He needed to hide. Soon, there would be drones in the air, and squads of MPs searching for him. Maybe the civil authorities would be called in to help contain him. The only thing Jack knew for certain was that Space Command wouldn't give up. They would never stop trying to find Jack and bring him back under their control.

Inside the small building, he had gained access to a supervisor's office, the control center for both the processors and the cooling systems. The latter utilized liquid methane from an underground source, which was convenient with Titan's vast supplies of methane, but also required strict oversight and safety protocols. Methane was not only highly flammable, but it required precise conditions to keep it in the liquid state. A minor leak would allow the methane to convert to its gaseous state, which could replace oxygen in an enclosed environment, like the processing facilities.

There was also a breakroom, a workshop with tools and a locker room with more of the thick coveralls. It seemed most of the people employed at the server farm were for facility maintenance. Jack found a pair of the coveralls and was slipping into them when someone caught sight of him.

"Hey, who are you?"

Jack turned around and saw a man in coveralls with a tool belt and a thick wool cap.

"Me?" Jack asked.

"Don't play dumb with me," the man growled. "This is my shift."

"Oh, yeah, I know that," Jack said. "But my old lady kicked me out, and I've been bouncing around just waiting for my shift. It's freezing out there, man. I figured I could just hang out here."

"You're day shift?"

"I'm actually a floater," Jack said. "Just hired on a couple weeks ago."

"You've been in training then," the man said. "Diego treating you right?"

Jack felt a bit of relief as the man seemed to relax. His threatening demeanor eased significantly.

"Oh yeah, he's great."

The man had a name badge sewn to the front of his coveralls. It said Pritchet and he moved with surprising speed. He turned slightly, still smiling in a friendly manner, but his hand reached out and grabbed the front of Jack's coverall. At the same time, his other hand drew out a heavy adjustable wrench.

"There ain't no Diego works here," the man said. "And you're wearing Baker's coveralls. I know Tim Baker, don't know you."

Jack was caught off guard, but not frightened. In fact, he felt a surge of anger.

"Listen, pal, I ain't looking to cause trouble," Jack said. "But I am not the guy you want to mess with."

"You threatening me?" Pritchet demanded as he held up the wrench.

"That's right," Jack said. "Let me go and walk away, or I'll fold you up and stuff you into one of these lockers."

The man brought the wrench close to Jack's face. "Mister, I don't know who you are, but you broke into the wrong place."

Jack didn't think about what he wanted. Since arriving back on Titan, nothing had been what he desired. Nor had he been given the time to consider what he wanted in regard to the changes in his body. A rising tide of frustration welled up inside him and he reacted to it.

His move to grab the wrench happened so fast it caught the worker off guard. His eyes opened wide with surprise, then narrowed in anger. He was taller than Jack and thick through the chest and shoulders. With a heave, he tried to yank the wrench out of Jack's hand. To his shock, it didn't move. He tried again, heaving with all his strength and a grunt of effort, but he still couldn't budge the tool.

"I warned you," Jack said.

Pritchet let go of the coverall Jack had put on, but not the wrench. With his free hand, he tried to push Jack backwards, but the smaller man didn't budge. Then he grabbed Pritchet's hand that was against his chest and twisted. His arm rotated and he yelped in pain, letting go of the wrench and twisting his body. The big man went down on one knee, trying to relieve the pressure on his wrist. Jack let go of Pritchet's arm and hit him with a tight little hook that connected with the big man's jaw. His head whipped sideways and he fell over onto his side.

Jack dragged the worker into the bathroom and left him there, but took the man's ID badge. His next stop was the break room. There was coffee. Jack filled a cup, dumped in some sugar, and stirred it with a tiny plastic straw. It wasn't bad. When he looked into the control room, he found a couple of guys inside. They weren't paying much attention to the screens and controls. There were no cameras on the outside of the buildings or even at the entrances. Everything was focused on the servers and the cooling system, which was understandable. The server farm didn't have the kind of valuables that would tempt thieves. Nor was there any kind of threat from competitors or domestic terrorists on Titan. The moon was, for most intents and purposes, still a frontier colony. It was a depository of valuable minerals, specifically the kind useful in producing energy for industries that relied on a large amount of it. The server farm hosted several AI programs and a manufacturing plant that used robotics and three-dimensional printing machines. While it had backup power and auxiliaries in case the back-ups failed, what mattered most was keeping the electricity flowing and the servers functioning.

"Where's Pritchet?" One of the men in the control room asked.

Jack shrugged. "He called in sick, I guess. I'm filling in."

That answer satisfied the men, who went back to their conversation. And Jack, realizing he had an hour until the day shift arrived, went to the supervisor's office. It was locked, but Pritchet's ID card worked in the scanner. The door popped open and Jack went to the computer on the supervisor's desk. He brought up Titan's Information Network and then got a map of Prime City on the screen. Memorizing the city layout between the server farm and the nearby space port, Jack closed out the program and logged off the network.

When he came out of the supervisor's office, one of the men from the control room was helping Pritchet out of the locker room.

"Hey, I don't know who you are and I don't care," the man from the control room said. "Just leave, okay. The police are on their way."

"What?" Jack asked.

"We called it in after you left Control, pal. It's protocol. Pritchet ain't sick and you ain't no floater. I don't care what you want, but leave us out of it."

"Unreal," Jack said as he headed for the door.

Anger was boiling up inside him. Why couldn't people just let him be? Maybe he needed to stop giving them a chance to stab him in the back. It was unreasonable to think that a security team wouldn't call in if a stranger showed up. They were just doing their jobs, and Jack didn't fault them for that. But he was angry that he had given them the chance. His goal of slipping unnoticed to the space port was ruined.

He should have turned to the right, but instead he went left. If the police were coming, it wouldn't be long before Space Command showed up as well. The space port was the obvious destination of choice, which meant that Jack had to lead the authorities in the opposite direction. If he just disappeared, they might shut down the port and start searching every ship. That was a risk he couldn't take.

As he hurried back through the cluster of buildings, he thought about Dr. Zeldin and Astra. No matter how much he might wish otherwise, they couldn't go back to their old lives. They were conspirators in his escape, which made them fugitives from Space Command and, maybe, wanted suspects by the police. Jack had no way of knowing if they had been picked up or if they had successfully slipped away. If the Commandos were paying attention, they would have realized after the fact, if not before, that the couple had come out of the same room where Jack had been found. In all likelihood, they were nabbed as soon as they got far enough from the motel that they couldn't be seen. Jack wished they had found some way to communicate. And if they weren't picked up immediately, then he had to believe that agents were sent after them the moment that Jack was rendered unconscious.

He hadn't forced them to do anything, or even asked them to. It had been their free choice, and yet he felt guilty for getting them into trouble just the same. And he wasn't in trouble for doing something wrong. Space Command was to blame. They were acting unethically, both in how they were treating Jack and by not giving him a choice in the matter. In fact, unethical wasn't strong enough a word. What they were doing was evil, but they were still the authority and no one on Titan would stand against them. No one but Jack.

And that's when he realized where he had to go and what he had to do. He turned north toward the Space Command campus and started walking.

30

The darkness was his advantage. There were no walls around Space Command, but there were large buildings that faced in toward the middle of the campus, with loading docks and parking garages that formed long barriers around the perimeter of the campus. There were even a few guard shacks on the main roads leading into the property.

Jack targeted one of the guard shacks. It was a standard booth, with surveillance feeds to a set of low monitors, a computer with a wireless ID scanner, and bulletproof glass on all sides. Most of the traffic coming through was hovercraft, and there was a set of metal stairs on the back side of the booth that led up to a platform on top. Normally, the booth would be manned by two MPs. But the word had gone out that Jack had been spotted nearby. Police had gone to the server farm, but only a couple of patrol vehicles. Local law enforcement hadn't been put on alert regarding the importance of finding Jack, just that he was a person of interest to Space Command. The cops would alert Space Command if they saw him or detained him.

But Space Command was responding just as Jack expected them.

Every able body that could be mobilized quickly was being called up. That left one guard in the booth and Jack watched him from the shadows.

There were two cameras facing the street and the back of a large building on either side of that street made it impossible to circle around the guard shack. Jack knew the moment his face was caught on camera, the computer would run a scan to identify him. He needed to get to the guard shack without attracting the guard's attention or getting pinged by the security's AI facial recognition system. If he could get past the guard shack, there was an entrance to the Marine barracks in the big building just beside the guard booth. Space Command kept no regular presence on Titan, but the building was often used as Marines arrived at the moon, either preparing to deploy or just returning. It might have been more efficient to have the Marines rally at a space station, but Space Command liked to put their Marine force on the ground between deployments. It was supposed to be for morale, but in reality, they simply wanted to give the Marines a chance to spend as much of their pay as possible, preferably in places owned and operated by Space Command.

The PX, bars and clubs on the Space Command campus offered goods without the usual taxes. That meant a visiting Marine or crewman could stretch their credits a bit farther. But with all that running around, drinking and getting high, it was imperative to keep people unarmed. The weapons that each Marine was equipped with before a mission had to be turned into the barracks armory for the duration of their stay on Titan, and Jack meant to take advantage of that.

He waited until the guard was sitting down. While Jack was concealed by the shadows, the guard was visible inside the booth. He was hunched over a monitor, maybe reading a message or perhaps watching the force build up nearby. Jack sprang into action. He couldn't sprint, but his jog was as fast as most people could run. He put his hands on his face, covering his nose, mouth, and jaw. Only his eyes and the top of his stubbly head were visible.

The guard looked up just as Jack reached the booth. The MP was shocked and tried to get his rifle to bear on the situation, but Jack was too fast. There were no cameras inside the booth. He raced in, grabbed the guard's rifle barrel, and held it away from him.

"You're—"

Jack drove a powerful palm strike straight up into the underside of the man's jaw. He hit the guard so hard it lifted him off his feet. He crashed back into the wall of the booth, then slumped down. Jack unhooked the guard's rifle sling and set the weapon against the counter. One look at the computer console showed that no alarms had gone off. His hands on his face had been enough to throw off the AI security system. Phase one of his plan was complete.

There were a variety of useful items in the booth. Jack took the guard's uniform, including his coat. There was a heater in the shack and the unconscious guard wouldn't get too cold. Jack put on the uniform, including the gun belt that held a High Energy Laser Pistol in a holster that strapped around his thigh. In the booth was a pair of stun batons and several sets of plastic restraints. He put a pair on the guard's wrists, then watched on the surveillance feed as a large group of MPs gathered at their rally point near a set of official Space Command transports. There was no need to reveal himself while so many MPs were geared up and on the premises. He watched them load into the transports, each one in light combat armor and carrying a variety of non-lethal weapons.

That was another advantage in Jack's favor. They didn't want him dead. In fact, it seemed they were willing to put their own people in harm's way just to ensure he wasn't killed. That didn't mean he couldn't make a mistake and get himself injured or killed, but if they wanted to use non-lethal munitions, he wouldn't be mad about that.

A few minutes into his vigil, the guard started to wake up. Jack drew his sidearm, checked to ensure it was on the lowest possible setting, then shot the guard in the leg. The energy blast at close range had the capacity to burn skin and tissue. And while every member of Space Command was officially his enemy, he wasn't a murderer. He had served Space Command in combat and had killed in that capacity. He had killed one of the researchers in his attempt to escape, but he was certain that in both of those situations, his actions were justified. He had killed in war and he had killed in self-defense. But he would not kill if he didn't have to. He was no villain, after all. He was the victim by any definition of the word and, while he was willing to die rather than return to the tortures of the R&D division of Star Command, he didn't want to harm the MPs or Marines who were just doing their jobs.

He waited for nearly fifteen minutes after the MPs had left before setting out. He took the unconscious guard's cap and pulled it low so that the bill of the cap was right above his eyes. As he left the booth, he pretended to adjust the cap and further shield his face until he was far enough from the cameras not to get picked up and identified by the security program.

The door that led into the Marine barracks was made of metal, with a bolt lock that fed into the metal doorframe. There was no doorknob, just a U-shaped handle below the bolt lock. Jack had taken the guard's ID, but there was no scanner on the lock. It was an old-fashioned security device that utilized a metal key. Jack didn't have a key, but he took hold of the handle with both hands, put his good foot on the wall next to the door and pulled.

It was the first time since his accident on the alien world that he had really put all his strength into a task. At first, the door didn't budge. Jack could feel the muscles in his thigh and across his back. They bunched, the muscle fibers expanding. His heart increased to supply more oxygen and give his body everything it needed to accomplish the task.

As he pulled the metal, the bolt groaned and the insert it fed into bent. There was a pop, loud as a gunshot, that echoed between the tall buildings. But if anyone heard it, they made no obvious reaction. Jack looked both ways as the ruined door opened. The bolt housing had failed, as had the metal frame that was supposed to hold it in place. It still stuck out of the door, but at an angle. Jack slipped inside and got his bearings.

He was in one of the maintenance hallways. The Marines looked after their own facility, but the cleaning supplies were stored in closets, and there were trash carts that had to be emptied. Jack went down the maintenance hallway and came out into the main corridor. There were large rooms to either side. Those to his left were filled with bunkbeds. The rooms on his right were for platoon meetings and recreational space. Jack wasn't interested in either of those. His focus was on the heavy door that led to the armory. It was a secure room. Only people with the proper ID that were entered into the security system would be able to open the lock. And unlike the door Jack had ripped open with his strangely enhanced strength, he wouldn't be able to repeat that feat with the armory door. It was more like a hatch on a spaceship. The locking mechanism was as thick as Jack's wrist, and there were three of them. He was strong, but he wouldn't waste his time or energy trying to break into the armory that way. Instead, he went to the pass-through window. It was situated a few steps from the door and was three feet wide and three feet long. At the bottom was a shelf that stuck out nearly twelve inches. Jack had passed similar pass-throughs multiple times in his life, either checking in his weapon or checking it out. The room was filled with rifles and ammunition of all types, including laser weapons and extra power packs.

There was no need for anything fancy. He walked right up to the window and waited for the Staff Sergeant on duty to turn toward him. Then Jack shot him with his stun pistol. The report wasn't like a gunshot. It was more of an electric sound, followed by a high-pitched whine as the capacitor inside the weapon recharged for another shot. The Staff Sergeant on duty dropped to the floor. Jack looked both ways inside the armory. There was no one else on duty. Like the MPs, the Marines who weren't carrying out essential functions were sent out to look for Jack.

There was no one in the main corridor either. If anyone heard the laser shot, they weren't concerned about it. Jack hopped onto the pass-through shelf, twisted around, and dropped inside the armory. He took a few seconds to check on the staff sergeant. He was unconscious but breathing steady and his pulse was fine. The floor inside the armory was bare concrete. The guard would certainly have a headache, maybe even a concussion, but he would survive. Not everyone Jack encountered that night would be so lucky.

Jack found what he wanted in a locked cabinet. He used the Staff Sergeant's ID card to unlock it. Inside was a HE-MAN rifle, so named because it was heavy and bulky. Most laser rifles were lightweight and small, with an effective range of about a hundred feet. Beyond that, the laser bolts lost enough energy to no longer be of much use. A HE-MAN rifle had a bigger power supply, which made it heavy, and four separate laser activators that allowed it to shoot rapidly like a machine gun firing projectiles. The laser blasts from the big rifle were deadly at five hundred feet. Jack replaced the tactical rifle with the HE-MAN gun, which was no problem for his improved strength to handle.

But what he really wanted were the grenades that were locked in a metal box with an old-fashioned combination lock on the front. Jack snapped the lock with his bare hands and got all twelve grenades from inside. He put them into a stretchy belt with loops for grenades and rifle magazines. He slung the belt over his head and adjusted the rifle so that it was comfortable and ready for use. Then he left the armory and headed for the R&D building.

Normally, a Marine carrying weapons on a military facility was not alarming. But Space Command HQ on Titan was staffed with mostly logistical and administrative service members. Few had ever seen combat. Jack got some strange looks, but he wasn't the only person in an MP uniform running across the Space Command campus. Everyone knew something was going on, even if they didn't know the specifics.

It took Jack almost seven minutes to run the mile from where he had entered the campus to where the R&D building was located. He had never seen the front of the building. It was where the offices of the researchers were located. Unlike the rear, which was connected to a wide parking garage, or the interior of the building where the laboratories were, the front was all glass and molded concrete. The entrance was wide and the lobby had polished tile floors and golden sconces on the walls. Jack looked around. There were some people coming and going from the other buildings, but no MPs were in sight. Nor were there any Marines. Jack flicked off the safety on the HE-MAN rifle and aimed at the glass front, ground floor of the R&D building. The laser rifle didn't chug or buck up. It just spewed high-power focused energy blasts at a steady rate that shattered the glass and burned holes through the walls. The elevators were damaged, and the decorative plants were destroyed. The artwork was knocked off the walls and ruined. Then Jack raised the rifle and fired at the row of offices on the floor above the lobby. It took a full minute to blast through all the offices. Jack didn't know which researchers were caught in the carnage. Some might have been innocent, but they worked with the sick bastards who had cut and burned him without mercy just to see if he would heal. They rubbed elbows with the barbarians who shaved his entire body and left him without clothes to wear, or blankets to huddle under at night. They, by their very presence in the Space Command Research and Development division, endorsed the hateful torture that led to him being strapped on a metal table, starved and humiliated, not even allowed to use a bathroom, much less receive medical help, by the so-called medical researchers. And so, they would share in the fate of those sadistic pigs, Jack thought.

There were alarms sounding, but none were as loud as the klaxon or rage ringing in Jack's ears. He let the heavy automatic laser rifle dangle from the sling across his chest while he pulled out a pair of grenades from the belt over his shoulder. The pins came free easily, and he tossed them on the first floor above the lobby. By the time he got another pair free, the first two had exploded. He walked the width of the building, tossing the grenades in and devastating the facility. By some miracle, it wasn't destroyed completely, but the entire face of the building was a smoking husk with no vestige of its former glory.

Jack hit the release on the HE-MAN rifle to release the battery. He knew the advanced power supply cost more than a new hovercar. But he didn't care, any more than Space Command who ordered them by the hundreds for the Marines they sent to do their dirty work. He had one replacement, which he slid up the stock and locked into place. The power indicator showed full ... and Jack was ready for more mischief.

He had made his statement, but he still needed to get away. There was no doubt in his mind that if he was captured, the torture would start again. He hadn't gone looking for the exceptional abilities that had suddenly been bestowed on Jack. But nor did he feel that it was right that he should suffer because of it. He felt good. Despite the injuries that hadn't fully healed, Jack felt strong. While the authorities were reeling from his surprise attack, Jack dashed through the destruction that was once the R&D Department, headed for the garage and his best chance for escape.

31

Evander Royce was an early riser. Up at 0430 every morning, he was in the office no later than 0530 and could often get more done before his secretary arrived at 0800 than many people accomplished in a full day. In those glorious, uninterrupted two and a half hours, he took care of the things he considered the most important. As Admiral of the Fleet, there were always urgent matters, but urgency didn't equate to importance. And at 0530, urgency could wait a few hours.

And every day, right at 0800, his secretary would arrive. She was a petite woman named Gina who possessed a beautiful speaking voice, but who could stare down the most pushy, obnoxious officers and, even worse, politicians who felt they had a right to interrupt Royce's day. She would bring him a latte in a thermal mug that stayed warm on his desk for a full hour while he savored every sip. They often met in his office and stood silently side by side, sipping their respective beverages and staring out across the Space Command campus for a full minute before the constant demands and interruptions began pouring in.

They were there, side by side, appreciating their moment of

peace, when it was shattered. No call was needed. They heard the explosions from nearly a mile away at the R&D building. Royce nearly dropped his latte.

"What was that?" Gina asked when the first two grenades went off.

"Trouble," Royce said. "Initiate a lockdown, Gina. Go, now! Then get to the bunker."

The bunker was under the admin building. It existed for the very threat posed by Sergeant Jack Hammer. He was attacking Space Command, and for all anyone knew, the administration building was next.

The bunker consisted of two facilities deep underground. The first was reached through the reinforced stairwell. It was located three stories below the basement level, and had enough food and water to sustain every person in the building for two weeks. It also had emergency power, water, air circulation, and communication lines. The reinforced walls and ceiling were eight feet thick. If the entire building fell right on top of the bunker, it would still hold up.

Connected to the bunker was the Vault. It had two entrances, one was a massive steel door on a set of mechanically activated hydraulic hinges. Once it was closed and locked, it could only be reopened from the inside. The other entrance was via an elevator shaft that connected directly with the Admiral of the Fleet's office. It looked like a shower stall, but once inside, Royce could insert his ID, which had a one-of-a-kind magnetic chip that would activate the emergency elevator. He could then dial what appeared to be the water controls. When they were turned from the off to the fully hot setting, the elevator would drop down the chute and into the Vault.

Everyone else, including the Chiefs of Staff, had to reach the Vault via the stairwell and through the bunker. Evander Royce went to his desk after giving Gina the order to put the building on lockdown and opened the top right drawer. Inside were a few office supplies and a couple of portable battery chargers. He put them in his pockets, then pulled open a trap in the bottom of the drawer.

There were three items inside. One was a fully mechanical .9 millimeter semi-automatic pistol with eighteen hollow-point rounds in the clip and another in the firing chamber. Royce picked it up, checked the safety, then tucked it into his waistband. Beside the gun was an emergency phone and a bottle of high-potency Fentanyl capsules, enough to kill sixty people in the event that suicide became necessary.

Royce's hand shook as he picked the pill bottle up and put it in his pocket, then he rushed to his private bathroom as explosions continued to rock the building. He had never activated the emergency elevator. But once he did, it went down so swiftly that his knees nearly buckled when it slowed. When the doors opened, the only people in the Vault were two members of Space Command's protective detail. They were standing by the massive door. Both were in full battle armor and armed with tactical laser rifles.

"What's happening?" Royce demanded.

"An attack from inside the campus," one of the men said.

They were faceless behind the dark front of their helmets, which didn't give Royce much comfort.

"Reports are of a lone gunman," the other said. "Perhaps using grenades."

"Grenades," Evander Royce said the word as if it were a curse. "How the hell did someone get grenades on this campus?"

It was a silly question. Space Command wasn't a hippy commune or a progressive liberal university. It was a military complex, but it still seemed outrageous that someone might have dangerous explosives so close to where Royce lived and worked.

People were already flooding into the bunker. It was a large space, intended to shelter the nearly two hundred people working in Space Command's Senior Command building. But Royce wasn't interested in seeing who had made it down to the bunker. He went instead to the communication console that was set up in one corner of the Vault. It consisted of two large curved screens. The upper screen had surveillance footage from the cameras around the campus. The lower screen had news footage from local, planetary, and system-wide news sources.

Royce focused on the upper screen, trying to catch sight of the perpetrator.

General Homer Ulysses Mortimer Fink was head of the Space Command Marine Corps and one of the only senior officers who didn't rush to the bunker for safety. His face appeared on one of the communication screens, and Royce brought it up on the main display.

"Sir, I'm here in the campus security command center," General Fink said.

"Tell me who the hell is attacking my facility?"

"We have a seventy-nine percent match to Sergeant Jack Hammer, sir. He's a Marine, but I can't find him on the active duty roster, sir. There's a block on his file, Top Secret, Need to Know Basis. I'm guessing you'll have more luck—"

Royce cut him off. "He's the rogue Marine we've been searching for."

Everyone at Space Command knew that Sergeant Hammer was wanted. And though his file may have been classified, everyone had a pretty good idea as to what was going on. Not the specifics, but the gist was common knowledge. General Fink wasn't giving the Admiral of the Fleet a report; he was making an unofficial complaint. There had always been a power struggle behind the scenes between the Admiral of the Fleet and the General commanding the SCMC. It was petty, but all too real, even bearing fruit while they were under attack.

"Pardon me, Admiral. I had no idea."

Royce found that hard to believe, but he didn't have time to play games.

"Do you have eyes on him?"

"He went into the R&D building, which was his target," Fink said. "At this time, I have no reports of him attacking anywhere else."

"We have to find him," Royce said. "Get people in that building."

"I would, sir, but unfortunately, all my MPs and the Marines on temporary station here were handed over to Captain Kittle for some exercise with local law enforcement."

Royce was furious, but he couldn't let it show. He put his hands behind his back and clapped his right hand over his left wrist. Standing perfectly still, he stared at the screen that showed General Fink. The man was thick, his muscular frame more fat than muscle. He had a tiny little mustache on his upper lip and his eyes seemed to droop, as if his eyelids were retreating from his forehead. Royce hated everything about the man.

"Call them back," he said through forced calm.

"I would, sir, but it seems this Captain Kittle has a special command and only takes orders from you, sir. I'm afraid you'll have to do it."

Royce realized the General was right. He reached out and cut the communication with Fink. The general's image disappeared on the view screen. It wasn't a slap in the face, but Royce still felt good about cutting the pompous general off. He initiated a call via comlink to Captain Kittle.

"Captain, we have a situation," Royce said. "Your target is here. I repeat, Sergeant Hammer is on the Space Command campus. He just attacked the R&D building and is currently inside that space. Get your people back here, ASAP. Over."

"Roger that, Admiral," Captain Kittle said. "I've got assets on their way to you now, sir."

When Royce turned around, there were half a dozen senior officers in the Vault. He focused on Admiral Kathryn Ross. "It's Hammer," he said. "He attacked the R&D building. He's gone inside. I want you to coordinate with General Fink. We have assets on the way to stop him. I want regular updates and no more excuses. This has gotten out of hand."

"Aye, Admiral," Kathryn Ross said. "Is there any word on Vice Admiral Duncan?"

"Should there be?" Royce asked.

"He was meeting with a team of munitions researchers today, sir. I haven't heard from him."

"Time will tell, Admiral," Royce told her. "Carry on."

She nodded and hurried past him to the communications console. Royce took a deep breath, tried not to think about the people who had undoubtedly been slain in the attack. It was impossible not to think about how close it came to almost being him. If Sergeant Hammer had attacked the Senior Officers' building instead of R&D, he might be lying in a pile of rubble. Fear ran an icy finger down his spine. It wasn't even nine o'clock in the morning and already Evander Royce needed a drink.

32

Jack was acting on instinct more than any plans. He had run into the R&D building with the thought that he would get to the garage and steal a hovercraft. But with the power down and the building half destroyed, it wasn't a simple matter of strolling through the once bright and wide corridors.

He climbed over a mound of rubble and found himself in a small lab. There was a technician trying to lift a steel beam off one of the researchers. The beam had crushed the man's leg, and Jack thought he knew exactly how the man felt. He stopped in the shadows, watching as the researcher sent the tech to fetch what looked like a small sword. The device was strange. It was about three feet long, with a curved metallic handle, but the rest of the object looked like a flat piece of wood. In fact, it reminded Jack of the yardsticks his father sometimes brought home from the lumber store. As a child, Jack had battled many imaginary enemies with a yardstick sword.

"Turn it on... but be careful," the researcher said, his voice strained with pain.

The tech powered the device on and the narrow edges of the flat object began to glow a dark red color.

"C-c-cut it... c-cut the... beam," the researcher stammered.

There were other tools in the lab. Jack recognized some of them. There was a portable power drill used for placing explosives in solid objects, several battery packs of various designs, a plasma cutter and a robotic digger. And there were things that Jack didn't recognize as well. Most were in cases, but some had fallen to the floor.

The tech slid the wooden end of the strange tool under the steel beam, with the red edge touching the metal. He pulled up, and Jack thought he was using the tool as a lever until he noticed the red edge had actually cut into the metal.

"I can't," the tech said breathlessly.

"It will work!" the researcher insisted. "The molecular disruptor is made to cut through anything!"

There was a loud bang nearby and the hiss of some compressed gas. Jack realized there were things in the building that were probably volatile.

"Sorry," the tech said, obviously coming to the same conclusion. The tech ran out a side door.

Jack had every intention of following the technician, but he stopped in the lab long enough to get a closer look at the strange device. The researcher looked at Jack and must have recognized him.

"P-p-please," he said. "D-don't hurt me."

Jack ignored the man and took hold of the metal device. It had cut through the beam, but not with heat. He pulled on the device. It was stuck in the metal, but Jack didn't give up. He pulled harder and, to his surprise, the object came straight up through the steel beam.

"Oh... thank you... thank you," the researcher said as the pressure on his shattered leg was relieved. He even managed to push the remaining part of the beam off his leg completely.

"Don't mention it," Jack said as he pressed the activator button with his thumb. The red edge on the material disappeared. Jack looked closer at the object. It wasn't wood at all, but some sort of composite material. It was too gloomy in the lab for a normal person to see clearly, although Jack's eyes took in everything. He reached up and touched the flat part of the composite material. It wasn't hot.

"What is this?" Jack asked.

"It's a carbon fiber slat with specially designed covalent atomic bonds," the researcher said. "They form a tetrahedral lattice, like a diamond. It's what makes a diamond one of the hardest substances in the universe."

"It won't break," Jack said.

"No, and the handle is called a Modis," the researcher said. "It uses electricity to create a band of electostatic force around the edge of the slat that causes positively charged protons to repel one another. In theory, it can cut through anything."

"Nice," Jack said.

"Please, can you get me some help. I'm seriously hurt," the researcher complained.

"Oh, yeah, I guess you heard about that Marine they were testing on here just a few days ago."

The researcher recoiled as if he had just seen a snake.

"I-I-I h-had n-noth-nothing to d-d-do with that."

"But you knew about it," Jack said in a casual manner as he waved the modis through the air. "You knew they were cutting on him. I'm a little surprised they didn't use this."

"It hasn't been cleared for use outside the laboratory."

"This is all you care about?" Jack asked, waving the modis at the ruined lab.

"It's my life's work. I heard what the med people were doing, sure. But that's not my field. I c-c-couldn't have stopped it."

"How do you know? Did you try?" Jack asked, looking down at the researcher for the first time.

"No," the man said, his voice barely a whisper.

"Then maybe you didn't deserve this," Jack said, waving the modis at the researcher's leg. "But you know what they say, lie down with dogs and you'll get up with fleas."

He left the lab, but kept the modis. The HE-MAN rifle had a rail on top for clipping on a scope or other tactical tools. Jack managed to fit the handle of the modis to the rail, so that the experimental device fit right on top of the big laser rifle.

He had to wind his way through the R&D building. Some of the labs had sealed up, probably to contain dangerous pathogens. Others were leaking substances that Jack didn't want to go near. He was almost to the garage space, which was built onto the back of the R&D building and stretched across to the structures on either side, when an explosion ripped through the building's upper floors.

Jack stepped into a doorway and waited for the rumble of the explosion to stop. He didn't know what was happening or if he would even survive. Strangely enough, that thought didn't frighten him. At least if he was dead, they couldn't hurt him anymore, although he did have a sense of revulsion at the idea of what the Space Command researchers might do with his body once they dug it out of the rubble.

But the upper floors didn't collapse down on the lower ones. Nor did the explosion reach him. Dust fell as the walls shook and the floor shuddered, but he survived, and before everything was still again, Jack was in the garage.

He didn't know much about automobiles. He could shoot and march in formation, and put a mean polish on his dress shoes, but he didn't know how to replace an alternator or repair a faulty repulser lift. But he did know that most personal vehicles had activation fobs, which were carried by the driver. The fob connected wirelessly with the vehicle's computer and gave it permission to operate. And Jack knew that it was human nature to leave such devices in the vehicle. It wasn't smart, and most people wouldn't do it, but he only needed one absent-minded researcher. He went to the first car he came to and checked the door. It was locked, and he moved on to the next. He checked door after door. They were all locked, and he was beginning to think he was wrong, but on his sixth attempt, the door opened. He couldn't help but grin. He was a wanted man, still in pain from the grievous wounds inflicted on him by barbarous researchers, and undoubtedly being chased by scores of armed military police, but he couldn't help but smile. It wasn't because he was right about the carelessness of people or because he felt that he was about to escape scot-free, but because it felt good to have something, even a little thing, fall in his favor for a change.

He sat down in the driver's seat and hit the start button, but the vehicle beeped at him and a warning flashed on the dashboard display screen. **Activation Fob Not Detected.**

Jack pulled himself out of the car and continued his search. Three cars later, his luck paid off. The vehicle, a luxury model with leather seats and a large, vertical display beside the hovercraft controls, started right up. Jack unsnapped the HE-MAN rifle and stuck it into the floorboard in front of the passenger seat.

"Now, we're talking," he said.

A green button next to the red Engine Start button said Repulser Activation. He pushed it, and the car rose up eight inches off the garage floor. He carefully backed the vehicle up, then angled it in a turn toward the garage exit. The interior of the garage was dark and starting to get smoky. Somewhere a fire was burning. Jack turned the car toward the square of light at the garage exit just in time to see a large transport land just outside. He turned the vehicle again and accelerated toward the ramp that led to the next level. If the MPs were back blocking the exit, he would just have to take the luxury vehicle off the garage's upper deck. The only problem with his plan was he didn't know if the hovercraft had an altitude limit. He might sail off the garage and fly away to safety or he might plummet to his death. There was only one way to know for certain.

33

D r. Zeldin and Astra stood in the shadow of a large utility structure. It was taller than the doctor, a big, dark box that hummed slightly. Beyond the shadows where they stood was the space port. It was essentially long rows of landing spots filled with cargo shuttles. There were hundreds of ships in the port, all positioned side by side, with refueling and energy cables running between them. From the wide cargo hatches came crates, pallets of goods and large containers. They were moved by four-wheeled vehicles that were small but clearly powerful, with hydraulic forks that lifted the various parcels. The ships in port weren't just being unloaded. Some were taking in loads that would be hauled back up to large spaceships in orbit.

At intervals all through the space port were light poles. Not just tall structures with lights attached to them, but the poles themselves were made of round bulbs that cast light in every direction. They were tall and narrow, filling the space port with so much light that it was like a bright, sunny day around the cargo shuttles. The light also revealed groups of soldiers. They were Marines from Space

Command. Dr. Zeldin had no doubt they were there to apprehend him.

"What should we do?" Astra asked.

"Is your friend here?"

She pointed to one of the many shuttles offloading cargo. "That one, with the red stripe, RM4227."

It was a rugged-looking shuttle with grime built up near the exhaust ports and more than its share of dings in the thick, metal hull. There were a lot of ships that looked much better than RM4227, but not many that looked worse.

"I don't think there's much chance of getting to it without being noticed," Dr. Zeldin said. "The best we can hope for is to look like we belong and go straight to the shuttle. Will they let us board?"

"That's what I was told," Astra said. "They take on cargo and passengers. If you can't pay, you can work for your passage to Veta Madre."

"Alright," Zeldin said. "The way I see it, we've got two choices. We could go together and, maybe, they're not looking for a couple. But the odds are good they are looking for me. If that's the case, you'll be guilty by association."

"You don't think they know about me? I rented the room in the motel, after all," she pointed out.

"Did you do that under your real name?"

"No," she said. "I told them my name was Lacy Montral."

"It would take work to track down your identity," Dr. Zeldin said. "Eventually, they'll get it, but probably not yet. Even if the people in charge have discovered your involvement, I'm betting the Marines out there on guard duty haven't been given a description. My guess is they're looking for me, but a woman probably isn't on their radar yet."

"And what happens if they take you in?" Astra asked.

He unzipped his duffel bag and pulled out a small box. He handed it to her. The box was heavy.

"What's this?" she asked.

"Gold," he said. "About fifty thousand credits worth. Mostly jewelry, but there are some coins in there, too. If something happens to me, you can use that to get a clean start on Veta Madre or wherever you decide to go."

"I can't take this," Astra said. "It's your money."

"Yeah, well, if they take me in, I won't be needing it. And if I do make it to the ship, you can give it back to me."

"Is it... illegal?"

"No," Cal said. "I had some money saved up. I used it at a pawn shop to get that stuff."

"You had a lot to lose," Astra said. "Why'd you do it?"

"I took an oath, the Hippocratic Oath, when I became a doctor. I swore that I would do no harm."

"You weren't the one harming Jack, were you?" she asked.

He shook his head. It was true, he hadn't carried out the vile experiments, but he had done testing on Jack while they were on the *Intrepid*. Just blood samples and med scans mostly, tracking the progress of his healing and physical changes. There was nothing wrong with that. In fact, it had been his obligation to carry out the work of isolating and identifying Jack's unique physical condition. But it had led to a much worse place. Cal had even taken Jack into the Space Command R&D building and turned him over to the so-called experts for testing.

"I wasn't, but I was involved in what was being conducted. As the physician who discovered his abilities I was entitled to remain connected to the testing and subsequent discoveries made. I had no idea what they would do to him at Space Command, but I felt responsible for having taken him there."

What he said was nothing new. They had both repeatedly questioned themselves and one another. Why blow up your life? Why throw away everything a person had worked for? Cal Zeldin had come to learn that there were times in a person's life, perhaps rightly called defining moments, that required he take action, no matter the consequences to himself personally.

"I respect your principles, doctor," she said, before stuffing the box of trade-quality precious metals into her own backpack. Then she lifted the bag to her shoulder. "Good luck."

"You too," Cal said.

She stepped out of the shadows and walked confidently toward the shuttles. Cal meant to watch the Marines, but he found himself drawn to Astra. She was wearing baggy pants and a sweatshirt over an insulated undershirt. Her hair was down, and she had pulled it to either side of her face to make it harder to identify her. Cal wondered if she felt the same pull toward him that he felt toward her?

When he turned back to the nearest group of Marines, he felt his heart drop into his stomach. They were clearly speaking with their superiors, and that had to mean they had identified her. He felt his heart rate increase and sweat prickled on the skin between his shoulder blades despite the cold weather. Would he run to her aid if the Marines tried to apprehend her? Was it better to use her apprehension as a distraction to aid him in getting to the shuttle? No, he knew he couldn't do that. And trying to free her from Space Command was an exercise in futility. But if they went after her, he would do it, if for no other reason than to prove to her he had been willing. At least, they could be arrested together, even if it was a small comfort.

Astra hated being exposed. As a woman, she knew the fear of being alone. Walking across the open space under the bright lights made her feel like an easy target. Every instinct she had told her not to walk but to run. She had a nearly overwhelming desire to get to the ship as soon as she could. But running would only attract more attention. She kept her head up, and her face pointed toward the shuttle, but her eyes were locked on the group of Marines just a hundred paces from where she was headed. There were six of them, all in combat gear with faceless helmets. She had no way of knowing if they were looking at her or not.

Then one turned, holding a hand to the side of his helmet. He was gesturing with his free hand, but not to his companions. Astra didn't know what it could mean. He was clearly talking to someone and, if not the other Marines, then maybe to the officer in charge. Her insides felt like water and her knees felt weak. She kept walking, but it felt awkward, like she had forgotten how to walk normally. Every joint felt shaky, every movement was forced. Her hands were sweating. There was no doubt in her mind that she would be arrested. She had never been in trouble before. She was less than fifty paces from the shuttle. She could see a pair of men directing one of the forklifts to its next pallet of ore to offload. She wanted to run to them, but she had no idea if they would help her or not. If the Marines came after her and she could somehow outrun them, the spacers would certainly not intervene. What reason would they have to put themselves and their livelihoods on the line? None that Astra could think of. There was a sinking feeling that she had made the biggest mistake of her life and, once again, she asked herself why she had done it. There was no answer that came to mind. Helping Sergeant Hammer seemed naive. Breaking free of the limitations on herself seemed indulgent. If she wanted a better life, there were a thousand ways to do that without throwing her future down the drain.

Despair seemed thick around her. Why even continue, she wondered. Why not throw herself on Space Command's mercy and beg forgiveness? It wasn't like they weren't getting what they wanted. She would be fired, of course. And without work, she would lose her apartment. But better to be homeless than to be locked up. After all, what she had done wasn't so bad. She could even argue that she didn't know what was going on, just that Dr. Zeldin had asked her to help Sergeant Hammer. What was the crime in that? She could make the argument that she had no idea who he was or what was happening, with an emphasis on the fact that she had no idea he had gone AWOL. Was that a crime? Did it even matter? No, she realized, it didn't matter. No matter what she claimed, no matter what was right, the truth was, Space Command would do whatever they wanted with her and no one would care.

Dr. Zeldin was just about to make a move. Perhaps he could distract the Marines long enough for Astra to get away? If he had to make that sacrifice, he could live with it. But just as he started to step out of the shadows and wave his arms to get their attention, the Marines turned and hurried in the other direction. He felt such a wave of relief that he didn't notice that Astra had stopped walking. She had turned and was staring at the Marines, her hands over her mouth and nose as she sobbed.

Cal looked both ways, then hurried toward her. By the time he got there, she had turned back toward the shuttle, but she wasn't moving yet.

"Are you okay?" he asked.

"I don't know," she confessed. "What just happened?"

"A miracle," Zeldin said with a nervous chuckle. "I don't know why, but they left. Now's our chance. Let's get out of here."

They hurried over to shuttle RM4227 and were met by a man in thick work pants, square-toe boots, and several layers under his parka.

"Help you?" he asked.

"We're looking for passage off Titan," Cal said. "Are you with the *Rosa Maria?*"

"I'm first officer," he said. "You got ID?"

"No," Cal said. "Is that a problem?"

"Might be," the officer said. "We don't take thieves or rapists."

"We're neither," Astra said.

"Our contention is with Space Command," Dr. Zeldin said. "We're willing to work."

"That's good. Everyone on the *Rosa Maria* works. You got skills?"

"I'm a doctor," Cal said. "Or was. She's my nurse."

"Not much call for that these days," the first officer said.

"We're not shirkers," Astra said. "We'll pull our weight."

"Alright, I'll take you up to see the captain, but he has final say in who comes aboard the ship. Till then, stow your gear in that compartment and start stacking those empty pallets. We'll be taking on provisions soon and you can get it sorted and locked down."

"Thank you," Cal said.

"Don't thank me yet," the first officer said. "Wait till you see the work, and then you can thank me. This ain't no luxury space cruiser, doc."

Zeldin had no illusions. As he helped Astra up the ramp, he knew his life was over. Dr. Cal Zeldin was no more. He cast one last nervous look over his shoulder, but the Marines were no longer in sight. He wondered briefly if Jack had something to do with it. There was no way to know for certain, but he felt it was highly likely. The man Dr. Cal Zeldin had set out to save had somehow saved him, instead.

34

Jack knew what was waiting for him on the garage's upper deck. He could feel a sudden increase in radio waves coming from above him. Through the narrow open spaces along the backside of the parking garage, he saw lights moving. He kept going just the same, only he rolled his window down and the passenger windows too. Then he opened the sunroof on the luxury hovercraft and pushed the HE-MAN rifle up onto the front edge just before taking the last ramp up to the rooftop.

Just as he crested the top of the ramp, they appeared. Dozens of Marines, not MPs, but regular combat fighters. His own people had come for him. Maybe they didn't know who he was or that he was also a Marine, but it didn't matter anymore. He couldn't hold back. With one hand up on the rear pistol grip of the laser rifle, he squeezed the trigger. The laser rifle spewed out death and destruction. At the same time, he smashed the accelerator to the floor. The luxury car's powerful repulsers sent the vehicle racing forward.

Jack couldn't really aim the big gun. But he turned the hovercraft, making a tight circle around the ramp that led back down into the garage. Going down was the safest bet, but he would only get trapped by the Marines above and below him. Instead, he continued firing and taking fire. The Marines were armed with non-lethal weapons. They fired rubber bullets, beanbags, and stun beams. But they couldn't just open fire at once. They were nearly all around the rooftop. More were on their way in, rappelling down out of their transports on thick ropes. If they all fired at once, they risked hitting one another and overwhelming their target. Too many non-lethals became lethal. Their commanders were shouting orders. Some were shooting at Jack, others diving for cover. His shooting was wild and a bit high. It was hard to hold the big laser rifle level. It wanted to slide across the roof as he turned. Rubber bullets and laser blasts ricocheted off the car. It was a bit like driving in a hailstorm. The owner, if he or she hadn't been killed in Jack's barrage against the R&D building, would be furious at the luxury car's condition.

And while the HE-MAN rifle had a large power supply, Jack used it indiscriminately as he raced around the roof looking for a way off it. The entire parking garage had a four-foot safety wall. When the rifle ran out of power, Jack pulled it back inside and pushed the repulser altitude adjustment higher. The hovercraft rose up and rocketed toward the back edge of the building. There were Marines in front of him. The windshield was cracked under the barrage from their weapons, but none got through to Jack. He knew it would have been a different story under regular combat conditions. But he used their need to take him down alive to his advantage. The Marines in front of him had to dive out of the way as the hovercar flew off the top deck of the garage.

For a moment, he felt like time was standing still and he was moving in slow motion. The hovercraft immediately started to descend, and he rose up in his seat for an instant of weightlessness. Then he was falling, and he pushed the repulser altitude as high as it would go. But the luxury car had a lot of mass, too much for the repulsers to overcome. Thirty feet from the parking garage, in one of the Space Command green spaces, was a tree. The car hit the top of it, crashing down through the branches, with the repulsers screaming and Jack feeling like his life could end at any moment. When it broke free, it fell the last twelve feet and hit the ground hard. Jack felt the impact knock the wind from his lungs just as all the vehicle's airbags deployed and saved him from smashing his face into the steering wheel. The engine stopped, the repulsers were destroyed and the tires all exploded from the collision with the ground.

Jack took a deep breath in, his chest hurting from the effort, and his eyes watering a bit. Then he snatched the Modis off the HE-MAN rifle and threw open the door. He was near a street light, and there were shouts from above him. Speed was the only asset that remained. He flung himself out of the car and sprinted for the nearest alley. Pain flared in the back of his mind, but there was no time for it. He ran into the darkness, somehow avoiding the fire from the Marines on the rooftop. He wasn't sure where to go or what to do. As he peeked back around the edge of the building, he could see the Marines making their way down. He knew he was in a jam, just not how to get out of it.

And then, without warning, something inside the R&D building blew up. Not just a canister of gas, but a heavy explosion that rippled through the building with enough force that it ripped the tree Jack had crashed into out of the ground, and flipped the car he had abandoned over. He barely managed to pull back into the alley as the shock wave smashed through the building he was behind and sent dust billowing all around him.

The explosion was not just a single, fast pop, but a loud rolling thunder. Added to that was the total collapse of the building and the parking garage. The buildings on either side of the R&D building went down, too. And it was from nothing that Jack had done. The researchers had obviously been at work with some powerful agents, the kind of research that was supposed to be carried out in posts in places far from population zones. Jack didn't have time to think about the ethics of what Space Command was doing or what laws they might have been breaking. He knew they were bad. But he also knew they would never give up. They would come for him and, if he let down his guard, they would take him back for more cutting and burning ... and who knew what else?

The dust cloud hid Jack, who jogged through it, holding his sweatshirt over his mouth and nose. He hurried down the alley, turned onto a city street he didn't recognize and continued his flight from the scene.

Captain Kittle was back in the flying command craft. He had been watching his forces after ordering them to take positions in the parking garage. The plan had been to send a few squads into the R&D building in search of Sergeant Hammer. Captain Kittle was not only surprised to learn he had returned to the Space Command campus, but had also attacked the R&D building. He felt that Hammer was up to something, not just exacting revenge. Maybe he was running interference for his co-conspirators or drawing the military force out of the town for a reason.

Then he had seen the attack. Large video monitors showed the live feed from the aircraft's external cameras. It was the only way to see what was happening directly below them. He watched the luxury car racing around, blasting away with a heavy laser weapon. Where he had gotten it, and the munitions to use on the R&D building, were a mystery that would be solved in the after action reports.

He watched the car race to the edge of the rooftop.

"Does that model have an altitude limit?" Kittle asked.

His officers were fresh, including the pair of computer specialists. One had already done a search on that very question.

"Sir, it comes standard with a twelve-foot altitude governor. Anything over that exceeds the vehicle's safety features and voids the manufacturer's warranty."

Kittle didn't care about the warranty or what would happen with the vehicle. But if Sergeant Hammer was killed in the crash ...

He held his breath as the car smashed into the tree. It was a terrible sight to behold and, yet, he couldn't look away. The vehicle tore apart the tree limbs and then dropped to the ground, with a crash that kicked up little clouds of dirt all around the vehicle.

"Move all forces to ground level," Kittle said.

"Sir, surely that crash did the target in," the communications officer said.

"You don't know what he's capable of," Kittle said. "Let's roll medics to the location. Have everyone stand by. If anyone fires on the target now, they will face a court-martial."

As the orders went out, the door of the vehicle swung open, and Hammer raced away. Kittle heard several audible sighs from his officers. They hadn't understood what the target could do, but they were starting to get the picture.

"How's he so fast?" one man said.

"How's he still alive after that crash?" a woman asked.

"Have all units move to ground level and spread out," Kittle said. "We can't let him escape."

They were high enough to see into the alley where Jack hid. He couldn't get far, Kittle thought as the troops already on the ground level of the garage came jogging out, their weapons held ready. Sergeant Hammer was fast, but he was still just one man. Kittle had four platoons of Marines, plus over a hundred MPs, making their way back from the server farm where they had been searching for him.

"Get me Colonel Mankins," Kittle said. "We have to alert him to the target's position. I want his MP's spread out on th—"

The explosions shocked everyone and sent the airships reeling. It was only five hundred feet above the R&D building and the shockwave went up - as well as out - in all directions. Alarms sounded and Kittle was nearly knocked off his feet. He managed to grab onto the back of his chair and pull himself into it. There were shouts and screams in the command portion of the aircraft.

"Remain calm!" he shouted before pressing the comlink activator on his chair's control pad. "Pilot, can we remain airborne?"

There was a pause with no answer. Kittle was just about to ask the question again when a voice replied, "Captain, we've got multiple alarms. We are putting down at the spaceport. I repeat, this is an emergency landing. Keep all your people strapped in for their safety."

Kittle glanced around the room. There was no need to repeat the order. Everyone was already strapped in tight. The captain wasn't worried about crashing or dying. He had survived emergencies in space, which was much more dangerous than mere gravity. Being a starship captain required that a person trust their equipment to do what it was designed to do, even in an emergency. Kittle was confident the command aircraft was designed to endure an emergency landing while preserving everyone on board. What bothered him was losing contact with the target. For all Kittle knew, Sergeant Jack Hammer had been killed in the explosion. If that were the case, Kittle's career was over. He would have to find the target and confirm whether he was alive or dead. As the command craft struggled to make a safe landing, the captain was busy plotting his next move.

35

"Sir, the Zyromite," Kathryn Ross whispered.

They were staring at a surveillance feed from nearly two hundred feet away from where the R&D building had been. Anything closer was destroyed and the feed from the cameras on the other side of the campus had been lost. Admiral of the Fleet Evander Royce had told someone to find out why, but he guessed the hard lines from the far end of their property passed under the R&D building.

"It's a total loss," Admiral Dyer said from across the room.

Royce couldn't be sure, but he thought he detected a smirk on the younger man's face. Of course, Admiral Dyer was just one of many senior officers who had designs on rising to replace Royce. And, given the gravity of what had just transpired, there was little doubt that Royce's tenure as Admiral of the Fleet would end very soon.

"How the hell did that happen?" Admiral DuBlaine shouted. "There's no way someone brought that much explosive material into our facilities by himself."

"He didn't bring it," Dyer said. "It was already there."

"The Research and Development division works with some

powerful materials," Kathryn said. "It's exactly what they're tasked with doing."

"Munitions research isn't supposed to be done in highly populated areas," Dyer crowed. "It seems the Admiral doesn't have control over what is being done right in his own backyard."

"But a cork in it, Dyer," Admiral Hawkins said. "A lot of Marines were just killed. And workers in those buildings, too."

"He's right," Royce said. "You want my job, Dyer? Come and get it. But for now, we have to keep level heads. There's a madman out there and we have an obligation to find him. General Fink has MPs stationed around our building. I think we can all take a breath and trust that we're safe here."

There would be inquiries and special prosecutors. The heat would be on Space Command and, specifically, Admiral of Fleet Royce. He had no illusions of keeping his role. It was never a permanent assignment. But, had he served well, he could have retired and taken a very lucrative position with one of any number of arms manufacturers or made the leap into politics. That future was gone, blown away by the same shock wave that had been sent out by the explosion that destroyed the R&D building.

Zyromite was just one of nearly a dozen black projects. There was always off-the-books research being done. At times, it included materials that were considered unsafe for research in standard settings. Zyromite was a powerful, new chemical compound. Munitions developers were looking to add Zyromite to existing warheads. It was extremely stable, unlike many other explosives. It required heat to set it off. The threshold was over a thousand degrees, although Royce didn't remember the specifics. What made Zyromite unique was the concussive power unleashed when it exploded. It was ideal for secondary detonation on penetrating, hard vacuum ordinance. A missile, fired through space that could punch into another vessel, and then blow up with enough force to rip the ship apart, was very attractive to Space Command. Developing such a weapon wasn't wrong, but doing it at the Space Command HQ facilities on Titan was. Yet Royce was prepared to take the blame. And, as luck would have it, with the R&D building in ruins, none of the other unsanctioned projections would easily come to light.

Despite what had happened, no matter who was ultimately to blame, the priority of the day was still the same. And perhaps, if the organic samples taken from Sergeant Hammer had been destroyed in the blast, it was more important than ever that they get him back. To that end, Royce used his personal satellite phone to contact Captain Kittle.

"Where are we?" he asked as soon as the captain answered his call.

"We had eyes on Hammer," Kittle explained. "But we were forced to make an emergency landing at the space port."

"Is he alive?"

"Very much so," Kittle said. "I just reached the last location he was known to be at the time of the explosion. He is not here."

"Finding him is still the highest priority."

"Then I need assets," Kittle said. "The Marines were caught in the explosion and General Fink ordered all his MPs back to Space Command HQ."

"Right," Royce said. "We don't have a lot of options. What about the Spec Op team that caught him before?"

"They're recovering," Kittle said. "I'm not sure what their status is."

"They can't be in that bad of shape," Royce said. "Get them back on the job."

"Copy that, Admiral. Do we rope in the locals?"

"Negative," Royce said. "This is on you, captain. You've got one last chance. Get what you need, then find him. Pretty soon, I'll be unable to help you, so this is your only shot. Don't waste it."

"Aye, Admiral, I won't."

Royce ended the call and nodded toward Kathryn Ross. She looked like she might be sick. There was no doubt in her mind that Royce's time at the top of the Space Command hierarchy was coming to an end. Whoever took his place would certainly send her packing. She was in charge of logistics, including the Space Command HQ. Under that banner was R&D, but with Rear Admiral Duncan missing, it would be Kathryn who got the axe. Unlike Royce, she hadn't yet solidified her post-military career. She was too young to retire and didn't have enough assets to support her yet. Unfortunately, her reputation would be tarnished by the attack and she doubted that she would fare well in the private sector.

"What?" she asked in a tremulous whisper.

"We've got one last shot," Royce said. "Get Oscar Team ready to roll."

"They're still in medical," Kathryn said. "I'm not sure what their status is."

"And I don't give a damn what it is," Royce said. "Have them gear up. Kittle is on his way to pick them up."

"Is that the way to go?" she asked.

"Listen to me," Royce said, putting his hand on her shoulder. "If there's one thing we need right now, it's motivated actors. Oscar team had Hammer and he put them down. I guarantee you, every single member of that team wants revenge. Let's see that they have a chance to get it. And trust me, if we can leverage the rejuvenating abilities that Sergeant Hammer is blessed with, nothing else that's happened will matter."

Kathryn considered the Admiral's belief and found it to be valid. She gave him a confident nod, then went to give the orders to mobilize Oscar Team.

36

Jack wasn't the only person on the streets, but he was the only person in uniform. He knew he needed to get a disguise if he was going to avoid detection for very long. In one of the alleys was an old man lying in what looked like a nest of trash.

"Hey, pal," Jack said to a man with a thick beard and a ratty coat. "Want to trade?"

Jack pulled off the military coat he had taken from the MP in the guardhouse. It was thick and warm, with a tall collar and reinforced elbows. The man Jack was talking to sat beside an electric transformer behind a large building that was part of the university complex. He smelled of booze and body odor, but Jack had no money and no other options. He needed distance from the explosion, but in the military gear, he stood out like a sore thumb.

"What do you want?" the beaded man asked.

"Your coat."

The man nodded, then stood up. He was dirty and clearly cold. They traded coats, and the bearded man wrapped the military coat tight around his frail body and settled back next to the electric unit.

"That thing keep you warm?"

The bearded man shook his head. "Keeps me alive," he said. "Whiskey keeps me warm."

From the narrow space between the electrical unit and the wall of the building, the man pulled out a bottle of cheap liquor. It was only half full of dark liquid. He pulled the cork, took a sip, then sighed.

Jack pulled on the coat and slipped the modis just inside. The tool, or weapon, Jack couldn't decide what category it fit into, felt good against his body. There was something about the rigidity of it that made him feel a boost of confidence. Not that his life was necessarily going in the direction he would have chosen, but he wasn't helpless either.

"Good luck," Jack told him, then, with his new coat, he set off through the city.

His destination was the space port, but he couldn't go straight there. It was the most obvious place to look for him. What Jack needed was to be seen in other places. Not by people, but by the system designed to keep track of every person on Titan. The facial recognition AI that Jack knew the people searching for him would surely tap into. And why not? It was the simplest way to find a person.

He also needed food. Jack had no money, but he had the military ID from the guard and from the staff sergeant in the armory. He couldn't utilize the IDs, which only had access to the Space Command property. But there were people who might pay for such goods. Jack was no expert in criminal matters. But after a few hours of wandering through alleys and doing his best not to be seen, he finally spotted a dealer.

He approached the man who stood against the wall of a building, his arms crossed, eyes sweeping from side to side. The street lights in the area around the man were out, but that didn't stop Jack. He strolled up and leaned against the wall just a few feet away. The man was watching him, but didn't respond.

"I have something that you'll be interested in," Jack said.

"Beat it," the dealer said.

Jack pulled the ID of the guard out of the coat pocket and held it out. The dealer glanced at it, but no interest crossed his face. Jack withdrew the ID.

"That's from an MP, corporal. I've also got a Marine staff sergeant ID. They won't get you in the senior officer facilities, but just about everywhere else."

"What makes you think I want that?" the dealer said.

"I doubt you do," Jack said. "But your boss, maybe his boss, could put it to use."

"Doubt it," the dealer said. "You want some rock?"

"No, I need food," Jack said.

"I ain't buying you no food," the dealer sneered. "Go drown yourself in a bottle, wino."

"I don't need you to buy the food," Jack said. "Just give the word to one of the businesses you protect. I'm just looking for whatever they can't use, before it goes in the dumpster."

"Who the hell are you?"

"Just a guy," Jack said. "Look, I gotta get some food. Do you want the IDs or not?"

"Let me see," the dealer said, showing interest in what Jack had for the first time.

Jack handed over the MP's ID. The dealer pulled out his phone and used the light from the screen to inspect the ID. Then he made a call.

"Yo, Diz, let me speak to the man."

Jack stayed silent, just listening.

"I got a lead on somethin', seems legit... yeah, don't know, never seen him before... wants food. I was thinking 'bout having O'Dell give him what's left from the morning rush... Yeah, I'll send you picks, then ditch this unit... You know it."

He ended the call, then took a picture of the ID. Without asking, he just held out his hand. Jack gave him the other ID. The dealer took pictures of them both, front and back, then slipped them into his pocket.

"Come with me," he said.

Jack did, keeping his head down, watching the dealer's shoes so that he didn't get tagged by surveillance cameras. It wasn't a foolproof plan, but it was like keeping one's head down in a firefight. It just made sense.

They didn't have to go far. Around the corner were several small café-style restaurants. They went into one, and the dealer led Jack through the small space where customers waited in line to order food, and past the open grill area where a big man was cooking several items at once. The man looked at the dealer and sneered.

"You're early," the big man said.

"Ain't here for that. Feed this man."

"The hell you say?"

"I didn't say it. Salt made the call. You want I should tell him you refused?"

"Whatever," the big man said. "I'll see to it. You get on out of here."

The dealer chuckled and shuffled back out. Jack didn't move. He didn't feel like he could. For the first time in his life, he was on the verge of out of control. Just the smell of the fresh-cooked food was so tantalizing that he felt he might react violently if he couldn't eat something. It was like an animal's instinct. Or the way sharks respond to blood in the water.

"You go back there," the big man said, pointing with one of his spatulas to the back room. "You can eat whatever is left from breakfast."

"Thank you," Jack said.

The big man just grunted and kept cooking. Jack went through a doorway and into a dark space. There was a little desk with a computer. Opposite that was a stack of vat-grown meat boxes and crates of soda cans. There was also a big trash can that was nearly overflowing. On top of the meat boxes was a wooden tray with almost half a dozen burritos wrapped in foil. Jack picked one up. It wasn't hot, but there was a bit of warmth left in the food. He unwrapped it and took a bite. It was filled with egg, onions, cheese, peppers, and a spicy sausage that Jack couldn't quite identify. He devoured the burrito and tore into the next one. Just as he was finishing the second burrito, the big man came in and stared at him.

"Who the hell are you?"

"Nobody," Jack said.

"That right? Don't look like a nobody."

"Who do I look like?"

"Look to me like you might be a Marine," the big man said. "I served, twenty-year vet. You got that look."

"Not me, not anymore," Jack said, picking up a third burrito.

"Once a Marine, always a Marine," the man said, thrusting out a hand. "My name is Dexter O'Dell."

"I'm Jack."

"Guess you heard what happened at SCHQ?"

"I heard something," Jack said, still eating.

"Question is, you running cuz you guilty, or what?"

"The less you know, the better," Jack said.

"They say lots of Marines got killed today," O'Dell said. "You got to square that with me, Jack. If you was involved, we can settle that right here, right now."

A big knife came from a sheath that was tied to the back of his apron. He held it easy by his side.

"Best start talking, Jack," the big man said.

"I'm not the guy you want to fool around with," Jack told him. "I was involved, but that explosion wasn't because of me."

"I don't know who you are, or how you got mixed up with Salt. But a Marine is a Marine for life. And a lot of good people died today. So, I guess you best turn around, Jack, put your hands on your head."

"I'm not going to do that," Jack said. He reached over, pulled a soda from one of the crates, and opened it. The can made a pop as the pressure inside was released. Jack took a sip, then set the soda down next to the half-eaten burrito.

"You finished?" O'Dell asked.

"For now," Jack said.

The big man moved faster than he had any right to. He lashed out at Jack, punched him hard with a left hook that connected square with Jack's cheekbone. The blow would have knocked most men out cold. Jack turned his head in the same direction as the punch, then slowly turned back to look at O'Dell, who was nursing his broken hand.

"You can still cook with one good hand," Jack said. "You keep this up, and you'll have to hire someone to cook for you."

"Screw you," the big man snarled as he thrust the knife straight at Jack's throat.

The movement was fast, but Jack was faster. He twisted slightly and made a circular motion with his hand. The knife thrust missed, and Jack's block connected, wrist to wrist. But Jack's block was so hard it knocked the knife from O'Dell's hand and snapped the big man's radius just behind the wrist. It made a slight snap sound that was almost pedestrian, but the look on the big man's face as he pulled his hand back and cradled it against his chest was pure shock and pain.

"I warned you," Jack told him. "I'm not your enemy, O'Dell. I appreciate the food. Just know that whatever you hear about that explosion, it ain't the truth."

The big man reared back and lashed out in a powerful front kick that should have sent Jack crashing into the metal door that led out into the alley behind the building. Instead, Jack caught O'Dell's size fifteen boot and shoved him back. The cook toppled back through the swinging door and landed hard on his back in the middle of his kitchen. Jack picked up the last two unopened burritos and put one in each of his coat pockets. Then he picked up the half-eaten burrito and soda. After taking a bite, he stepped to the back door and opened it. There was no one in the dark alley, which was littered with trash, food containers and big vats of used grease. He stepped out into the night and started walking. His foot hurt with every step, but the food was helping and, if he was lucky, he might just slip off Titan before he had to kill anyone else.

37

"Oscar team in place, over." Lieutenant Caffrey said, utilizing his helmet's comlink.

"Copy that, Oscar One," came the almost instant reply. "We are tapping the city's surveillance systems now. Stand by."

Lieutenant Caffrey was inside the hull of a cargo shuttle. The Starfire 88c hadn't moved in years. It sat empty while ships around it came and went. Across from him sat his special forces team. They were not completely recovered from their last clash with Sergeant Hammer, but Caffrey knew that no team was ever really one hundred percent healthy. And then there was Specialist Sil. She had some bumps and bruises, but compared to most of the team, she was in great shape. Yet she had refused to go after Sergeant Hammer. Their conversation when Kittle called them up still echoed in Lieutenant Caffrey's mind.

"He's not the enemy, sir," Tina Sil had said.

"That's not our call to make," Caffrey told her.

"I won't do it. I can't."

"This is what we do. If you are unable to perform your duties,

Specialist Sil, I will have no choice but to remove you from Oscar Team with a full report of your insubordination."

It was a bluff. Caffrey didn't want to lose a good member of the team. And knowing what happened with Sil, how Hammer had saved her from falling out of the transport, he thought he understood her reticence.

"If that's what you have to do, sir."

"Come on, Tina, you're a vital part of this team. You know what we're up against. We need you."

"It's not right, sir. He's not the bad guy."

"How can you say that? He attacked Space Command."

"I know that, sir. I still won't take part in bringing him back. I don't know why he attacked Space Command, but he's a Marine and he saved my life."

Caffrey hadn't pushed her further. He knew his people well enough to understand when they had made up their minds that there would be no changing them. Fortunately, she was the only member of Oscar Team who refused to bring the rogue sergeant in. Even if they weren't completely healthy. In fact, Lieutenant Caffrey knew they were fortunate not to get sidelined. He, for one, was anxious for another shot at Sergeant Hammer.

"My head is killing me," Haskins said.

"Drink more water," Riggs told him. "It's like a hangover. You've got to rehydrate."

"Worst hangover ever," Haskins grumbled.

"Where would you rather be?" Caffrey asked. He knew they would all rather be somewhere else, but they all wanted payback, too. "I know what I want and I won't get it at the med facility or lying in my bed. If that's what you want, Corporal, by all means, don't let me keep you from it."

"No, sir," Haskins said. "This is where I want to be."

Lasko didn't say a word; he just shook his head. They were in full armor this time and with a full understanding of what they were up against. They might not feel good, but they were still capable

Marines. Besides, Lasko knew that complaining wouldn't help anything.

"Good, because this team has never failed before, and I don't want us to ever fail again," Caffrey said.

"We didn't have the intel last go round, sir," Sergeant Preston said. "The rogue sergeant won't be so lucky this time."

Inside the Starfire was a containment unit. Once they had Sergeant Hammer in restraints, he would be locked inside the containment pod where his vitals would be measured at all times. If he woke up inside the pod, they could gas him back to unconsciousness before he got a chance to break free. Captain Kittle had assured them that gas had been used on Sergeant Hammer before and he was confident that it would be enough to keep him docile during transport.

Unlike most of his squad, Lieutenant Caffrey hadn't been stunned. In the fight with Sergeant Hammer, he had been knocked unconscious. The blow could have been worse, he knew. His helmet had taken the brunt of Hammer's vicious punch, but it still rang his bell pretty good. Bright lights caused stabbing pain in Caffrey's head, which had a constant, dull ache. His neck was painfully stiff. He could feel the muscles in his shoulders and the back of his head were on the verge of cramping up. He needed rest and muscle relaxers. His medical scans showed two bulging disks in his neck, but nothing would keep him out of the field with his team. If Sergeant Hammer was going to stop Caffrey this time, he would have to kill him.

"I've got a feeling he ain't showing up here," Corporal Armena said.

"Where else is he going to go?" Riggs asked. "This is the only space port in the city."

"Maybe he's got a connection with someone off grid?" Specialist Olinski suggested.

"No, I don't think so," Caffrey said. "This guy doesn't have a plan. I'm not even sure he's mentally stable."

"If he's crazy, isn't that more reason to believe he won't do the logical thing and try to find a ride off-world?" Armena asked.

Caffrey wasn't sure how to answer that question.

"Doesn't matter," Staff Sergeant Riggs said. "This is where we were told to wait for him. Maybe the brass has the hounds on his trail, pushing him into the trap."

"And we're the trap," Haskins said.

"Damn straight," Riggs declared.

"He killed a lot of people," Specialist Amy Farmer said. "I don't think we should underestimate this guy."

No one spoke up in reply. They had heard the reports. Over two hundred Marines, technicians, and researchers were confirmed dead, and they had only been working on removing the rubble for a few hours. Most of it was still so hot it couldn't be handled yet. Everyone had their own opinion about the explosion. Lieutenant Caffrey understood that Sergeant Hammer hadn't set it off personally, but he had attacked innocent people and destroyed a sensitive Space Command facility in the process. In Caffrey's mind, the blame for what happened lay squarely on Sergeant Hammer's shoulders.

"All the more reason for us to bring him in," Caffrey said. "We do our job and he won't be able to hurt anyone else."

There was another pause, then Haskins asked the question that was on everyone's mind. "Why do they want him alive?"

Lieutenant Caffrey couldn't see the faces of his team. His command helmet gave him access to their vital signs and allowed him to speak to them all at once or one-on-one. But he couldn't read their expressions. Likewise, the full battle armor masked their body language. But the silence following Haskins' question told him they all had reservations.

What they knew for certain was that Sergeant Hammer had enhanced physical traits. He was stronger and faster than a normal man. He had more stamina as well. The fact that it had taken four stun blasts to render him unconscious was on the verge of scary. Add to that was the fact that he woke up less than an hour later and sprang into action, which not only incapacitated four Spec Op commandos, but he also survived a thirty-foot drop from a moving vehicle. There was no doubt in anyone's mind that Sergeant Hammer was part of Space Command's search for troop augmentation.

It was that knowledge that gave them all some pause in their feelings about the target. Rumors of what happened to the volunteers of the so-called Super Soldier programs were rampant and none of them were good. Then there was the fact that Sergeant Hammer attacked the Space Command R&D building. What he hoped to accomplish was anyone's guess, but no matter what his beef, Lieutenant Caffrey didn't think it was right that innocent people had died because of Sergeant Hammer's actions.

Still, it added to the mystery. And then there was the admonition to bring Sergeant Hammer in alive at all costs. The only reason any of them could imagine for that order was to finish whatever the scientists had started on him. If what they started drove him mad, or caused him to harbor so much hatred for them that he attacked the R&D building, a person had to wonder just what they were doing to him in the name of scientific research.

"Doesn't matter," Lieutenant Caffrey said without much conviction. "We don't need to know all the whys and hows. Our job is to complete the mission. Setting the rules of engagement is above our pay grade."

"Ooorah," Sergeant Von Lasko said in a quiet response.

Caffrey didn't know if he was being smart or actually agreeing, but before anyone else could respond, Captain Kittle's voice came through Caffrey's comlink. The LT held up a hand while he listened, then said, "Copy that. Oscar team is moving into position now."

Everyone in the empty shuttle turned toward Caffrey, who explained, "He's headed this way. A retail camera caught sight of him through a storefront window."

"And they're sure it's Hammer?" Riggs asked.

"There's only one way to find out," Caffrey said. "Remember the plan. Wait for visual confirmation. We don't know which ship he's trying to reach, but when he's in the open, we strike. The old maintenance building is the only place to run. If he makes it that far, we'll use the gas grenades. He might be armed, so watch yourselves. Let's move."

"You heard the man, three by three," Riggs barked. "Move, move, move!"

The hunt was on. The trap was set. The hunters were moving into position. All they lacked was their quarry ... and Sergeant Hammer was on his way.

38

Jack wished he had another burrito. He had already eaten the two he had taken from O'Dell's cafe. The food was like fuel to his body, which felt more like a furnace than an organic being. He had been on the move all day. It had been nearly five hours since the explosion. And for the past four hours, he had been moving from shadow to shadow, avoiding open spaces and surveillance cameras.

There was no doubt that O'Dell had called in the assault. In fact, Jack had heard the sirens not long after leaving the restaurant. But considering the fact that nothing had been stolen and no property destroyed, Jack didn't think the police would put up much of a search. Nor had they, but he was glad for the report just the same. It would be picked up by the people hunting him and maybe they would believe that he would keep moving in that direction.

He had turned back toward the space port, but had moved in a long, curving route that enabled him to avoid detection and mask his intent. Of course, the space port was the logical destination. It was the best way off world. If Jack had more resources, he would avoid it, lie low and try to make a connection with someone who had the means of getting him off-world by another method. But he had no resources and no help. Added to that harsh reality was the explosion of the R&D building. Jack hadn't planned to destroy the whole thing. In fact, he hadn't really thought it through at all. He just wanted to create a distraction and maybe get a little revenge. He hadn't targeted anyone with the laser rifle, but he knew that it was inevitable that people would get hurt in his attack. He justified that because they were involved in Space Command's unethical and torturous experimentation on him. He hadn't volunteered for it and didn't agree to it; therefore, in his mind, Space Command had no right to do it. Anyone working with those monsters was guilty by association, at the very least.

But the guilt of knowing that people had died weighed on him more and more with each passing hour. Hundreds of Marines just doing their job, carrying out orders they had nothing to do with, had died. And he knew he hadn't directly caused the explosion that destroyed everything and killed so many innocent people, but indirectly...

Jack shook off the guilt as he had time and again, but it always returned. The only thing that helped was to focus on the mission. His next objective was to get off Titan. But that was easier said than done. Little did he know that he stopped in the shadows beside the space port in the exact same place his friends had occupied hours earlier. In fact, RM4227 was still in port. The provisioners were running behind. The news of the explosion at Space Command had slowed everything down. People were watching the news, wondering what had happened. Was humanity under attack? Was the explosion an act of terrorism? Should they seek shelter? These were all pressing concerns and work was not so important.

As Jack stood and watched, he saw dozens of shuttles being loaded and was thinking he would have to ask someone for help when he spotted a familiar face.

Astra was in the cargo hold of one of the shuttles. Jack was surprised he had noticed her, but she appeared to him in that moment like food to a starving man. With a bit of concentration, he was able to zoom in his vision on her. There was no doubt it was Astra; she was helping cinch down a cargo strap. Jack felt a surge of hope. He gave one last glance in both directions. There were plenty of people moving around the space port, but no sign of Space Command officials or Marines. He took a breath and made his move.

At first, he felt foolish and completely exposed. Walking under the bright lights, he would be seen, probably recognized. There were undoubtedly cameras that would catch him on video and analyze his facial features. An alarm would sound, and the police would notify Space Command. MPs would be mobilized, and soon, the space port would be crawling with officials in search of Jack. That fear eased after the first few paces, and he did a good job of convincing himself that he could make it to the shuttle. And he was halfway there when he caught sight of movement in the shadows. He turned, saw the glint of light off a rifle barrel, and dove to the ground.

There was a flash of laser light, but the stun beam missed him. There was no time to be sad that he had been discovered or that his plan to escape had been thwarted. He had to move or they would catch him.

Jack rolled to his feet and into a sprint. The only good thing he could say about his plight was that his foot was nearly healed. It was still sore, but he could run on it. And run he did, back toward the edge of the spaceport where the shadows were deep. But out of them came a trio of Marines in full battle armor. They had laser rifles that were pointed his way. Jack turned one way, then back, and raced for the only place of safety he could reach. It was a building made of cut stone, with a low, sloping roof, and one missing - or open – man-sized door. The interior was pitch black and Jack raced toward it.

The first stun beam hit his sore hip and knocked him down. But Jack didn't stop moving. More stun beams sizzled off the tarmac where he had fallen, but Jack immediately rolled to the side, ignoring the buzz of fear in his head and the aching pains in his body. He sprang up, as agile as any gazelle, and sprinted for the building. More laser shots sizzled past him. He was almost to the building when a second stun blast hit his shoulder. It knocked him into the wooden door frame, where a rusty nail was only halfway into the wood. The butt stuck out an inch and a half, where it tore through the flesh on Jack's chest and shoulder. Blood flowed as he hit the dusty concrete floor inside the old building. Ignoring the pain, Jack shimmied backward, the modis and its carbon fiber slat dug into the skin on his side. He had it tucked into the top of his pants and hidden under the long coat he had traded with the homeless man for.

He came up to his feet with one hand on the chest wound. It burned like fire across his chest and shoulder. Hot blood was gushing from the wound. He pressed against it, ignoring the pain, as he backed into the darkness of the room.

There were a few laser blasts that were fired inside. They all missed him. The Marines weren't getting close. The fact that they didn't follow him inside the dark building was a clear sign that they had a plan. He had nothing. But he could see in the dark. His new ability had made traversing the city much easier. He could hear better and sense things like radio waves. The cold didn't bother him as much and what would be incapacitating wounds like the gash across his chest and shoulder didn't keep him from doing what he needed to do. The first order of business was getting out of the building. There was a rear and a side door. He went to one, found it locked, then tried the other. He started to pull against it, hoping to rip it open like he had done at Space Command, but the pain in his chest when he pulled made that impossible.

"Sergeant Hammer," an amplified voice called to him. "You have no way out. The doors are welded shut."

Jack looked and saw the weld beads in the corner of the metal doors. They were in metal frames, which were stronger than the wooden one he had crashed into. It seemed his luck had run out.

"Lay down on the ground with your hands on your head, and you won't be harmed," the amplified voice said. Jack thought he recognized it, but couldn't be sure.

"This is your last warning."

"Screw you!" Jack shouted.

They had him cornered and he moved just inside the doorway, expecting the team to breach the room at any moment. But they didn't come inside. Instead, a canister was thrown in. It bounced twice, rolled a short distance and began to hiss.

Jack knew he only had a few moments before he was taken down by the gas, whatever it was. He drew out the modis and activated it. The red light along the edges of the carbon fiber slat lit up. He dashed to the rear door and stabbed at the metal with the modis. It punched through the metal and stuck there. Jack pulled it down, using his weight to help pull it through the steel door. It moved, coming down close to the hinges. He cut until the modus was at the bottom of the door, then he pulled the slat free and pushed on the metal door. It groaned as it bent backwards. Jack didn't wait; he threw himself into the gap, pushing on the door and struggling to squeeze through it. The clean air outside the building was a relief, but he was wedged so tight that he almost couldn't breathe. Then, with a final surge, he managed to squeeze through the opening.

After deactivating the modus, he propped it against the back of the building. He pulled off the old, tattered coat and dropped it on the ground. Then, with a quick twist, he uncoupled the modis from the carbon fiber slat. The handle went into his pocket, but he held the three feet long harden carbon rod close to his body, and he hurried around the building. On the far side were crates. He waited by them. The workers that had been moving around on the space port had taken cover when the Marines began shooting. All he could do was wait and prepare. If he was going to escape, he had to fight.

The Marines waited a full minute, then breached the old building. Jack couldn't hear their communication, which was contained within their battle helmets. But he could hear their boots as they moved on the concrete floor. They spotted the ruined door, and some approached it. That was Jack's signal. He rushed around the front of the building and charged into the open doorway.

It was the last thing any of the Marines expected. They were focused on the back of the building, trying to understand how their plan went wrong, when he appeared. Jack roared in pent-up rage and threw himself into the fight. He used the carbon fiber slat like a club. Its edges were dull, but the structure was rigid and strong. He hit the nearest Marine hard enough to send him flying into another. They turned, trying to discover what was happening, but Jack moved like a tornado through their midst. He was so fast it was hard to track his movement, turning, sliding and swinging the club.

It hit Haskins in the face, cracking the corporal's helmet and knocking him unconscious. He fell back, crashing into Sergeant Lasko, and they both fell as Jack charged into Staff Sergeant Riggs. He shoulder-blocked the NCO so hard that Lasko smashed into the wall and collapsed.

Jack was not an expert at any single form of hand-to-hand combat, but like most Marines, he had trained in several styles. But he gave no conscious thought to his movements and attacks as he swept through the room. His body moved with fluid grace and such speed that within a few seconds, four of the Marines were on the ground. By that time, someone thought to fire their weapon. The laser blast missed Jack and hit Amy Farmer, who once again was knocked out of the fight by friendly fire. Jack swung his club at the shooter's rifle, batting it aside and allowing Jack to kick the Marine's knee. His shin connected with the side of Otto Olinski's knee and bent it inward at an angle it wasn't built for. He screamed loud enough that Jack heard it through the man's battle helmet as he dropped his rifle and fell to the ground holding his injured leg.

Someone managed to jump onto Jack's back, but he twisted and flung them off before dropping to a knee on their back. A laser blast flashed over his head and Jack ripped the downed Marine's sidearm from its holster. Then he dove to the side, rolled over and up onto one knee. Other than speed, the real advantage Jack had was his eyesight. He wasn't blinded by the flashes of laser light. Meanwhile, the Marines were utilizing night vision inside the building, which wasn't the best of optical situations. And with each laser blast, they were blinded for a few seconds.

Lieutenant Caffrey was barking orders, trying to get his Marines to stop shooting, but Jack joined in the shootout. He blasted the lieutenant in the chest. The sudden flood of energy scrambled the systems in his command helmet, but didn't render him unconscious. Lasko struggled back to his feet and charged at Jack, intending to club him with his rifle, but Jack saw him coming, jumped toward the Marine and they crashed together with brutal force. Lasko was knocked backwards and completely senseless. Jack, with his greater muscle mass and dense bones, shook off the collision and kept fighting.

Sergeant Preston was stunned by a shot from the laser pistol, and Corporal Armena was clubbed in the side with Jack's carbon fiber slat. The corporal went down with three broken ribs and a punctured lung. He coughed blood inside his helmet, which sent a warning to Lieutenant Caffrey, but the officer's smart helmet was malfunctioning. He pulled it off and tried to look around, but it was too dark.

"Retreat," he shouted. "Back outside!"

"They can't," Jack replied, his voice coming out of the darkness like a nightmare. "You're the last man standing, LT."

"You go to hell," Caffrey snarled. "I've already been there. It's called Space Command R&D."

Caffrey turned toward the doorway and got two whole steps before he was hit in the side by a heavy body and smashed into the wall. The pressure didn't let up, and the lieutenant was pinned.

"Did they tell you who I was?" Jack asked.

"No," Caffrey said. "But I know you're a killer."

"I'm Sergeant Jack Hammer, Rifle Brigade, Bravo Company, Third Platoon. Enlisted number 07382901, most recently of the *Intrepid*. I got hurt on some nameless planet no one's ever been to before. My platoon pulled me out of a hole and loaded me on the last dropship leaving that rock. Only we were hit with a gamma surge from the system star on our way back. Everyone else died, sir. My entire platoon, even the crew of the drop ship. Radiation sickness got them, sir, but not me. Instead of dying, I got better. And Space Command wanted to know why, so they could make you and your team better fighters."

"That's the job, Marine," Caffrey growled.

"Like hell it is," Jack replied.

"That why you blew up the R&D building and killed all those Marines?"

"I bloodied their nose, but I didn't blow up anything," Jack said. "But I'll admit, I didn't consider what else they were cooking up in their house of horrors."

"You need to surrender, Marine."

"And go back to Space Command? Sir, they cut me just to watch my body heal. No pain meds, no treatment. They cut me and then they burned me. God only knows what they would have done if I hadn't escaped."

"You're lying," Caffrey said.

"No, sir, I'm not lying. That's what they did to me. They took tissue samples, organ and bone biopsies, blood samples, and flayed the skin off my body. When I fought back, they strapped me to a table, refused to feed me or even let me go to the bathroom."

"You're delusional."

"No, sir, I'm not. And I'm going to let you go, now. I'm going to let you go so that you can look into it. You do that and you'll see that I'm not lying."

He eased off of Lieutenant Caffrey, who twisted around. There was just enough light coming in through the open doorway that the officer could see Jack's face. It was rugged, with a wide jaw, thick black hair, and piercing blue eyes. Jack stepped back, raising both hands. There was a dark stain of blood on his torn shirt.

Lieutenant Caffrey was in shock. His team was down, and the perpetrator was just letting him go. His hand went to his sidearm in pure instinct. He saw Jack's eyes narrow, then he spun around as Lasko slashed at him with a big knife. The blade ripped across Jack's cheek. The angry Sergeant had abandoned the idea of bringing Jack in alive.

"Lasko! Stand down!" Caffrey shouted as Jack backpedaled toward the doorway.

But Von Lasko was in a frenzy. He rushed at Jack, who sidestepped the knife thrust and drove a powerful upper cut into Lasko's ribs. The crazed sergeant grunted in pain but slashed at Jack with his big knife. Jack stepped through the doorway and the blade smashed into the wooden frame where it stuck fast. Jack hammered down on Lasko's hand with the side of his fist. The blade of the knife snapped in two, leaving Lasko with just the handle. He threw it at Jack, who spun out of the way and then delivered a powerful spin kick that connected with Lasko's chest. The angry sergeant flew backward, straight into Lieutenant Caffrey, who had come up behind him. Both men collapsed onto the floor of the old storage building.

Jack sighed, then turned. He took a single step before a laser blast hit his shoulder and knocked him down. He wasn't completely stunned, but he was exhausted, and his head seemed fuzzy. Where had the laser blast come from? Were there more Marines?

He was trying to figure it out when Captain Kittle came into view. The man was blurry, but Jack remembered him. He had seen the captain a time or two on board the *Intrepid*. He liked to make surprise inspections and was not well-liked in the Marine section of the ship.

"You were close, Sergeant Hammer. Very close," Kittle said. "That was a strategically brilliant move, luring the Spec Op team into the building. I didn't know you could see in the dark."

"Lots you... don't know," Jack said, trying to regain control of his limbs, but they were sluggish and felt unnaturally heavy.

"Oh, well, I know enough. I know you're back where you belong, Sergeant. There is something incredibly unique about you and I plan to get it, even if I have to cut it out of you myself."

Jack wasn't entirely sure what happened. He heard the roar of a propane-powered forklift. Saw Captain Kittle, who was smart enough to stay out of Jack's reach, turn and fire his rifle. Then he was hit by a forklift with a pallet of ten-pound rice bags on front. His body was sent flying by the impact and the forklift rolled to a stop.

"Jack, you crazy bastard," Dr. Zeldin shouted. "I don't know how you're alive."

"Me either," Jack said, as the doctor helped him up.

Jack looked back. Captain Kittle lay in a bloody heap, but he was still breathing. It crossed Jack's mind to finish the old officer off, but he was having trouble walking.

"You're just in time," Zeldin said. "We're about to take off."

"Saw... Astra," Jack managed to say.

"She's waiting. We've got you now. Don't worry. Everything is going to be okay."

It was what Jack wanted to hear. He was helped onto a shuttle, which almost immediately took off. He was taken to a compartment where Doctor Zeldin patched up the cut on his chest and shoulder, as well as the gash on his cheek. Astra was there too, with food and water. Half an hour later, Jack was feeling better and as they broke into orbit above Titan, everything began floating around their cabin.

The shuttle landed inside a massive cargo freighter. The three Space Command refugees were tired, but for the first time since breaking Jack out of the R&D building, they felt safe. But that feeling didn't last long.

After being told to wait in the shuttle, it took over twenty minutes for the Captain to arrive. He was a short, thin man with large eyes and a short, brown beard.

"That's him," the first officer said, pointing at Jack.

"Is there a problem, Captain?" Dr. Zeldin asked. "We're just looking for passage to Veta Madre."

"Sure you're not looking to escape Space Command?" the captain asked. He had a gravely voice and his teeth were stained from tobacco.

"We aren't looking for trouble," Astra said. "Just a fresh start."

"I don't get many deserters," the Captain said. "My name is

Avery. This is my first officer, Commander Rudd. He tells me you've got some special skills."

"I'm not sure..." Jack said.

"I seen ya fight a whole squad of soldiers by yourself," Rudd said. "They was all armed and everything."

"Looks like you're not too much worse for wear," the Captain said. "If it's Space Command that wants you, there's no place you can go where they can't follow. But, if you're willing to help me with a little situation I've got, I can get the *Rosa Maria* moving and out of the system in a few hours."

"What kind of situation?" Cal Zeldin asked.

"There's some people on Veta Madre. Call themselves La Garduña. They want to take over my ship."

"La Garduña, as in organized crime?" Cal asked.

"As in the kind of people who threaten a man's family," Captain Avery said. "Ain't nobody willing to stand up to them. But maybe you are?"

"That's crazy," Zeldin said. "We're trying to avoid trouble, and you're talking about getting us into something even worse."

"They're dangerous people," the Captain said. "No honor, no mercy, that's the truth. But it seems like we could help each other. I'm not looking to run afoul of Space Command, but if you can help me with the goons trying to get my ship, I'll take you wherever you want to go."

"This is crazy," Dr. Zeldin said.

"Crazy may be just what we need," Jack said, standing up. He looked at Astra. "You okay with this?"

"I'm not the one putting my life on the line," she said.

"You did the moment you helped out Doc Zeldin here. And if I agree to help the Captain, we'll all be in danger."

"You don't like the terms, we can take you back down to Titan," Captain Avery said. "I've got four more shuttles waiting to be unloaded. Leaving now isn't ideal, but I'll do it if you can help me out."

"I can help you," Jack said. "How long until we reach Veta Madra?"

"A week. You can rest up. I've got some things that might help, but not much."

"It'll be enough," Jack said. "But you guys don't have to stick around."

"I can't go back," Zeldin said.

"And I don't want to," Astra said. "Maybe we can help."

"You already have," Jack said. "Go ahead, Captain. Let's make tracks before Space Command gets organized enough to try and stop you."

"I had a feeling you would say that," Avery said with a chuckle. "I already gave the order to start out of the system."

"Out of the frying pan and into the fire," Zeldin said.

"I've got a gift I didn't ask for, doc," Jack said. "We might as well put it to good use."

EPILOLGUE

"What's his status?" Admiral Royce asked Doctor Reed Sagan.

"Multiple fractures," Sagan said, "ribs, hip and pelvis. We had to remove his spleen and open his skull to relieve the pressure. He's in a coma now. With traditional care, he's looking at a six to nine-month recovery, depending on how much damage was done to his brain. And that's if he wakes up at all."

"What's the alternative?"

"I've developed a serum," Sagan said. "It's based on what we got from Project Hammer."

"I thought we lost everything."

"We lost all the samples," Sagan said. "But not the knowledge. His genome and enhanced cell structure were in the cloud. We have a lot of information that we can put to good use. We need time to test it and put the serum through the normal protocols, but if you want, I could try it on Captain Kittle."

"It could kill him?"

"It could. But the alternative is pretty grim. He'll be in pain the rest of his life, with multiple physical problems to overcome and/or live with."

"And the alternative?"

"If it works, a full recovery. The regenerative possibilities are extremely promising."

"And the side effects?"

"We won't know until we try," Sagan said. "I think we've got an amazing opportunity. The serum only works on a body that is in extreme distress. To test it, we have to hurt someone or find patients in that state. Captain Kittle is an opportunity that I don't think we can afford to waste."

Royce sighed. Under different circumstances, he would disagree. But he was on his way out of command. There was simply too much opposition for him to hold on, even though everything that had happened on Titan was done for the good of Space Command. And despite what his rivals might say, Evander Royce cared about the good of Space Command. He knew the future was within their grasp. Whoever took his place would be cautious. They might even squander the opportunity to learn as much as they could from Project Hammer.

"Do it," Royce said. "Top secret, of course, but use the serum. Do it now before someone else tries to stop you."

"I'll have him moved to the *Valiant* where I can treat him personally," Dr. Sagan said. "Thank you, Admiral."

"Don't thank me, just finish the work, Doctor. That's all that matters, now."

Dr. Reed Sagan, former medical researcher and the sole remaining member of Project Hammer, smiled. "I couldn't agree more."

COMING SOON

Nomad (Jack Hammer Adventure)
  – book 2 coming Summer 2026

SURVIVORS (SSG VANHORN BOOK 1)

4.5 stars with over two thousand ratings on Amazon

SURVIVORS
SAMPLE PROLOGUE

Looking back, I can see why we lost. When you're lying in a medical pod, with more painkillers pumping through your veins than blood, you end up with a pretty clear retroactive perspective.

It wasn't a tactical defeat, but rather a political one. Maybe every veteran of war says that, though. In the end, the politicians blame the commanders, the grunts on the ground blame the politicians, and, more likely than not, the commanders blame themselves for not standing up to their superiors, even if they knew the plan was faulty right from the start.

I'm not complaining; I'm alive, after all. Still, even now, the fight comes back to me in flashes. I don't remember much. It's like my mind doesn't want to admit that such horror was real. Or maybe it's the meds—I can't say for sure, just like I can't say for sure what happened on our mission. What I do remember is the flight to Luyten C in the Gliese system and the fear that seemed to gnaw at me beneath my armor.

Don't get me wrong: I *wanted* to fight. I was a Terrestrial Advance Combat grunt, or what the old Earth-based military called Force Recon. Luyten C wasn't my first combat drop, either, but the Orrkasi had never attacked anything so close to our home world before. Even after a century of exploration and colonization, the Sol system was still our most inhabited sector of space. If the Orrkasi had managed to establish a base on Luyten C, they would have been able to launch attacks deep in our system. The consequences were dire, and we all knew the stakes: it was kill or be killed. I managed a little of both.

At this point, the only things I know for sure are that I am still alive and that I somehow made it back to the naval hospital on Titan. I deduced where I am when I realized I could see Saturn's rings through the window when my vision finally cleared. I knew I was alive because of the pain—so much pain that I wish for death, although the med droids won't let me die.

My injuries are severe enough that I've been trapped in a medical pod, with nothing to do but think. If I ever get out of here, which is a really big *if*, I'll be permanently maimed. That means I won't be on a TAC team ever again. My team should have left me on Luyten C. The old samurais had it right: it's better for a warrior to die in battle than to live with the knowledge of all they've lost.

And it seems to me that I've lost it all.

SURVIVORS
SAMPLE CHAPTER 1

"Next!"

I stepped up to the counter at the logistics station. My orders had come through after what had seemed like a lifetime of rehabilitation. They should just call it torture since, in my opinion, that's what it is —torture and disappointment. I handed my slate to the sergeant behind the counter. He took the shockproof computer tablet that every Marine carried and scanned it.

"Staff Sergeant Vanhorn," the bored clerk said without looking up at me. "Let's see...I've got you going out on the *Rihla*. Gate D, docking bay eight."

"Thank you," I said, taking back my slate and stepping aside to let the next Marine have access to the clerk.

I slipped my hand-sized slate into the cargo pocket on my thigh, then hefted my loadout bag, thankful for its tiny wheels. I wasn't sure that I would need all the gear inside the bag, as I wouldn't be going into a combat zone again. The scar tissue on my left side had ended that possibility. I could finally bend my rebuilt left knee without screaming in pain, but running was impossible. The surgery on my back that had fused most of my spine into a solid chunk of bone, scar tissue, and rigid med-grade plastic left me stiff. The pain was constant, as was the feeling of something foreign in my left eye —laughably impossible, since my left eye had been too damaged to save. The surgical droid had removed it, yet I felt the constant need to rub it and remove the imaginary speck of grit that seemed to be agitating it.

I shuffled off toward the people mover, a moving walkway that would take me through the installation until I found the right gate. It seemed strange to be back on active duty after nearly a year of surgeries, rehab, and recovery time. Worse still, I couldn't even talk about what had happened, since the operation on Luyten C was classified. The brass didn't want the public to know how close the Orrkasi had gotten to infiltrating the Sol system. While I'd been just as ignorant as anyone else during my slow recovery, I knew more about that fight now. I'd even received access to the after action report filed by my squad. They claimed I had saved their lives, although I didn't remember it. Their truth was undeniable: buried somewhere in my kit was a little box with a purple heart and silver star, medals earned in combat against a vicious, enigmatic enemy. Still, all the decoration in the world couldn't compensate for the hurt I'd endured. I still couldn't be sure if I was grateful that my team had carried me out of that hellhole or not; I had lived in a state of almost constant suffering every day since.

Upon finally reaching Gate D, I started the long walk down the docking arm toward the ship that would be my home for the foreseeable future. I knew nothing about the *S.F. Rihla,* only that the word meant 'journey' in Arabic. I was familiar with the type of exploratory vessel, as TAC teams were commonly stationed on them. I was unofficially 'TAC team 13,' the slang term for non-combat personnel. They hadn't booted me out of TAC, but I was relegated to a support staff position. I wouldn't find out what desk they would tie me to yet— that would be explained once I was on board the *Rihla.* Even without that knowledge, I couldn't imagine a worse way to finish my enlistment term. I had two years remaining in my standard ten-year TAC term, and it was clear that for the whole time, I would be stuck doing whatever scut work no one else wanted.

From the docking arm, I walked along a long, enclosed boarding ramp, experiencing the short transition to artificial gravity. At the ship, I passed through a wide airlock and entered the main concourse, making my way straight to the deck officer.

"Staff Sergeant Vanhorn," I said, saluting the deck officer. "Reporting for duty."

"At ease, Staff Sergeant," said the second-grade lieutenant, a woman clad in naval uniform identical to the space fatigues I wore, save for their dark blue color. The name stenciled on her chest read 'HOLLY, J,' and her smile was genuine. I couldn't help but notice she was very pretty. "You'll be working with Lieutenant Bass down in the Marines section of the ship. That's level B, section eight."

"Thank you, sir," I replied.

"Welcome aboard, Staff Sergeant."

I moved past her, mentally taking note of her name. The flight deck where I had boarded was busy with technicians and machinists servicing the drones and passenger craft stored on the ship. I crossed the wide space, inhaling the smells of metal, chemical lubricants, and ozone generated by the plasma wielders. This three-story deck was on the lowest level of the ship; above it were six other decks built on an oval structure with an open center. It reminded me of an upscale shopping center, only instead of stores, the levels were filled with berths, offices, chow halls, and unit-specific areas. In the very center was the command and control area, an enclosed pod large enough for the senior officers to observe the ship's systems and pilot the vessel. I had spent the majority of my adult life on ships just like this one, but I was fuzzy on how they actually operated. I knew that the entire vessel was powered by a fusion reactor and used an anti-gravity propulsion system. Beyond that, it was a mystery.

I climbed a flight of stairs from Alpha deck to Bravo, then made my way around to section eight. The offices of the Marines were a suite of rooms that could have been in a business center on any number of worlds—the navy liked to keep their ships sparkling, and I'd heard that a full quarter of the ship's crew spent their days polishing and cleaning the ship so that it looked brand new. In this area, the walls were made with a transparent polymer that looked like tinted glass and were framed in chrome, matching the metallic shine of the handrails and other fixtures. Glossy white panels comprised the deck, and the ceilings glowed in a spectrum of light.

It was beautiful, but it couldn't distract me from what was to come. Stepping into the staff office area, my heart sank, and I felt a twinge in the pit of my stomach. The thought of polishing a seat with my ass for the next two years made me feel ill.

A man with gray stubble for hair greeted me as I entered. His face was a mass of wrinkles, and he wore what I suspected was a perpetual frown. The rank on his shoulder showed him to be a master sergeant. I pulled out my slate once again and handed it over. The master sergeant took it and scanned it with a device that was connected to his computer, then huffed before handing it back.

"Lieutenant Bass has requested that you see him before reporting to your duty station," the master sergeant said. He spoke slowly in a deep voice. "You'll be berthed in with the rest of the staff NCOs in section two. Ship schematics are being downloaded to your slate, along with a duty rotation. Chow hall is on Delta. You can wait on the lieutenant over there."

He pointed to a row of chairs that folded down from the wall. With a nod, I moved over, propping my loadout bag against the chair on the end before I eased my way down. My leg hurt, my back was stiff, and the scar tissue up the left side of my body was tight and made movement awkward. I settled onto the chair and stretched out my leg, although I refused the temptation to rub my knee. It was impossible to hide the damage, but I didn't want to draw unnecessary attention, either.

On the wall behind the master sergeant was a display that slowly rotated through the names of the Marines on board the *Rihla*. Following the standard rule of three, there were two rifle platoons and one TAC platoon. I knew that the TAC platoon would consist of two combat squads and one staff squad, the latter of which would oversee the logistics of the combat teams. I assumed I would be part of this squad in some capacity.

I didn't have to wait long for Lieutenant Bass, who soon stepped out of his office and greeted me.

"Staff Sergeant Vanhorn?"

I rose to my feet as quickly as my mutinous body would allow and came to attention.

"At ease, Staff Sergeant. Why don't we step into my office?" Bass said.

He was a short man, muscular and obviously fit. I couldn't deny the pang of envy at how deftly he moved. After I followed him into the little office, he shut the door with the push of a button and waved me toward the single guest chair in the small space.

"It's not too often that we have heroes on board," Bass said. The nameplate on the desk showed his first name to be Oliver. He didn't sit down, instead choosing to lean against the side of his desk. It was too small and cluttered to sit on, but he clearly didn't want to sit behind it.

"I'm no hero, sir," I replied.

"Nonsense—you saved your squad on Luyten C. The entire corps was talking about it last year."

"I thought the op was classified."

"The mission details were; your actions on the battlefield weren't."

I knew the corps had no qualms about making examples of people, even embellishing stories to help meet their recruiting quotas. Still, it didn't set me at ease to think that people were speculating about what had happened on Luyten C. I had been too dazed to even realize that any of the details had been released.

"We lost an entire fire team," I said. "Was that in the report? Corporal Dallas, Lance Corporal Green, Private First Class Choi, and

Private First Class Honrey. Killed by the Orcs. I don't even know if we were able to recover their bodies."

"Every battle has casualties," Bass replied. "You led that squad through scores of Orrkasi. We don't have a solid number, but I've heard rumors that there were over a hundred."

"That's an exaggeration," I said, with some uncertainty. I knew I had never seen so many of the enemy Orrkasi, or Orcs, than I had on Luyten C. Most people called them Orcs because they so resembled the fantasy creatures from books and movies, both in their looks and in their animalistic ferocity. I hadn't expected any of the Marines in my squad of thirteen TAC operators to survive that day, including myself. I still wasn't sure I was thankful that I had.

"You're being humble," Bass said. "You and your team showed everyone what TAC is all about. Your actions turned the tide on that battle…and you've got the stripes to prove it."

Without him coming out and saying it, I knew he meant my scars. My missing eye burned, but I refused to touch the black patch that covered the pit where my eye had once been. There was nothing there but puckered flesh, and even after a year, it still made my skin crawl to think about it.

"Well." Bass broke the momentary silence, standing straight before moving around to his side of the desk and picking up his slate. He made it look easy; for him, it was, in a way it would never be again for me. I did my best not to let my envy turn to bitterness. "I'm glad to have a man with your background on board. Our TAC platoon is untested in combat. They're well trained and ready, but we haven't seen the enemy yet. I'm hoping that changes on this cruise."

In that moment, I realized Bass was a climber. The quickest way to advance in the corps was through combat, and the quickest route to combat was the command of a TAC platoon. Little did he seem to know that facing the Orcs in battle was nothing to wish for. They were savage fighters, ruthless, hard to stop and even harder to understand. I had seen them resist oncoming fire, and I had seen them use stealth and cunning to ambush humans. It wasn't something I hoped to ever see again, and in my state, I doubted I would—unless, by some horrible turn of events, they managed to turn the tide of the war.

"Yes, sir," was all I could think to say. I knew better than to try to correct a commissioned officer.

"We'll need you if it does! Staff Sergeant, you're to be our master-at-arms on this cruise," Bass explained with more gusto than I thought possible. "We have a full armory. You'll have three Marines under you. Everything is ship-shape in there, and we have a simulator and live fire ranges. Those are overseen by Gunny Patel. Your job is to keep everything ready for combat operations, if we get the chance. We'll have a full platoon meeting at oh-seven hundred hours tomorrow. In the meantime, get the lay of the land and make sure you can find your way around. It'll get hectic once the ship is under-way, and I believe we're scheduled to leave port at fourteen hundred hours tomorrow."

"Yes, sir," I repeated, thankful for the armrests on the seat. I used them to push myself up, ignoring the spasm of pain in my back as I stood. "Is there anything else?"

"No, no, I just wanted to meet you," Lieutenant Bass said, extending a hand. I shook it, noting the clamminess of my commanding officer's palm.

"Thank you, sir," I replied.

"If you need anything at all, Staff Sergeant, you know where to find me."

"Yes, sir. Thank you, sir," I repeated.

Bass sat down and pressed an icon on the top of his desk. The door whooshed open, and I made my way out. My loadout bag was waiting for me to grab as I left the suite of offices.

From the walkway around Bravo deck, I could look up and down the entire core of the ship. Two decks above, the command and control center was outlined with lights that made it gleam like a gemstone. Beyond it, I could see decks Echo, Foxtrot, and Golf high above. It was a beautiful ship, but I hadn't expected anything less. I made my way around to section two and found my berth. It was a standard NCO cabin, which meant I shared the space with someone else. In this case, it was Gunnery Sergeant Patel who was in the little room when I entered.

"Welcome, Staff Sergeant," my new roommate said from his seat in a comfortable chair, where he was watching a replay of a sports broadcast from Earth. The cabin must have been a little larger than what he had shared on other cruises, I realized. I knew that he had been promoted to staff sergeant after the battle on Luyten C. Before that, he would have shared a barracks-style berth with twelve other Marines on board the naval vessels he'd been assigned to. A semi-private cabin must have been a welcome change.

It wasn't a bad situation for me, either. The room was large enough to have a lounge space, with two of the plushy chairs positioned directly across from the wall display on which the gunnery sergeant was watching the game. There were also two small desks on either side of the room and sleeping nooks built into the wall, outfitted with privacy curtains. In the kitchenette was a refrigeration unit, a tiny reheating oven, built-in cabinets, and a sink. I could see that there were already a few heavy metal tumblers in a rack by the sink.

"Thanks, Gunny," I replied.

"Call me Pat, at least in here. No need for formalities in our own space, yeah?"

I nodded in agreement and propped my loadout bag against the locker on what I guessed was my side of the room.

"You've got space for personal items," Pat said, pointing to the cabinet that was built around the refrigeration unit. "The fridge only has two shelves, but one is empty if you need it."

"I didn't think to stock up before leaving port," I admitted. In truth, I'd never had the luxury of keeping my own victuals in my cabin before.

"You can place an order from the commissary," Pat supplied helpfully. "They'll deliver it to the ship."

"Good, thank you," I said.

"Of course. We have to look out for one another." Pat paused the game and turned in his chair to give me his full attention. "I'm in charge of the simulator and live fire range. What have they got you chained to?"

"Armory," I said. "Sorry in advance—I may end up smelling like gun oil and soldering smoke."

"I've smelled worse," Pat replied. "You need help with that kit?"

He pointed at my heavy loadout bag. I shook my head. The truth was, the bag was heavy, and with my injuries, lifting the entire thing was difficult. Right now, though, I didn't need to lift it with all my gear still inside. I set it down and slowly settled onto the bed in my nook.

My cautious movements didn't escape Pat's notice. "Looks like you've seen some action."

"Yeah," I replied vaguely, trying to evade the question. "I've been in convalescence and rehab for the last year."

Unfortunately, he'd already espied my full name printed on my loadout bag. "Vanhorn...I know that name," Pat said. "Were you with the TAC team on Luyten C?"

I nodded reluctantly.

"Holy shit, you're *that* Vanhorn—the sergeant who saved his entire platoon!"

"No." I shook my head. The names of the Marines I had lost passed through my mind. I knew I would never forget them, nor did I want to, even though remembering them was more painful than all my injuries combined. "I didn't save everyone."

"Ah," Pat said, a little awkwardly. "I didn't mean to pry."

"Forget it," I said, hoping to have a good relationship with my roommate. "It's in the past. I don't really remember much about it. I was on a lot of meds for a bit after that op. Everything around then is more than a little fuzzy now."

"Oh, I understand that," Pat said. "I like a drink or two, so I've lost a few wild nights myself."

Very different, but I was willing to let it go with a smile. I began to unpack my bag. The clothes were all neatly rolled and arranged already; beneath them were some personal weapons I had taken to carrying into combat, some old-fashioned projectiles and boxes of ammunition. It didn't take long to get my personal effects stored in the wide locker, including a close-quarters tactical shotgun, which I fastened to the inside of the door with maglocks.

"You came prepared," Pat noted wryly. "Does that thing work?"

"Absolutely," I said.

"Once a TAC team Marine, always a TAC team Marine, I suppose."

"You ever tangle with an Orc?" I asked.

"No," Patel said, glancing down. "I was in logistics right out of basic."

"You've seen the vids, though."

"Of course. I've run the simulator on the *Rihla* for over a year. I can hold my own."

I didn't point out that facing a living, breathing Orrkasi warrior was nothing like drilling tactics in a simulator. The Orcs were taller than humans and almost twice as broad. They had huge heads with wide lower jaws and pointed teeth that stuck out at odd angles. They were built like gorillas: short legs, thick chests, huge shoulders. They weren't all that fast, but they were hard to stop. The standard flechette-firing sidearms issued to Marines were worthless against an Orc. Most TAC team members I knew had ditched these unreliable, weak pistols for old-fashioned revolving slug throwers, now called hand cannons or penetrators.

"Then you know that if they get close, the bastards are hard to stop," I said. "I've seen them leap on a person and use their teeth, too. When it comes to that, I prefer something with more stopping power."

"Makes sense," Pat said.

I pulled out my revolver. It was a long-barreled pistol, stainless steel with a black rubber grip. It was chambered for .357 magnum loads, and I had three boxes of soft lead ammunition and four speed reload cylinders. I took out the empty cylinder that was in the gun and loaded in six fresh slugs, but I didn't return the cylinder to the weapon. Instead, I put it all on the shelf of my locker. I could get to the gun and click one of the fast-load cylinders in place in just two seconds. At that point, the weapon would be ready to fire and hard to control, but at close range, it could stop an Orc with just two shots.

After loading everything into the locker, I set the biometric lock and shut it. The only item that remained was the bag of pills I kept with me. They were powerful painkillers, but I only used them when absolutely necessary. I hadn't needed them in nearly two months.

"Will having these in the cabinet be a temptation to you?" I asked Pat.

"What are they? Narcotics?" He shook his head with a chuckle. "No, I prefer liquid painkillers."

He returned his focus to the game. I settled into the seat beside him and pulled out my slate. It only took a few seconds to sync with the ship's network, and I found the page for the commissary easily enough.

"You from Earth?" Patel asked.

"A long time ago, yes," I said, thinking of my home in Alaska. I hadn't been back since completing basic training over a decade before. "You?"

"Mars," Pat said. "My folks were water farmers. But I love American-style football."

"Can't fault you there—I don't mind it myself," I replied.

"You have a favorite team?"

"No," I said. "It's too hard to keep up on deployment."

"Tell me about it," Pat commented. "This game was played last year. I've got dozens more on file to watch. I hope you don't mind."

"Not at all," I replied honestly. "This is a nice setup."

I spent the next half hour ordering snacks from the commissary. The space station where the *Rihla* was docked was essentially a huge refueling port, and the commissary had everything from civilian clothing to alcohol, gaming systems, and entertainment credits. I bought some sheets for my bunk, knowing that the standard-issue bedding on board a ship was nothing desirable. I also managed to get enough junk food to fill my side of the pantry cabinets. Mixing liquor with the narcotics I was sometimes forced to take was dangerous, so I opted for soft drinks instead.

Once I had placed my order, I slipped my slate back into my pocket and got to my feet.

"Going to check out the armory?" Pat asked.

I nodded. "I want to find my way around early."

"Roger that. You want a guide?"

"No, that's not necessary. Enjoy your game."

"Always," Patel said with a grin.

I left the cabin and made my way around to the training section of the ship. The TAC team occupied Bravo deck, while the two Marine fire teams were on Charlie. Since the TAC team took up less space, the physical training facility, simulator, and live fire range were also on Bravo deck. The simulator was standard, just a simple room with forty omni-directional virtual training stations, enough for an entire platoon to train together. The live fire range was smaller, with just four firing lanes and programmable targets.

After exploring Bravo, I went up to Delta to find the chow hall and the armory. The armory was a simple place: a long room with racks of weapons and drawers filled with ammunition and batteries. In the center was a long, narrow workbench with various weapon mounts. The back wall held a rack full of tools. As I walked through the space, I felt a sense of both comfort and immense relief. I had been afraid that I would be assigned to an administrative post, and typing reports or making schedules wasn't my idea of fulfillment. Working with tools, on the other hand, was something I could see myself doing. While tiring and painful at times, being on my feet would also help my recovery. Sitting down only made my bad leg more stiff; I needed motion to keep the blood flowing to my joints and the scarred muscles.

While the ship was in port, the armory was locked down, but my biometrics had already been put into the system. This gave me access not only to the room, but also to the guns themselves. I pulled down one of the standard-issue laser assault rifles, called LARs. It was a simple weapon, with pistol-style grips at the stock and along the barrel sheath. On top was a rack for mounting different tools, like a scope or flashlight, depending on what was needed for a given operation. The batteries loaded easily into the stock's pistol grip, and a quick inspection showed almost no barrel degradation. Still, the weapon was only marginally serviced. It needed a full breakdown, cleaning, and rebuild.

"At work already?"

I turned to find Lieutenant Holly, the deck officer who'd welcomed me aboard, at the open entrance to the armory, leaning casually against the doorframe.

"Just getting my bearings," I replied.

"What do you think of your predecessor's work?" she asked.

It was a loaded question. I had no idea who the previous master-at-arms had been. For all I knew, it could have been Lieutenant Holly's best friend, and something about her made me want to avoid any offense to her if I could help it.

"Well, there's some work to be done," I admitted. "But I'm glad. I need to keep busy—I'm no good sitting around all day."

"I think the former MA was just waiting out the last few months of his enlistment. A lot of Marines see this type of post as a dead-end job."

"I nearly ended up dead, period," I said. "I'm grateful for anything I'm able to do at this point."

"Well, don't work too hard," she said, "or you'll run out of things to do."

She flashed a smile that was hard for me to interpret. The problem, I realized with a jolt, was that I found her pretty, and that messed with my head. I didn't know if I was reading too much into the gesture. *She probably smiled at everyone*, I thought.

Yet something inside me wanted desperately to believe that she could see past the scars, the missing hair, the eye patch, and the limp—all superficial—and understand that there was much more to me than met the eye. Physically, I wouldn't have said I was a catch even before Luyten C, and I was still trying to accept that my body would carry the burden of that experience for the rest of my life. I didn't want to think that I would be forced to live out these days in solitude as well.

Lieutenant Holly walked away, and I replaced the LAR in its rack. Continuing my inspection, I saw cases of weapons, ammunition, and even explosives. There was also an emergency lever on the wall. The armory was a vital station in the ship, but it was also dangerous. The lever could seal and eject the armory so that the munitions didn't damage the rest of the ship in an emergency situation.

I had used the armories on other ships, but that had only involved going to the window and checking out gear. In all honesty, I had always taken the armories and the Marines who worked in them for granted. Now I felt I could contribute to this space. As master-at-arms, not only were there things I could do, but with a little effort, there was much that I could do *well*. It gave me a sense of comfort to know that I was in a secure role where I could make a difference. While I continued to work on my body and its recovery, I would have a sense of purpose; and that was a feeling I'd feared I might never have again.

I was just about to lock the armory back up when my slate vibrated in my pocket. I pulled the device out and saw that I was wanted on Alpha: my treats had arrived. With those in my possession, I could truly make myself at home on the *S.F. Rihla*.

SURVIVORS
SAMPLE CHAPTER 2

The chow hall was the same on every ship. There were large food prep machines, each with a variety of dinning options. I picked mushroom and cheese ravioli in parmesan cream sauce with reconstituted broccoli and chicken flavored protein loaf. On my first night on the *Rihla*, I ate dinner alone, then returned to my cabin to change my clothes before walking down to the physical therapy center. There was a large cardio section, which hurt my heart a bit: I had always prided myself on staying fit, but my injuries made running nearly impossible. I couldn't use the cardio machines or most of the resistance equipment. Instead, I used bands and focused on increasing my range of motion. My left arm would only rise as high as my shoulder and ached when I tried to go any higher. I worked carefully but with a quiet intensity, focused on regaining a semblance of my old self. The PT center was mostly empty, save for a few Marines putting in the work to keep their bodies ready for whatever the corps might throw at them.

I did the same exercises my former physical therapists had put me through, pushing my artificial joints until exhaustion took hold. After an hour, I was sweating more from pain than exertion. With that pain came the sense of pride that a good workout always gave me. I enjoyed the fact that I strove to demand so much from my body, even when no one would judge me for taking an easier route or throwing in the towel completely.

After my workout, I showered, then made up my bed with the new sheets from the commissary and climbed into my bunk. Pat was still watching football. I slid the light-blocking, noise-dampening curtain closed and quickly fell asleep, worn out from both the physical and emotional strain of the day.

The next morning and first platoon meeting felt like they arrived only seconds after I'd shut my eyes. At 0645, I was dressed and waiting in the designated briefing room on Echo. There were a few other Marines waiting with me. They all looked hungover and exhausted, which wasn't surprising: most of the platoon had leave, and the Pathfinder had an entire wing filled with bars, clubs, restaurants, and other forms of entertainment.

Within ten minutes of my arrival, the entire platoon was present and waiting for Lieutenant Bass. The TAC squads were exactly as advertised, two groups of cocky, hard-charging Marines. I had once been part of them, but I could see the disdain in their eyes whenever they glanced my way. In the culture of the Space Fleet Marine Corps, the TAC teams were the elite fighters, the superstars. Everyone else was beneath them and, to most members, not worthy to share the same space.

I sat in the back with Pat, along with the rest of the support staff that made up the third squad of Lieutenant Bass's first platoon. I had three Marines working under me, Sergeant Nathan Bridger, Corporal Kelly Farris, and Lance Corporal Beatrix Finnegan. They had all said hello and not much else—likely out of some sense of internal embarrassment, I knew. By this time, I was used to the looks of fear and uncertainty my appearance often evoked; and the fact that they would all be answering to me once the platoon meeting was over only made them more apprehensive. I was their new boss, and they had no idea if I would make their lives miserable or not.

A first sergeant barked an order, and we all stood to attention as Lieutenant Bass entered. He looked fresh and excited as he stepped to the podium. Whatever the plans were for the *Rihla's* cruise, he evidently approved.

"Welcome aboard the *Rihla* and to the First Platoon," he said. "Most of you know me, and you know what I expect. Do your job, always be prepared, and we'll get along just fine. All right, at ease— let's get down to business. I've just received word from the captain that we'll be making a cruise to the Leonis system."

For nearly half an hour, the lieutenant gave a formal lecture about the system. Leonis B was a planet in the habitable zone of its system. Our ship would make orbit, launch mapping satellites, and essentially lay claim to any resources in the system. It used to be a mundane task to explore new star systems before the Orrkasi had crossed our path. They were eager to extend their own reach, and we had been engaged in almost constant warfare ever since. There was no reason to believe that the Orrkasi had invaded the Leonis system, but there was always a chance, and Lieutenant Bass was hopeful that the TAC teams he commanded would see action. I couldn't help but wonder how he would feel if he had the first clue just how horrible the Orcs were.

For a moment, it took an effort to push back the terror of my own memories. It hurt just as much that my experience was so tainted by those nightmarish recollections. I loved being on a TAC team, standing shoulder-to-shoulder with men and women I respected. The bonds formed during countless hours of training and experiencing the horrors of combat together made them like family. It hit me that I was no longer part of that world. My job was simpler, and, for the first time in my adult life, that was a blessing to me.

When the platoon meeting ended, I got to my feet slowly and shuffled down the aisle. The members of the TAC teams were crowded around the door, blocking the way. I stood back, in no real hurry to leave. My little group of gunsmiths was waiting for me, but we weren't required to staff the armory until noon. Before that, we would just be going over a shift schedule and assigning roles. The responsibility of being the senior NCO of a ship's armory was in many ways simpler than managing fire teams and making sure a squad was ready for combat.

I was almost to the door when a big man bumped into me. The blow knocked me off balance, and I ended up leaning against the wall to keep from falling. The last thing I wanted was to look weak in front of the Marines of the TAC teams. The man who bumped me was a sergeant whose name badge identified him as Theo Barker. He glanced over at me and flashed a wicked grin before turning back to his companions without commenting on his rudeness. I knew the type: he wore the TAC team designation of a screaming eagle on his uniform, but there were no ribbons for combat drops. Some Marines thrive in training but can't handle the rigors of actual combat. Despite this, I could tell that Barker thought himself superior to me; I doubt he even saw that I formally outranked him. Still, I let it go, reminding myself that there was no need to start a feud. Barker's rudeness wouldn't affect how I did my job.

Pat, who was standing nearby, didn't see it that way. Given what I knew of his background and the pecking order pervasive in the military, perhaps it was because he had endured years of disrespect from combat operators who looked down on him as a logistics officer.

"Sergeant Barker!" Pat snapped. "Don't turn your back on Staff Sergeant Vanhorn. You owe him an apology."

I raised my hands, hoping to wave off the need for an apology. Barker turned, glanced at me, and grinned again.

"Sorry, I didn't see you there, Staff Sergeant," he said, his voice dripping with condescension. "I'll have to be more careful. I didn't realize I was in a handicapped zone."

He chuckled as he turned away. Pat took a deep breath, clearly offended by the flagrant insult. I knew he was about to explain to the room exactly who I was and why—at least in his eyes—I deserved their respect. It was commendable, but I didn't want people to think I considered myself a hero. The truth was, I felt exactly the opposite. My job on Luyten C had been to accomplish the mission objectives and get my Marines back safely. I'd only accomplished half of that. I would pay for my failures with pain, probably for the rest of my life. Almost getting myself killed didn't merit any special treatment.

"Don't," I said quietly to Pat. "It's not worth it."

"He can't treat you like that," my cabinmate fumed.

"It's fine, really. I hate to admit it, but I used to be the same way," I said. "Guys like Barker have to believe they're invincible. They can't second-guess their actions, not on the battlefield."

"But we aren't on the battlefield," Pat argued as we left the briefing room. "And nothing gives someone the right to disrespect a superior. It's bad for morale."

"We'll let it slide just this once," I told him.

I took my time descending the stairs to Delta. The jocularity of the TAC teams had made my own self-consciousness much worse. They were strong, and I felt weak; they moved quickly where I was still slow. More than anything else, they were full of hope, while my future was tainted with despair. The corps had given me the tools to rebuild my body, but my mind was still struggling to accept this new normal.

On Delta, I shuffled around to the armory, where my new team was waiting. The door was standing open, a clear violation of protocol: the armory was a secure facility on the ship, and that security was not to be compromised. Since the ship was in port, however, I had no obligation to chastise my team; and it was soon apparent that they had left the door open for me.

"Ten-hut!" Sergeant Bridger announced as I entered.

My three fellow Marines all came to stiff attention and saluted, even though that wasn't customary, as salutes were usually reserved for officers and as a show of respect. I returned their salute with a smile.

"All right, cut that out," I said.

"Just wanted you to know we're excited to have you, Staff Sergeant," he said.

"Well, I'm glad to be here," I said. "Did you all work with my predecessor?"

"Corporal Ferris and I did, Staff Sergeant," the young sergeant explained. He was short man with a clean-cut face and the beginnings of a potbelly. "Corporal Finnegan came on a few days before you."

"Well, the first thing you need to know is that I prefer to be called Van," I said. "We work together, and I prefer proficiency over protocol."

"Understood," he said. "I go by Nate."

"Kelly," introduced one of the two women. She had a round face and dull brown hair twisted into a complex braid that was wound into a bun at the back of her neck. She looked to be about my age, but it was difficult to know for certain.

"Trix—it's short for Beatrix," the lance corporal added. Trix was the youngest member of our little team. She was thin, with blonde hair cut short and bright green eyes.

"Very good," I said. "I'm guessing you already had a schedule in place, Nate?"

"We did," Nate confirmed. "Six-hour shifts."

"Was it acceptable?" I asked.

"Yes."

"Good, then we'll keep it. What are your specialties?"

"I've got experience in power supply management," Kelly offered. "I would be glad to keep up with the batteries and charging rotation."

"Very good," I said. "Nate?"

"I'm a bit of an inventory nerd. I love lists."

"Great. You can keep track of ammunition. Trix?"

"I don't really have a specialty yet," she said. "But I'm good with my hands. I build models, or at least I used to."

"Where did you serve before this?" Nate asked.

"I was an administrative assistant at the Lunar base," she said.

"I can teach you everything you need to know to service these weapons," I told her. "You and I will do a complete check of every weapon in here. I'll take charge of the explosive ordinance personally. If you have an issue with anything or anyone, you come to me. I don't care what the issue is—I'm available day or night."

As if to emphasize my point, the slate in my pocket buzzed. I pulled it out and glanced at the screen. The message turned out to be a summons to meet with the ship's captain.

"Looks like you're a popular person," Nate said with a grin.

"Do you have other requirements for us?" Kelly asked. "PT? Training?"

"No," I told her. "Just keep in mind that we'll be on this ship for a long time. Do what you need to do to stay sane. Other than that, no one is allowed in the armory other than senior officers and the four of us. If someone wants a weapon with live ammo and the ship isn't on alert status, they need authorization from their CO. Let's keep it simple. I'll be back and take the first shift here while the rest of you get squared away."

I left them to work out the rotation schedule. It didn't matter to me when I worked. Life on board a ship was all about routine. There was nothing to differentiate night and day—it was all the same. The easiest way to deal with the stress of a military vessel was to create a routine and stick to it. I cared much more about the happiness of my team, so once they had their preferred slots in the rotation, I would build my daily routine around it. I also planned to spend more time with each member of my team during their time in the armory. The best work environments, in my experience, were both professional and friendly.

Checking my slate, I saw that the captain of the ship, Liza Dunning, had requested that I meet her in her office, which was directly across from the command and control center. When I made my way there, that part of the ship opened up, displaying a small waiting area just inside. To my surprise, I found Lieutenant Holly stationed at the tiny desk outside the captain's office.

"Staff Sergeant Vanhorn," she said with a brief grin; whether she meant it to be or not, I was enchanted. "Right on time."

"I was just in the armory," I said, cursing my inability to think of anything else to say.

"I'll let the captain know you're here," she said, tapping some of the icons on a large tablet-sized slate. "You can sit down. She's on a video conference at the moment. There's no telling how long that might last."

"Do senior officers always serve out here?" I asked, waving at the captain's office.

"You may not have noticed, but I'm actually a junior officer," she said, tapping the gold bar on the collar of her uniform.

"I've seen you all over the ship," I said. "I just assumed you were second in command."

She laughed. "I'm Captain Dunning's gopher. But I don't mind— I plan to be in her chair one day, and when that day comes, I want to know everything about the ship...even the armory."

"I can tell you everything about it," I said, glad for the opening. Flirting wasn't the best idea—after all, she was an officer, and not even one in the corps—but there was something about her that I couldn't resist.

"Is that so?" she asked.

I cherished the hope that she was flirting back, while telling myself that it didn't really matter if she was or not. In that moment, it just felt validating to believe she was. It had been a long time since anyone had looked at me with anything but pity or revulsion.

"Absolutely," I replied. I was about to say more when her slate beeped.

"That's Captain Dunning," she said. "She's ready to see you now."

"Thanks," I said, glad that I hadn't sat down. I didn't want Lieutenant Holly to see me struggle with something as simple as standing.

The captain's office had double doors that slid apart as I approached. Where Lieutenant Bass's office had been small and utilitarian, the captain's large office held more creature comforts than any other place on the ship that I had seen so far. That might have been customary; never having been summoned to a captain's office before, I had no way of knowing for sure. Until my promotion to staff sergeant while still recovering on Titan, I was an average grunt who never went near senior officers if I could help it. I still felt an undeniable sense of apprehension as I walked into Dunning's workspace.

She was seated behind a wide desk, the surface of which showed three holo-projectors. I could see that she had two pages of information projected, and the third projector showed the command interface of her computer. As I walked forward, trying not to limp, she passed her hand over a switch to deactivate the holograms. She waved at one of the chairs across from her desk.

"Have a seat, Staff Sergeant," she said. "I take it you've gotten settled and met your team."

"Yes, Captain," I replied. "Everything is in order."

"And the armory?"

"It's in passable shape," I said honestly.

"I expect things to be tip-top, not merely passable," she said.

"I agree and will see to it personally," I assured her.

"That's what I want to hear. We've got a full load, and we haven't had to use anything in my last two cruises, other than the ammunition fired at the range."

I nodded. The common weapon was a laser blaster, which didn't fire ammo, but there were other weapons that fired flechettes, tranquilizers, non-lethal rubber bullets, and even some depleted uranium rounds. There were probably more that I'd find once I'd done a more exhaustive inventory of the armory.

"As you know, we also have explosives on board," the captain continued, "and any personal weapons must be checked into the armory once we're on our way."

I knew that some captains let the Marines keep their personal weapons in their lockers, but it seemed that this one wouldn't. That's where I had stowed my revolver and tactical shotgun; obviously, I would have to move them to the armory. If they were fired anywhere but the range, it could cause major problems for the ship —and my career.

"Yes, Captain," I replied.

"I don't micromanage, Staff Sergeant. I simply expect excellence and efficiency from all my department heads. What I don't want is drama. I know that your people will work with the platoons to ensure that they have everything they need in a timely fashion, and without any issues."

"Yes, Captain."

"And I expect that the weapons under your care will remain in proper working order. If, heaven forbid, we run into the Orrkasi, lives will depend on the reliability of the weapons in your charge."

"They'll be ready for any event we encounter," I promised.

"Excellent," she said, standing up. I followed her example, trying not to show the pain that the movement from seated to standing caused. The spasms passed, and I began to move away from my chair. "I'm happy to have you on board, Staff Sergeant. Your reputation precedes you."

"I'm just a Marine," I said. "Nothing more."

She gave me a hard look, then nodded. "Very well, Staff Sergeant. Unless there's a problem, we may not see a lot of each other on this cruise, but my door is always open. Don't sweep any matters under the rug and let them fester."

"Yes, Captain," I said, coming to attention and saluting.

"Dismissed," she said.

I brought my hand down but couldn't turn on my heel the way I had been taught in basic training. Fortunately, Dunning had already returned her attention to something on her desk. I didn't stumble, even if I couldn't perform the crisp movements I wanted. The realization made me feel broken as I carefully exited her office.

"How'd it go?" Lieutenant Holly asked.

"Fine," I answered, trying to return her smile. I don't think I succeeded. In response, a look I hadn't seen before passed across her face.

"Staff Sergeant? Have you been up to the rec deck?"

"No," I said. "I haven't been above Echo."

"Well, I don't know what your schedule is, but I'll be on watch in the CIC at oh-four hundred," she said. "The best coffee on the ship is served up on the rec deck, and I like to get a cup about an hour before just to get my motor running. If you're around, I wouldn't mind a little company."

"Oh-three hundred, then?" I said. "I think I can make that."

She gave me a smile, and I felt my spirits lift. It wasn't a date—it wasn't even a flirtation—but I wouldn't pass it up either way. As I headed down to the armory, I thought that my luck might just be turning.

ALSO BY TOBY NEIGHBORS

End Times

The Four Horsemen

Surviving Wormwood

Three Woes

Wizard Rising

Magic Awakening

Hidden Fire

Crying Havoc

Fierce Loyalty

Evil Tide

Wizard Falling

Chaos Descending

Into Chaos

Chaos Reigning

Chaos Raging

Controlling Chaos

Killing Chaos

Elder Wizard

Lorik

Lorik the Protector

Lorik the Defender

We Are The Wolf

Welcome To The Wolfpack

Embracing Oblivion

Joined In Battle

The Abyss Of Savagery

The Vault Of Mysteries

Lords Of Ascension

The Elusive Executioner

Gryphon Warriors

Regulators Revealed

Avondale

Draggah

Balestone

Arcanius

Avondale V

Third Prince

Royal Destiny

The Other Side

The New World

Luck Holds

Zompocalypse

Spartan Company

Spartan Valor

Spartan Guile

Dragon Team Seven

Uncommon Loyalty

Total Allegiance

Kestrel Class

Jump Point

Gravity Flux

Modulus Echo

Zero Friction

Planet Fall

Charter

Jack & Roxie

My Lady Sorceress

The Man With No Hands

ARC Angel

Battle ARC

Broken Crucible

Hidden Kingdom

War INC

Carthage Prime

Cronus Team

Skandia Seven

Mercurial

Magnificus Prime

Incursio

Merlin Appears

Runners

Survivors

Infiltrators

Resistance

Conquest

Occupation

Extraction

The Signal

Battle Orders

Base Of Fire

Hard Site

Recall

Evade

Assault

Space Fever

Staying Alive

Fractal Cut

Blast Zone

Action Zone

Covert Infil

Armor Brigade

Havoc Squad

Thunderbird

Ghost Tactics

Quantum Combat

Infinite Threat

Shadow Threat

Evolving Threat

Lingering Threat

Latent Prowess

Gravity Masters

Gravity Storm

Daughter of the Night

Supernova

Artifact

Blood Moon

Renegade

Juggernaut

Retribution

Independence

Sons of Perdition

Iron Man

Brutal Planet

Hell Flyers

Foray

Conspire

Siege

Colossus

Dead Space

With Pete Garcia

Apocalypse One Percenters